Too late

She'd forgotten herself. She forgot who she was. Simply a captive. And more importantly, she forgot who he was. A merciless criminal who would stop at nothing to get what he wanted. So what if he wounded her with some ugly words? He could hurt her in far worse ways.

There was no sound save the crash of their breaths filling the space between them. She started sliding back a step, but his hand shot out. She squeaked and lifted her fists, prepared to fight him, however hopeless it would be against his greater strength.

His hand closed around the back of her neck, hauling her closer until all of her pushed against the lean length of him. It was like being pressed up against a living, breathing wall. A wall that radiated heat. Their angry breaths collided, mingled. Their gazes devoured each other. His cheek burned an angry red from her fist.

She realized his intent the moment before his head swooped down. His mouth crashed over her own.

By Sophie Jordan

HELL BREAKS LOOSE

A Devil's Rock Novel

SOPHIE JORDAN

WITHDRAWN

AVONBOOKS

An Imprint of HarperCollinsPublishers

HELL BREAKS LOOSE. Copyright © 2016 by Sharie Kohler. All rights reserved. Printed in the United States of America. No part of this book may be used or reproduced in any manner whatsoever without written permission except in the case of brief quotations embodied in critical articles and reviews. For information, address HarperCollins Publishers, 195 Broadway, New York, NY 10007.

First Avon Books mass market printing: August 2016

ISBN 978-0-06242373-3

Avon Trademark Reg. U.S. Pat. Off. and in Other Countries, Marca Registrada, Hecho en U.S.A.
Avon, Avon Books, and the Avon logo are trademarks of HarperCollins Publishers.
HarperCollins® is a registered trademark of HarperCollins Publishers.

16 17 18 19 OPM 10 9 8 7 6 5 4 3 2 1

For Rachel Vincent and Kimberly Derting:
Thank you for propping me up through the last half of this book with your brilliance and laughter. I wish I could bring every book into the world with you both at my side.

HELL BREAKS LOOSE

ONE

It's actually not that difficult to slip the Secret Service.

Or maybe it was simply that Grace Reeves was the last person anyone would expect to rebel. Everyone (and by everyone she meant the entire country) considered her the most boring, predictable, unexciting First Daughter to ever grace the White House. Ha! There was a pun she hadn't heard before.

In elementary school Grace never so much as received a U (for unsatisfactory) on her report card. In high school she never broke curfew or got caught making out with boys. In college she never went to any wild frat parties. No one would expect her to sneak out of a hotel and ditch her detail.

Even Grace could hardly believe she was doing it.

She cast one last glance at the panic button sitting on the hotel dresser. She had to leave it behind. It carried a GPS, and she didn't want anyone tracking her once they realized she was gone. She'd be back when she was ready. When *she* felt like it. The wholly selfish thought felt good. This rare moment of irresponsibility felt *good*.

She stepped carefully into the sitting area that separated the suite's two bedrooms. Holly's voice carried through the shut doors, weary with disappointment, as Grace eased past the sofa. ". . . She's hopeless. No matter how often we rehearse, she's awkward every time we stick her in front of people."

Holly thought she was napping after their busy day. It shouldn't sting to hear her personal aide talk about her. It was nothing she hadn't said to Grace's face. It was nothing Grace didn't admit herself. It didn't change the fact that Holly was her friend. Maybe her only one. Pathetic, Grace guessed, that her best friend happened to be on her father's payroll.

"It's even worse if cameras are present," Holly added. A *thunk* followed the comment and Grace could picture her sitting on the edge of the bed and kicking off her knee-high boots.

She knew she shouldn't take it so personally.

Holly wasn't being unkind and nothing she said was untrue. Grace sighed. It had been a long day. That was all. She was just being cranky and more sensitive than usual.

Breakfast with seniors at a local retirement community, a luncheon with a women's literacy group, and an afternoon speaking at a local university where college kids snickered and whispered about her behind their hands. It all added up to a typical day. A typically *miserable* day, but nothing she couldn't handle. Nothing she wasn't accustomed to doing for her father. Nothing that should send her running like she was now.

No. That was entirely because of the call.

Her father had taken ten minutes out of his busy schedule to Skype with her and let her know what "contribution" he expected from her for his re-election campaign. She snorted. That's what he called it, his face neutral and unassuming in the screen of her laptop. Like he wasn't asking for *everything* from her. A contribution. As though she were one of his constituents writing him a donation check. He'd asked a lot from her over the years. She'd put off grad school for him because he asked. He knew how important it was to her, but he'd asked her to put her dreams and ambitions on hold. Fortunately, they deferred her acceptance, but if she did this for her father . . . what were the odds she would ever get what she wanted out of life? She'd never be free.

She couldn't help remembering how she used to hide in her bedroom. In the narrow space between the wall and her bed, she would cover herself with stuffed animals and lay there buried beneath their soft weight, listening to the cadence of her breath as her parents entertained guests downstairs.

The clink of glasses, the hum of voices, and the burst of laughter had all sounded so far away. She'd hoped no one would find her. She hoped they would forget about her upstairs. Sometimes she got her wish. They forgot about her and she woke up buried beneath stuffed animals the next morning. Sometimes they remembered her existence and dragged her downstairs to play the piano. She would cling to a smile and hope she didn't mess up too badly. That she pulled off the role of happy, perfect child. She'd never been a very good pianist. Or perfect daughter. Then and now.

She wanted to hide under those stuffed animals again. Only she wasn't nine years old anymore. She was twenty-six and these days she didn't own a stuffed animal. A deep sigh welled up from her tightening chest. Her father would never stop dragging her out to perform.

Grace froze as Holly suddenly stopped talking, afraid she was finished with her call and would step out into the sitting area. Holly would insist on accompanying her—as would her detail. Thankfully, her voice started back up again.

"Five more days, baby, and I'll be home." She was talking to one of her boyfriends, then. Holly had several. Too pretty for her own good—she looked like a young Heidi Klum. She loved good-looking men. And sex. Holly frequently regaled Grace with her sexcapades. She would listen raptly, hanging on every naughty word with vicarious delight. Grace didn't get much action these days. Ironic, considering the bomb her father had just dropped on her. You'd think a woman on the verge of announcing an engagement got a little action.

Charles, her sort a boyfriend, was nice. Everyone thought so. If their chemistry didn't rock the charts, that was a minor complaint. Relationships thrived on less. True, not Holly's. But others. At least that's what her father told her when she complained that she didn't like Charles as anything other than a friend. Her mother said she should feel lucky to have a man like Charles. Her mother reminded her of that repeatedly. Harvard grad. Handsome. Thirty-four years old and already so successful. He was a catch. *He* was. Grace didn't miss the fact that her mother never said she was a catch.

Grace continued past Holly's room, glad at least that she wasn't talking about her anymore. They had moved on to sexy talk. Holly giggled. "Oh, you think I should wear the black teddy? I thought you liked the red one. What'd you call it? Easy access? You still have that toy you bought?"

Grace rolled her eyes. God, if she didn't want to escape before, she did now. The last thing she wanted was to hear Holly descend into phone sex. That was enough to make her ears bleed. It was one thing to listen to Holly's stories a day or two after the fact, she didn't want to sit in the audience while the show was playing.

Shaking her head, she unlocked the door and eased it open the barest crack. The suite had three doors that led out into the hall, and Carter stood in front of her room's door. A smile curled his lips as he glanced at the phone in his hand, snorting at something on the screen. It just confirmed what she already knew. She was a powder puff detail. No one considered her high risk. Because she wasn't.

Nothing ever happened to boring.

Even as preoccupied as he was, Carter would notice if she slipped out of the room and walked right down the hall in front of him. She closed the door softly. Biting her lip, she stared pensively across the sitting area. They were on the second floor.

Holly's voice carried. "You're so bad. I'm not going to do *that* . . . I don't care how long it's been since . . ."

Stifling a groan, Grace moved to the sliding glass balcony door before she could chicken out. Opening it, she stepped out into the chilly evening. She didn't need to bother with a coat. Winter in Texas felt like fall back home.

She peered over the railing. Not too far down. The hedge would break the fall. Shooting a quick glance over her shoulder to make certain Holly hadn't emerged from her room, she swung one leg over the side and then the next. Gripping the railing, she slid her hands down the iron rails until she was crouching, her butt sticking out in an undignified manner. She lowered one leg and then the other, dangling for a moment, the soles of her tennis shoes brushing the top of the hedge. Pressing her lips together to stifle any noise, she opened her hands and let go. She dropped. As hoped, the hedge broke her fall, swallowing her up. She thrashed in the bushes for a moment before gaining her feet.

Standing, she shook the hair back from her face

and climbed out of the bushes onto the pebbled path. Dusting off her jeans and wincing at the snags in her silk blouse, she looked left and right, verifying that no one was around. Her detail, most importantly, wasn't, but that wouldn't be the case for long. Even if Holly didn't figure out she was gone soon, Holstein, the special agent in charge, required routine perimeter checks. She needed to get out of there before the next one.

She skirted the swimming pool and circled around the back of the hotel, planning to make her way to the burger place she had spotted from the car earlier.

It almost seemed too good to be true. Walking outside—*alone*—on her way to get a hamburger. For a moment she felt almost normal. Normal and *not* someone being bullied into marriage with a guy who did nothing for her girl parts. She winced. She made it sound like she expected a guy Daddy handpicked for her to actually be the *one*. She'd gone along with dating Charles because it got her father off her back, and he was a genuinely nice guy. She could do worse. She'd thought maybe something could grow between them. Only lately had it become resoundingly clear that wasn't happening. She'd been contemplating ways to end it.

And now her father expected them to get married? She shook her head, feeling sick all over again. How could she go through with it?

Staying parallel to the hotel, she peeked carefully out at the street.

Agent Marshall and Agent Thompson stood in front of the building beneath the hotel portico. She pulled back, flattening her body against the brick wall. They chatted casually, looking slightly bored. They were probably waiting for Holly to notify them of their dinner plans.

Grace smiled grimly. She was going to dinner like a normal person. Without her personal aide/best friend. Without a security detail. Without a boyfriend who liked to call reporters ahead of time to make certain they were at the restaurant when they arrived. Charles was all about a great photo op.

Turning, she walked briskly, leaving the hotel behind and ducking down a back street. She held her breath, half expecting, half dreading a cry of alert. Nothing happened. She tucked her hands in her pockets and practically skipped ahead, imagining sinking her teeth into a big juicy burger. Maybe sweet potato fries, too. She couldn't remember the last time she had eaten something like that. Something so good it was bad.

The scuff of a shoe on loose gravel had her looking over her shoulder.

Two guys followed a couple yards behind her. She didn't know where they had come from. She hadn't noticed them before. Facing forward again, she buried her hands in her pockets and picked up her pace, trying to ignore the sudden hammering of her heart.

It was just a street. It was just two guys walking on a street. Apparently she'd watched too many episodes of *Criminal Minds*.

They didn't know who she was. They weren't following her. Her life was not that dramatic. It definitely wasn't that dangerous.

Just the same, her heart steadied with relief as she approached the end of the street. Two more steps and she would be free, out onto the busier thoroughfare, a block away from the diner she'd passed earlier.

A figure stepped out and blocked her, materializing out of air. She gasped and stopped hard, blinking up at the face before her.

"Hi there," he said, utterly normal.

"H-Hey," she stammered, not feeling similarly normal. Grappling for composure, she stepped to the side to move around him, but he matched her move, stepping to the right and blocking her again.

His mouth kicked up at the corner. He was toying with her and enjoying himself in the process.

"Excuse me," she said, her voice harder. It was her father's no-nonsense-my-army-is-bigger-than-yours voice.

He cocked his head as if considering her request. "Where you going?"

A sound behind her had her looking over her shoulder. The two guys from earlier had stopped directly behind her, crowding her, looking down at her and reminding her of her diminutive height. She felt every inch of her five feet two inches.

She shifted uneasily. She had never been in a situation like this before. Never felt threatened. Even before she was the president's daughter, no one had ever paid her special notice. She was the type of girl who went unnoticed. Most of the time she was simply invisible. Most of the time she wanted it that way.

She wanted it that way now.

Squaring her shoulders, she adopted that air of perpetual arrogance her father wore with such ease. She had certainly stood witness to it enough. "Let me pass."

The guy in front of her tossed back his head and laughed. "'Let me pass,'" he mocked, greasy strands of hair brushing his shoulders. "She sounds like someone used to getting her way."

Grace stifled a flinch. She couldn't remember the

last time she had gotten her way in anything. Quite possibly never.

Greasy Hair glanced over her shoulder at the two men behind her. "Don't you think so, boys?"

Her stomach bottomed out. He knew them. He was *with* them. They were together. All these thoughts clicked one after another in her mind. There was no denying it.

She was in trouble.

She lunged forward and tried to step around Greasy Hair. He grabbed her, wrapping his arms around her and squeezing her so tightly she couldn't catch her breath. His face was so close she could see the tiny flecks of gold in his hazel eyes. "What's the matter? You too good for us?"

She shook her head hard, her heart fierce and savage, threatening to break free from her chest. "Let me go."

"Such a disappointment." He tsked his tongue. "I thought the president's daughter would have better manners than this."

Oh, God. With those words, her fate was sealed. Her last scrap of hope that they didn't know who she was died a swift death. Grace's heart twisted, an aching mass in her chest. Longing to go back, to retrace her steps and order room service with

Holly, surged within her. She could be in her pajamas eating a mediocre burger and lukewarm fries watching TV. Maybe a *Modern Family* rerun.

Greasy Hair stopped smiling. His lips flattened into a thin line that peeked out of the patchy beard on his face. He looked utterly, frighteningly serious as he stared down at her. He reached out a hand and she flinched, trying to back away, but the two men behind her prevented her from retreating. She stopped. Nowhere to go. Nowhere to run. He fingered a lock of her hair as though testing its texture, marveling at its cleanness. Then he released it abruptly. Holding his hand midair, he snapped his fingers. "Take her."

They grabbed her, hard hands bruising where they dug into her arms. She struggled and opened her mouth to scream. The sound never escaped her lips. Something gouged into her ribs. For one terrified instant she thought it was the barrel of a gun.

A jolt of pain punched her. She went rigid as fiery-hot waves rippled over her. They didn't stop. Her teeth clamped tight. She couldn't move, couldn't speak. It was the strangest sensation. She was conscious of the men, their voices, their sweat-doused stink, a hard object digging into her side.

Tires squealed and a van peeled in front of her,

filling her vision. A sliding door swished open, revealing a dark gaping hole. She was picked up and tossed into that shadowy maw.

The door slammed shut and the pain suddenly stopped. The men crowded into the small space with her, the smell of them bitter copper in her nose. Her body went limp. Her jaw relaxed. She gasped for breath, intelligible words tripping from her lips. Shaking, sprawled on the hard metal floor of the van, she tried to lift her head to look around. The van accelerated, rumbling all around her.

There were high fives and triumphant exclamations. She felt her lips moving and knew she was speaking, but nothing sounded right to her ears.

A guy looked down at her and laughed. "You Tased the shit out of her, Zane!"

"Yeah." Greasy Hair laughed once. "Easier than I planned. Didn't expect her to stroll outside all alone."

Grace shook her head, fear like metal in her mouth. Her one and only act of rebellion and this had happened.

She reacted, her leg lashing out, managing to kick one of her assailants. Her efforts were rewarded with a slap to the face. Her head struck the steel floor of the van. Stars danced in her vision.

Whimpering, she lay there, the scald of tears filling her eyes. The men around her laughed.

Did anyone even realize she was gone yet? Was Holly still talking to her boyfriend, oblivious to her absence? For once, Grace wished that she had just stayed put and accepted her fate. Marriage to Charles wouldn't be so bad, she reasoned. She could do worse.

Because this fate? It was so much worse.

TWO

DEEP SHADOWS BLANKETED the hospital room. A dim glow radiated from the panel above his hospital bed, saving the space from complete blackness. Not that Reid minded the dark. He was accustomed to it. There weren't any nightlights in a prison cell. And his stints in the hole had shown him just how dark darkness could be.

Someone outside the room laughed as they passed his door. The footsteps faded. Otherwise the hospital was quiet, with that humming quality of a building that never shut off. Like him. He was wired tight. Tension knotted his shoulders as he reclined in the bed. He never shut down. Never turned off. He couldn't afford to. Not until he was a pile of ashes in a box. Then, he'd rest. Hopefully that wasn't happening any time soon.

Doctors, nurses, and other personnel worked the

six floors of Sweet Hill Memorial with seemingly little thought to the felon in Room 321. Exactly the way he wanted it. He'd been here eight days. Eight days since he was taken from Devil's Rock Penitentiary in an ambulance. In that time, he'd been an exemplary patient. He withstood all the poking and prodding without complaint. He slept and ate his fill. You could say whatever you wanted about hospital food, but compared to prison food it was five-star cuisine.

He'd used this time to store up energy and plot his next move. He had only one chance and he couldn't fuck it up.

He'd be sent back soon. He wasn't hooked up to any beeping machines anymore. His wounds had pretty much healed, leaving only the black lines of stitches and fresh, itching scabs. No threat of infection or continued bleeding. His arm sling could come off in a few days. According to the doctor, he was lucky to be alive. Half an inch to the left and the shiv would have hit his heart.

Reid had said nothing when the doctor told him that, looking at him so expectantly. As though he might express relief or gratitude. He might be alive and breathing, but he had died a long time ago. He was nothing but a walking ghost now.

A ghost with nothing to lose.

Still, starting that fight had been a gamble. He winced, recalling how quickly everything had escalated and turned into a full-on riot. He'd only meant to get himself injured. Instead, inmates had died. Guards were injured. He'd seen North go down in a shower of blood. He felt like shit about that. He'd promised Knox he would look out for the kid. After a few inquiries, he'd learned that North was in a room somewhere else in the hospital. Thankfully, he would recover, but that face of his wouldn't be so pretty anymore.

And that sucked. More guilt. More sins to heap at his feet. But it was done. He, better than anyone, knew you couldn't change the past. He just had to make sure it counted for something. That it wasn't for nothing. Then he could go back to rotting away for the rest of his life.

Reid took a deep, mostly pain-free breath as a nurse entered his room for a final bed check of the night. He was the last to be told anything concerning himself, but he knew what was coming. Even if he hadn't spied the paperwork on the doctor's clipboard authorizing his release, he knew. His time here was done. It was now or never. He had to act tonight.

"Are you comfortable? Can I get you anything? Another pillow?" Nadine asked as she adjusted the one beneath his head, bringing her chest close to his face. It was a game she liked to play. Tease the hard-up convict. Lingering touches on his body that didn't feel quite so clinical. It'd been a long time for him, but he knew when a woman was into him.

The guard who'd accompanied her into the room snorted. Reid leveled his gaze on Vasquez. The man clearly found her compassion toward a scumbag like him unnecessary. Unsurprising.

Reid looked back at the nurse. "I'm fine." He smiled at her. It felt a little rusty. He hadn't done a lot of smiling in the last eleven years, but it seemed to work. She smiled back.

He picked up the remote control with his arm that wasn't in a sling. "I might watch some television." The more noise coming from his room, the better.

He punched the on button and the TV flickered to CNN, the channel Landers, the day guard, preferred. It was a good thing Landers wasn't here tonight. He hung out in the room with Reid a lot so that he could watch TV. Vasquez, on the other hand, only entered the room to accompany the hospital staff. The rest of the time he stood watch outside the door.

"Don't stay up too late," Nadine advised. "You need your rest."

He nodded, training his gaze on the TV as if he cared about what was happening in the rest of the world.

Footage of a vaguely familiar female dressed in a boring gray suit rolled across the screen.

". . . an inside White House source reports that the First Daughter has been missing for over twenty-four hours, ever since Wednesday afternoon following a luncheon with the Ladies Literacy League in Fort Worth, Texas, where she delivered a speech on the . . ."

Nadine tsked. "Can you believe it? Someone abducted the President's daughter. What's the world coming to?"

He shook his head as if this was indeed something he gave a fuck about.

"She probably took off for a weekend to Padre Island," Vasquez grumbled. "Meanwhile, every law enforcement agency in the state is on full alert, wasting time and taxpayers' money searching for her."

The timing couldn't have been better as far as Reid was concerned. Deep satisfaction pumped through his veins, mingling with the swelling adrenaline. That meant they would care less about one escaped convict.

He didn't bother pointing out that the dark-haired female—who looked anywhere between the ages of twenty and forty—was the least likely candidate for a wild weekend at Padre.

"Haven't you been watching the news?" Nadine asked Vasquez. "They suspect terrorists," she pointed out with an indignant sniff.

"What does the media know?" The guard rolled his eyes. "Watch. She'll show up on Monday with nothing worse than a sunburn."

Nadine shook her head, clearly not in agreement, and looked back to Reid. "Good night."

Reid fixed a smile to his face as she slipped from the room, the guard close behind her.

The door clicked softly shut, and he sat there for a long while, letting the minutes tick past, letting the hospital sink deeper into night, his hand twitching anxiously at his side. It was hard being inactive for this long. If you were idle on the inside, you didn't last very long.

CNN streamed a constant feed of First Daugh ter Grace Reeves while reporting absolutely nothing new or enlightening. Graduate of some all-girls college. She looked uncomfortable in her own skin. She was dating the White House communications director, with rumors of an engagement imminent. Surprising, since she didn't look the type to be with the slick-looking guy mugging for the camera.

They flashed pictures and footage of Grace Reeves from a braces-wearing awkward adolescent to current day still-awkward-looking adult. You would think the President had someone on staff that could coach her on how not to look so pinch-faced. Maybe they could dress her better, too. Not like a middle-aged bureaucrat.

When the clock on the wall read 12:34, he decided he'd waited long enough. They had left him unrestrained. Injured and wearing a sling and with a guard standing watch twenty-four/seven, they deemed it unnecessary. Fortunately for him.

The trick would be getting out of the room—and out of the hospital—undetected.

He rose from the bed and slipped the sling over his head. Dropping it on the ground, he moved his arm gingerly, experiencing only a slight twinge of discomfort from the deepest of the lacerations in his chest, but not the arm itself. The arm felt good. He'd had worse.

He fashioned a lump under the covers, doing the best he could to make it look like a body. He turned off the light above his bed. It might pass for him if someone took a cursory peek inside the dim room.

Moving quietly, he slipped the surgical scissors out from where he'd stashed them under the mattress and moved a chair beneath the ceiling access panel.

A draft crept through the back slit of his hospital gown as he climbed up on the chair and lifted his arms, working two of the tiny screws loose in the panel. It swung down soundlessly.

Sucking in a breath, he pulled himself up through the panel, grunting at the strain in his still sore muscles. The square space was barely wide enough for his big body, but he managed to heft himself through, stretching to his full height.

Above his room, the space was dark and crowded with conduit pipes and hot water valves. He hunkered and ducked his head, walking on pipes, carefully choosing his steps so he didn't crash through the Sheetrock.

Light trickled in from another access panel ahead. Reid peered down between the slats, identifying the hallway outside his room. He kept going, looking through the square metal panels until he finally came to one that overlooked a break room.

He listened to the rumble of voices below and glimpsed the top of one man's balding head as he changed shirts. "See you tomorrow, Frank." A locker slammed shut. "Tell your wife to make some of those cookies again."

"They're supposed to be for me," Frank complained.

"I'm doing you a favor," the other guy laughed. "You're fat enough." He left the room and it was just Frank for a few more minutes. He was out of his range of vision, but Reid could hear him rustling around. Soon, another locker shut and his footsteps rang out as he strode from the room.

Reid waited a few seconds and then worked the screws loose until the panel swung open. He lowered himself down, clutching the edges of the opening until his feet landed lightly on cold tile.

He moved swiftly, starting with the lockers, hoping there was one whose combination lock hadn't shifted and would lift open for him. He got lucky on his sixth try. Even better, a pair of men's scrubs and a hoodie hung inside. Several dollars and loose change littered the bottom of the locker floor along with a pair of tennis shoes and a pocketknife. Reid grabbed it all and shut the locker. Arms full, he disappeared into one of the bathroom stalls to change.

The shoes were a little snug, but the scrubs fit. He tightened the drawstring at his waist and slipped on the hoodie, zipping it halfway up. Snatching up his hospital gown, he stuffed it into a trash can on his way out.

He walked out into the hallway like he belonged there. Squaring his shoulders, he slipped one hand in the pocket of his hoodie and immediately brushed the cold cut of metal. He wrapped his fingers around the clump of keys, thumbing the clicker. Sweet. Lifting a car would be simple enough.

Reid didn't pass anyone as he strolled down the hall. He dove through a corner door that led to a stairwell and hurried down the flights. Vasquez could check on him any time. He needed to be far from there when that happened.

The first floor had a little more life to it. An orderly turned the corner before him, humming a tune as he pushed a cart. A nurse passed him as he strode toward the front lobby. She barely glanced up from the chart she was studying. He felt the stare of the camera in the corner but kept walking. It was like he was invisible.

Later, they would study the footage and marvel at him walking bold as day down the hall. But by then it wouldn't matter. He would be long gone.

He passed through a set of automatic doors and sent a smile to the woman behind the circular counter of the admittance desk. She gave him a distracted nod as she spoke into a phone.

Only two people sat in the waiting area. One

dozed. The other stared at the TV in the corner where footage of the First Daughter ran in a constant loop.

His heart stalled and then sped up at the sight of the security guard near the door. His attention was focused on the television screen, too. As Reid approached, he looked up and locked eyes on him. This was it. If there was going to be trouble it would happen now.

"Evenin'," Reid greeted as he neared the door. Almost there.

The guard glanced him up and down before nodding. "Have a good one."

Reid didn't breathe fully. Not even once he stepped out into the night. Every bit of him pulled tight. He didn't let himself feel free. Not yet. It wasn't time to drop his guard. He still had a long way to go to accomplish what he needed to do.

Glancing around, he pulled out the keys from his hoodie and pressed the unlock button. A distant beep echoed on the night. He moved in that direction, weaving between cars. He pushed the unlock button again and this time spotted the flash of headlights.

He advanced on an old Ford Explorer and pulled open the driver's side door. Ducking inside, he adjusted the seat for his long legs then turned the ignition on and drove out of the parking lot.

He headed east for thirty minutes, stopping at a gas station to fill up the tank with the money he'd found in the locker. This late, the place was deserted. He kept his head low as he paid the sleepy-eyed clerk and avoided looking directly at the security camera in the corner.

Reid pulled around the back, where a lone car sat parked beside the Dumpster, presumably the clerk's car. He swapped license plates with it. The guy probably wouldn't even notice anytime soon.

He'd still have to get rid of the Explorer, but this would give him some time. He could ditch the vehicle after he got where he was going.

Satisfied, he hopped back behind the wheel and drove a couple more hours through the night, putting Sweet Hill far behind him. His adrenaline never slowed. He constantly glanced up at the rearview mirror, half expecting to see the flash of headlights. They never appeared.

The highway was dark, the passing car rare on this isolated stretch of road. He rubbed a hand over his close-cropped hair and settled into his seat. Desert mountains lumbered on either side of him, dark beasts etched against the backdrop of night. He flipped through radio stations. No news of an escaped convict. It had been a long time since he was this alone. He still didn't feel free, though. He doubted he ever would.

Eleven years had passed since he'd been out, but he expected to find Zane in the usual place. His brother was simple that way. He liked his routines. Reid would bet that the cabinet was full of the same cereal they ate as kids.

The cabin sat several miles behind the main house on 530 acres located outside Odessa. The land had been in his family for almost two hundred years, granted to them after the Texas War of Independence.

The authorities didn't know about the cabin . . . or the hidden dirt road that veered off the county farm road you had to take to get there. The old Explorer bumped along the unpaved lane. It was so overgrown with shrubs and cacti that it couldn't rightly be called a road, which was the point.

After an hour the road suddenly opened up to a clearing. The cabin stood there. Three trucks and a few motorcycles were parked out front, confirming that the cabin was still in use and far from forgotten.

The front door opened as he emerged from the Explorer. Several men stepped out onto the porch, wielding guns. He spotted Zane at the center of them. His chest squeezed. His brother had visited him a couple times his first year at the Rock. Nothing since then.

Time had not been kind to his younger brother. He was stockier, the baby roundness gone from his face. He was shirtless, too, and Reid marked the dozens of tats covering him that had not been there eleven years ago. Most notable was the eagle sitting atop a vicious looking skull. Most of the guys staring Reid down had the same symbol inked on their necks or faces. Once upon a time he would have been the one standing there wearing that eagle and skull. If fate hadn't intervened . . . if his eyes hadn't been opened.

If he hadn't gone to prison.

He swallowed against the acid rising up in his throat and fixed a smile on his face. "Hey, little brother."

It was a bitter pill. This was his baby brother. The reason he hadn't taken off for parts unknown when he graduated from high school was because of this guy right here. He hadn't wanted to leave Zane alone with their crackhead mother and a deadbeat dad who showed up every few months. Fat lot of good sticking around did his brother. He'd ended up in jail, and his brother was running with a bunch of low-life thugs. *His brother was a low-life thug now.*

"Holy shit," Zane declared, hopping down from the porch, still holding onto his rifle. "Son of a bitch! What are you doing here?" He slapped his thigh as if he'd just seen something amazing. Something like his older brother who went away for a life sentence standing in front of him.

Reid lifted his chin and tried not to stare too hard at the emblems of hate riddling his brother. He nodded at the rifle. "Is that any way to welcome me home?"

Zane hesitated a moment and then flung his arms wide. As if the past were forgotten. As if bad shit never went down. As if Reid could still be one of them again. "Welcome home, brother."

Zane embraced him, clapping him hard with his free hand. Reid pulled back and eyed the other men, meeting their dilated gazes head-on. Not a single one was sober. They were all high on something. Even so, several looked at him with distrust. Evidently not everyone had forgotten that before he went to prison not everything had been copasetic. They clearly remembered that he and Sullivan had grown contentious with each other.

Rowdy, his brother's second-in-command, wore a grin for him, though. Even if that grin did not quite reach his eyes, Rowdy reached out and clapped hands with him.

"Good to have you back." Rowdy looked him over. "Looking fierce, man. Guessing they didn't release you for good behavior."

"Nah. Thought I'd just go ahead and let myself out."

Zane and Rowdy laughed. "Same ol' Reid."

"You couldn't have come back at a better time." His brother's eyes glinted with excitement, reminding him of the kid he used to be, and that only made his chest ache harder.

"That right?" Reid asked.

Zane nodded eagerly, gesturing to the cabin. "Yeah." He shared a look with Rowdy and the other guys, and Reid got the sense that he was missing out on some joke. "Let's go inside and I'll tell you all about it."

Reid followed him inside and did a quick scan of the living room, noting how run-down the place had gotten in the eleven years he'd been gone. It had never been the Four Seasons, but now the house smelled of sweat and stale cigarette smoke. The upholstery on the arms of the couch had worn off. Dirty white threads tufted up as if trying to escape from the piece of furniture.

"We got something big going down, Bubba."

The sound of his little brother using his old nickname elicited a pang in his chest. He had a sudden flash of a little boy missing his front teeth chasing him around the trailer park. *Bubba! Wait for me!*

That boy was gone. Zane's eyes were bloodshot and dilated from God knew what drugs and a patchy beard hugged his cheeks. It was hard to reconcile him to the soft-faced boy Reid had last seen. *Get over it, Reid. That boy is gone.* Still. Easier said than done. His brother was the only family he had left.

"Yeah?" Reid looked at the men standing around him, a prickling sensation crawling up the back of his neck.

Zane chuckled lightly and scrubbed at the back of his neck under hair that fell long and greasy. He needed a shower. "Why don't I show you?"

Turning, Zane headed down the dark hall to the back bedrooms. The carpet was flat and matted beneath Reid's shoes as he followed his brother. He felt the other men behind him, crowding close like anxious dogs. Something was definitely in the air. Feral and testosterone-laced. He recognized it from prison. Right before a fight broke out. Blood was in the water and the sharks were hungry.

Zane opened the door to the master bedroom and stepped inside. Reid followed. He sucked in a breath as his gaze landed on the bed and the woman restrained there. His stomach pitched and a fresh wave of acid surged up inside him.

Her hands were bound together with a cord that extended to the brass headboard. She sat board-straight on the edge of the bed, her knees locked tightly together. Her eyes were red-rimmed and puffy. She had been crying, but now her eyes were bone-dry above the gag. She didn't blink as her wide brown stare flitted over him, assessing him before flicking to the men at his back. Her nostrils flared as if scenting danger. She would be right about that. They were the wolves and she their next meal. Of that he was certain.

She tossed her head and said something against the muffled rag stuffed in her mouth. Her dark hair was loose and tangled around her shoulders, trailing long over her cream-colored blouse. The shiny fabric was dirt-smudged and stained, but still looked expensive. Probably the most expensive thing in this cabin. A bruise marred the flesh of her cheek above the gag where someone had hit her, and something clenched in his gut.

Even in her condition, Reid had no problem recognizing her.

Fuck.

"Surprise!" Zane waved at her.

They'd done it. They'd abducted the President's daughter.

THREE

*S*HE'D STOPPED CRYING some time ago, but the urge returned in full force with the arrival of the new guy. He was bigger than the rest of them. He looked more ruthless. Something in his eyes, in the hard set to his mouth . . . there was no softness there. She wouldn't be able to appeal to any part of him.

He also seemed somehow more alert, more aware, more ready to snap than the rest of them. The rest of her abductors reminded her of children, anxious on their feet, unable to hold still. Their eyes, however, were dull and slow-moving. It was a strange contrast.

The sharpness of New Guy's hazel gaze could cut glass. She felt it slice through her as he stood there staring down at her with an empty expression on his coldly handsome face. She registered this with a swift sweep of her gaze. There was no denying he was sexy in a rough and ruthless kind of way. Even with a faint shadow of beard hugging his square jaw he was model-hot. Charles had nothing on this guy. Even Holly's hot boyfriend was somehow *less*.

Watching New Guy watch her, she lifted her bound wrists to her chest and attempted to twist her hands free. It pulled the cord tighter but she had to try. One of her abductors walked over and placed a hand on the top of her head, petting her like she was some kept animal. "We got fucking royalty here."

She yanked her head away and knocked at his hand with her bound hands.

He abruptly crouched down in front of her, propping his hands on the thighs of his ratted-out jeans, and she recognized him as the one who had hit her in the van. His eyes were dark, all pupils, as he gazed at her. "I like that you still have some fire in you."

"C'mon, Rowdy." Greasy Hair called him away. "Let's go talk."

Relief warred with the constant fear inside her as they filed out of the room. All except New Guy. The big one. He lingered, staring at her with that unreadable gaze. Maybe Greasy Hair wasn't in charge anymore. New Guy seemed so in control, so powerful, it was hard to imagine him taking orders from anyone else.

She held his gaze, hoping that maybe she was right. Maybe he wasn't like the rest of them. It was a flimsy hope, but she clung to it like a frayed ribbon in her hands. He hadn't been there when they took her. He didn't look happy to see her here. Maybe he could help her. *Maybe*. He was strong, well over six feet, his body hard and muscled beneath his shirt. He held some influence if they had thought to show her to him, after all.

She tried to speak into the rag, leaning forward in supplication. They locked eyes and for a breath she thought she saw something flicker in the depths of his gaze. Some kind of emotion. Then it was gone—if it had ever existed at all.

With a single shake of his head, he clasped the doorknob and shut the door, sealing her once again inside her prison.

REID'S HEAD WAS spinning as he made his way down the hallway and into the main room of the house.

The president's daughter.

They had abducted the fucking president's daughter.

The litany ran through his head like a bullet

train. He could hardly think of anything else, which was bad considering he came here for one thing and one thing only and it had nothing to do with Grace Reeves.

"Shit, man, I can't believe you busted out." Zane clapped him on the back again. At this point he would have bruises tomorrow.

The rest of the guys dropped off in various spots in the living room. No one was concerned with the presence of the gagged woman in the back room. He wondered if she had eaten. Or used the restroom. They'd had her since yesterday. Had they seen to any of her needs?

One guy immediately lit up a joint, while another one sat in front of the beat-up coffee table and started shaking cocaine out of a sack. Some things never changed. They were all still a bunch of drug dealing burnouts. That's what Otis Sullivan wanted them to be—what he had always wanted them to be. Mindless drones subject to him.

Reid glanced around, taking in the sagging mouths and dilated eyes of every guy present, including his own brother. They didn't have a care in the world or a thought in their heads. Not a single one sober and yet they were the most hunted men in America right now.

And he had just joined their ranks.

"What you gonna do with the girl?" he asked, trying to sound casual, as though it didn't matter one way or another to him. As though he couldn't still see her face, her eyes, in his mind.

"I don't know. We'll figure something out." His brother shifted on his feet and shot a cagey look at Rowdy. Instantly, Reid knew he was lying. They had a plan. For whatever reason, his brother wasn't partial to sharing that information with him. Apparently, some things had changed after all. Zane didn't fully trust him anymore.

"You got no plan? So you just grabbed her for the hell of it?" He moved to the rusted fridge in the kitchen and pulled it open, peering inside as though the question didn't weigh on him like a ton of bricks. Any minute this place could be swarming with FBI, and he was pretending the biggest concern on his mind was what he could feed his stomach.

Zane spoke up, an edge of defensiveness in his tone. "We gotta wait for word from Sullivan."

Of course. Sullivan. He still pulled all the strings.

"Yeah?" He took a breath, trying to play it cool even though what he really wanted to do was shake his brother for letting Sullivan call the shots. "Why'd Sullivan want you to grab her anyway?"

Zane considered him as he sank down on the

couch and accepted a joint from the guy next to him. He lifted a bottle of beer and took a long swig, still staring at Reid.

Rowdy bent over the coffee table and snorted a line of coke, tossing his head back with a deep gasp. The guy's nose was so red it looked ready to fall off.

"Don't know if Sullivan would want me to talk to you about this," Zane finally said. "You two didn't part on good terms."

That would be because Sullivan was the reason he went to jail. Guess Zane had forgotten that. Or he just didn't care. Hell, maybe all the drugs and booze had fried his brains.

Reid opened up a tube of tinfoil and sniffed at the burrito inside. "Come on, man," he coaxed, peeling back the tortilla and taking a peek inside at the questionable contents. "I'm your brother. Just busted out of jail and I came straight here. If I had any hard feelings, would I be here? Hell, no. I would have gone straight to Mexico."

Sniffing, Rowdy pinched at his nose as if his sinuses troubled him. "Got a point there."

Zane and Reid stared at each other for a long moment, unspoken words passing between them. Finally his brother shrugged and took another hit off his joint. "We're not going to kill her. At least not yet. Waiting for Sullivan to tell us what to do with her."

Reid put the burrito back in the refrigerator. "This is going to bring a lot of heat. Hope he comes up with something good. And quick."

"Sullivan's not a fan of the president," Zane explained slowly, as if still unsure how much to say.

Rowdy snorted. "Understatement. After donating a shit ton of money to his campaign, Reeves screwed him over," Rowdy offered, chafing his hands hard over his thighs, full of anxious energy and mind-altering chemicals.

"Yeah?" Reid asked. "How so?

"Remember Sullivan's nephew Jeremy?" At Reid's nod, he continued, "Well, he got sent to prison on racketeering charges."

"He talk?" Reid asked, because he knew the kid had been working for Sullivan. Any racketeering had been on Sullivan's behalf.

"Nah, he weren't no rat. Sullivan expected a favor from the president, or leniency at least, but Reeves wasn't having it. No favors from him. They gave the kid twenty years."

Reid whistled. He'd been in for eleven and that had felt like a lifetime. He remembered Jeremy. Sullivan had sent him away to some fancy college to get a degree in business or accounting. Something he could use to help manage Sullivan's empire. The kid was smart, but soft. And maybe not that smart if he got caught. Prison couldn't have been an easy transition for the likes of him.

"Gets worse," Rowdy chimed.

"He killed himself," Zane said with a shake of his head.

Reid blinked. Guys had killed themselves at the Rock. Of course. It happened. It was prison. You could almost mark the ones that weren't going to make it the moment they arrived. They stuck to themselves. They didn't make allies. A bad thing on the inside. You needed friends. They had a look. A desperate, shell-shocked expression that gradually faded to vacancy. They weren't even present anymore by the time they ended it.

In his second year at the Rock there had been a guy in the cell next to him who hanged himself. The morning after he'd watched through the bars, glimpsing the waxy gray face as the guy was rolled out on a gurney.

Zane continued. "Sullivan wants payback."

Now Reid understood. It was personal. He grimaced. Jeremy wasn't just some lackey. He'd been blood. Sullivan wanted the president to suffer, and he would make him suffer by hurting his daughter.

As if to underscore this, Rowdy suddenly stood,

his movements jerky and erratic. "Man, I need to fuck something. She ain't much to look at, but she'll do." He chuckled. "Maybe she'll thank me. The chubby ones are always grateful for it."

Reid froze for a fraction of a second, absorbing what was happening . . . what was about to happen. Grace Reeve's suffering was about to begin in earnest. He stepped into Rowdy's path, flattening a hand on his chest.

Rowdy glanced down at his hand and then knocked it aside, all friendliness lost. "You gonna get out of my way, man?"

Rowdy had always been a bastard when he was stoned. That much hadn't changed. "You can't have her," Reid said softly. He had seen a lot of people abused. Even before prison, but especially in there, where he'd seen grown men broken and reduced to tears. He thought about that terrified looking girl in the back room and how fragile she appeared.

He knew how Rowdy was with women. Even women that chose to be with him. He wasn't kind. He used ugly words and his fists flew with little provocation. Reid doubted that had changed while he was away. Grace Reeves wouldn't hold up well. After him, the others would take turns. An awful lump rose up in his throat. She might not survive it at all—she might not want to.

"Yeah, Reid?" Rowdy demanded. "Why not? I stuck my neck out there to take her. You weren't around, buddy. I earned it." He stabbed a finger down the hall. "She's the only chick here, and I want to fuck something."

"Not her."

"Why? You wanna bang her?" he demanded.

The question hung heavy on the air. Reid didn't shift his gaze even a fraction of an inch from Rowdy's face. Never break eye contact. Never show weakness. He felt everyone in the house watching him, waiting. Whether a roomful of men raped Grace Reeves was entirely up to him and what he did in the next few moments.

"Yeah," he finally said, accepting that it was the only thing these guys understood. As primitive as it sounded, it was about claiming. Possession. The rights of the conqueror. "Yeah, I do."

Rowdy's eyebrows arched high. "Then get in line. I go first." He moved to go around him.

Reid flattened his hand on Rowdy's chest, wondering how he ever considered this guy a friend.

Reid had been a different person all those years ago. Lost and broken himself. "I'm not taking turns," he ground out, his voice lethally soft, the same tone he used in prison, when he'd staked his claim on something and wanted everyone to know there would be no backing down. It was a warning. "She's mine."

A tight silence descended.

Rowdy inhaled, shaking his shoulders out and lifting his chest on a swell of breath. Reid recognized the move. He'd done that when they were kids, right before he was about to throw down. Reid always knew shit was about to get real when Rowdy took that breath.

He tensed, squaring himself, grounding his heels into the cracking linoleum, ready to stop him from heading down that hall.

He told himself he was doing this because he didn't want to add to his trouble. Because he didn't want to be an accessory to the rape of the president's daughter. But what was the point in lying to himself? He was already in for a life sentence. He knew, inevitably, he would end up behind bars again. He hadn't escaped Devil's Rock to stay out of prison.

He escaped to take care of some long overdue shit. No, it wasn't fear of reprisal that had him standing in Rowdy's way and stopping him from going in that bedroom. It was the simple *wrongness* of it.

He'd seen the girl. He'd read the terror in her eyes . . . *felt* it. He couldn't let any of them go back there and break her. He wasn't that indifferent. He wasn't that sadistic. And it bothered the shit out of him that his brother was. Zane didn't use to be like these guys. He had failed, Reid thought. He'd let his kid brother become this.

He glanced over at Zane, still sitting on the couch, nursing his joint like it was any other day. Like girls got raped around him all the time.

"You really want to go to the mat over this?" Rowdy challenged. "You just got back. Pretty early to already be pissing me off, ain't it?"

Reid faced him again and cocked his head. "Pissing you off has never been a big concern of mine."

He and Rowdy had been in the same grade. They'd scrapped as much as they got along. Growing up with parents that didn't give a shit about either one of them, there hadn't been much for them to do except raise hell. Especially after his grandfather died. Fight and get into trouble. That had been his life. Unfortunately, that existence was what led him to Sullivan.

Rowdy snorted. "Some things don't change, then."

He jerked his chin up. "So we gonna do this or what?"

Rowdy smiled. "C'mon, man, not like we never shared a girl before."

He suppressed a wince at the reminder and shook his head. "Not sharing."

Rowdy's smile slipped. "Now you're just being a selfish bastard."

Suddenly Zane was there, sliding between them. "Guys, go easy. It's all good. We're friends here. Remember? Family." Some of Rowdy's tension lessened. He didn't look quite so eager to pounce.

Zane looked back and forth between them before settling his gaze on Rowdy. "C'mon, bro. The guy's been in prison for years. He's got a right to be a little selfish. Let him have her."

Rowdy didn't react at first. His granite jaw remained locked. Reid was starting to think there was no avoiding it. They were going to throw down. Then Rowdy grinned.

"What the hell? It's been what . . . ten years or so? Shit, man, what have you been doing with yourself all that time?" He grimaced. "Never mind. I can imagine how you been getting off." He mock shuddered and then laughed with a shake of his head.

It took everything in him not to slam his fist into Rowdy's face. What Rowdy was thinking, what he was implying, had not happened, but it was no joke to him. He'd seen it happen to plenty of other guys at the Rock. When he closed his eyes he could still hear the grunts and cries echoing through the night. It wasn't the kind of thing one ever forgot.

He shouldered past the two of them, ignoring Rowdy's shout, "Have fun! We're gonna grill some steaks. We'll bring you one."

He held up his hand in a backward wave as he headed down the hall, eager to leave their company. Being around them made him almost long for prison. There was a rhythm there. A norm. He knew who his friends were. Who he could and couldn't trust.

It wasn't until he stepped inside the bedroom that he realized being in here alone with her presented its own form of hell.

FOUR

On HER SECOND year of college, Grace took a zoology course. She remembered the professor talking about apex predators, also known as alpha predators. They ruled at the top of the food chain. They killed and felt no guilt. The weak fell beneath them and that's just the way the world worked.

She was face-to-face with an apex predator. She knew this with surety. He stared at her for a long moment before moving forward—and that's when she noticed the knife in his hand.

That glint of a blade in his fist seemed to fit him. Everything about him smacked of danger, and she knew she would feel that way even if she wasn't crouching like prey on a bed before him, waiting to be devoured.

A tide of panic swamped her. She curled back as far as she could go on the bed, pushing into the headboard. She had nothing. No weapon of her own. Nowhere to go. No chance to run away. No chance at all. She was at his mercy. Vulnerable to him and whatever he was about to do, and it made her angry. Angry because she was always vulnerable, always subject to someone. Never free. Heat flushed through her. She twisted her wrists inside the cord binding, ignoring the pain.

Her stomach twisted sickly and a strange sense of calm descended. The kind of calm that comes with the realization that there was nothing left *to* do.

She remembered watching shows like *Dateline* and *48 Hours*, when police officers rattled grim statistics about the likelihood of survival once the victim was taken from the site of abduction. Well, she'd been taken. She'd let them take her. Hell, she'd made it relatively easy for them, and that burned her up most of all. She had become one of those grim statistics.

He stopped at the edge of the bed directly in front of her. Her gaze scanned up his denim-clad legs to his brutally handsome face, hard as granite, eyes like shards of green-shot amber stone.

After a pause, the long, lean line of him leaned over her. She flinched as his hands closed around her forearms and tugged her away from the headboard. He pulled her hands toward him. Her fingers worked on the air, groping helplessly. They'd gone numb and bloodless long ago from the tight cord at her wrists.

The blade flashed and she moaned into the rag, already imagining it cutting into her. Her mind raced. Would it be fast? Painful? God, don't let it hurt.

He tugged at the tight binding cutting into her wrists, forcing the restraints even tighter. He brought the knife down, snapping the thin cord. She looked down, certain he had cut her, too, but there was no flash of red.

Immediately the pressure eased and blood rushed back into her hands, bringing a fresh onslaught of pain.

He grabbed the rag sticking out of her mouth and held onto it, locking eyes with her. "I'm going to pull this out, but if you scream it's going back in." His gaze drilled into her. "Got it?"

She nodded and then the rag was gone. She worked her dry-as-cotton mouth and brought her hands to her jaw, gently flexing the aching muscles in her face with a whimper. She doubted she could scream if she even wanted to. Her mouth was parched as the desert.

Sudden shouts and laughter carried through the door and made her jerk. Her gaze darted in that direction, worry punching her chest, making her breath ragged. It sounded like a party was going on out there. She hoped it stayed outside and didn't find its way in here. To her.

He followed her gaze and then looked back at her. A long beat of silence crackled between them. "Take off your clothes."

"Wh-What?"

He repeated himself, speaking slowly, enunciating each word. "Take. Off. Your. Clothes."

She glanced down as if needing to reacquaint herself with the notion of clothes. She swallowed against the golf-ball-size lump in her throat. He wanted her naked? It didn't take much imagination to see where that would lead.

She flushed cold then hot and shook her head swiftly, loose hair pelting her in the face. She started to shake. Slow tremors that she couldn't control. The fear, that ultimate degradation that she had not permitted herself to even contemplate since the moment of her abduction, stared her in the face.

He leaned forward, his fists sinking into the mattress, springs creaking as he brought his nose into almost touching distance of hers. He was close. Too close, and her shaking just got worse.

"You and I are the only two people in this house

who aren't high as a kite." His breath fanned her lips as he spoke. He let that sink in for a moment. "If you want to keep them out there—" He nodded toward the door. "—and away from you, then you need to strip and get into this bed."

He was serious.

This was really happening. He was giving her a choice of sorts. Him. Or them.

Her mind raced beneath his unflinching stare. She could suffer him or deal with an unruly gang of men. She scanned him and her stomach knotted at his immense size. He could break her. And then she thought of the rest of them—rough and foul, with eyes that lit up when they hurt her. Her cheek still throbbed where that one had slapped her.

Another raucous shout went up from outside the room followed by the sound of glass breaking. She flinched and darted another glance to the door.

"That's right," he confirmed, his deep voice steady and guttural. She felt it like a touch. "They're not the most civilized boys. I had to tell them you're mine just to keep them off you."

Her gaze flew to his face. Lifting her chin, she hoped she looked a lot tougher than she felt. Inside she was shaking . . . screaming. "I'm not yours. I'm not property."

He waved a hand around the room. "Here, that's

exactly what you are. This isn't your world anymore, princess, and if you hope to survive, you
need to play by my rules and do exactly what I say."

She exhaled slowly, turning his words over in
her head. He meant to . . . help her. Could he mean
that? "And that involves me getting naked?"

He lifted one big shoulder in a shrug. "You can
keep your underwear on. If they come in here, they
won't notice that under the covers."

"How generous," she muttered.

He looked at her blankly. "It is."

Turning away, he tucked his knife back in the
pocket of his jeans. She breathed a little easier with
that out of sight. "So just to confirm, you don't
plan to . . . touch me?" She couldn't bring herself
to say rape. As though putting a name to it would
make it a possibility.

One corner of his mouth lifted in a smile that
did nothing to soften his expression. If anything
it made him look more sinister. "You're not my
type."

"Rape isn't about that." This time she had no
problem busting out with the word. She'd visited
with women's victims groups. She'd heard their
stories. She could see their faces in her mind right
now . . . their ravaged eyes.

He sobered again, staring at her as though

seeing her for the first time . . . and seeing something else, too. Something distant, visible only to him. "You're right," he agreed. "It's not. I don't get my rocks off breaking people weaker than I am. You'll just have to trust me."

Trust him? Was he kidding?

She stared at him. He looked back at her, his expression one of seeming patience.

She exhaled. "You just dabble in kidnapping, then?"

"I wasn't in on this."

"But your friends took me," she shot back. "I'm here because of them. And you're telling me to get naked. That kinda makes you complicit."

He chuckled. Reaching behind him, he grabbed the back of his collar and pulled his shirt over his head in one smooth motion. "Complicit." He shook his head. "College girls."

She could hardly process his words because his chest was all she could see. Broad, tan, and muscled, with ink crawling over one shoulder and bicep. It was an athlete's body. Or the kind of body you'd see in a Calvin Klein ad. She had never seen a man's body like *this* up close and personal before.

His hands landed at the waistband of his jeans and her gaze flew away, determined not to watch.

Heat crept up her neck to her face, burning her cheeks. She heard his jeans drop.

The bed dipped under his weight, and she sucked in a sharp breath and scrambled to the edge of the mattress, still refusing to look at the body radiating heat toward her. She felt like she was flying out of her skin.

"Easy there, princess. We just gotta make it look real."

Her eyes widened. Make it look *real*? "Wh-What does that mean?"

"Get under the covers. I would suggest you scream to make it sound legit to the guys in the next room, except you're so nervous I'm not counting on you being very convincing."

She wasn't so sure about that. She was freaked out enough that she could probably provide the soundtrack for a good old-fashioned slasher film.

He tugged at the comforter to get her to lift up. She readily obliged, hopping off the bed and backing away. His voice stopped her cold. "Nu-huh. Clothes off."

She touched the front of her badly wrinkled silk blouse, hesitating. It had been six months since a man saw her naked. And that had been a quick breast exam followed by a perfunctory pelvic exam. It hardly counted.

Charles might be her boyfriend as far as the world knew, but they had never slept together. Of course they had kissed for the benefit of the cameras. Nothing her mother would deem vulgar. Only chaste pecks. In private, however, they'd experimented, willing to give it a go since her father was so determined for them to be a couple. For all they had tried, the spark wasn't there. Making out with him was awkward. Two fourteen-year-olds fumbling together in a closet had more chemistry. Grace had put an end to it, sensing he would have gone all the way even as lackluster as they were together. And how humiliating was that? Charles would suffer sex with her.

No, Nathan from college had been the last real boyfriend to see her naked. They'd dated before her father took office. They broke up when he started grad school and she moved to DC at her parents' behest. Three years since Nathan. Since sex. And that had only ever been in the dark of her dorm room. Whenever Nathan attempted to turn on the lights she'd flipped them back off, too self-conscious.

She toyed with a button on her blouse. *Just pretend he's old Dr. Mattheson,* she told herself.

"C'mon." He sounded impatient. "It's the only way."

She looked at him then. Yeah, he so wasn't Dr. Mattheson. She carefully trained her gaze waist up. *Not going to look down there.* God, he might read that as interest. "You won't hurt me." Even though she phrased it as a statement, a question hung in her voice . . . a plea, and she hated that. Hated that begging for her safety was something necessary. How had this become her life? "What's your name?" she asked, hoping to reach him, to connect in some way.

He held her gaze, a muscle feathering across his clenched jaw. She refused to break eye contact and look away this time. Grace waited for him to say it. Needed to hear him say it.

"Doesn't matter."

She wet her lips. "I'm Grace Reeves."

A corner of his mouth kicked up as he slid between the covers. "Yeah. I know." Thankfully, the covers were now draped over him from the waist down.

"Of course." She shifted uneasily on her feet. The rough voices of the men carried from the other room. As he said, it was either trust him or put herself at *their* mercy. She felt her lip curl at that prospect. She already knew what they were like.

The naked man in the bed she had occupied only

moments before nodded toward the door. "Why don't you turn off the light and get into bed?" A question and not a question. A well-toned arm patted the space beside him like he wasn't asking anything out of the ordinary. "It's a big bed. We won't even touch."

She didn't budge. She doubted a bolt of thunder at her feet could get her to move.

He sighed. "My name is Reid."

It was something at least. A name. "Reid . . ." She said his name carefully, moistening her lips. ". . . promise me you won't—"

"I'll keep you safe, Grace Reeves." The swiftly uttered words crossed the space between them and wrapped around her like a double-lined fleece blanket. The words did their part and provided solace, but it was also his eyes. Steady and true. The guy could be in politics. If he wasn't a dangerous criminal. If he wasn't built like an MMA fighter and sporting tattoos and scarred knuckles. He had that mesmerizing quality that compelled trust. *And he was hot. Magic Mike hot.*

She gave herself a quick mental kick. Exhaling, she told herself that had nothing to do with it. Nodding, she moved to flip off the light. In the dark, she undressed with shaking hands, leaving her underwear on. Her clothes dropped, whispery sounds in the dark. The chilly air rolled over her skin, leaving a wash of goose bumps in its wake.

She walked barefoot across the room, rubbing at her tender wrists. She sank down on the mattress beside him, wincing at the squeak of the springs—beside *Reid*—and pulled the cool sheet up to her chest, tucking the fabric under her arms. Scooting to the far edge of the bed, she hoped that she wasn't wrong. She prayed he meant what he had said.

FIVE

It took all of five seconds to realize he might have been lying when he said she wasn't his type. He had gone a long time without sex and right now *female* was pretty much his type. *Young* female, even better—or in this case, worse. A female that smelled soapy clean and faintly floral and he was screwed.

He kept to his side of the bed, rigid as a slat of board, inhaling deep even breaths as he battled for self-control. He'd mastered the art of self-control in prison . . . for keeping his composure when everyone else went bat-shit crazy around him. This shouldn't be so hard. *He* shouldn't be so hard.

He wouldn't hurt her. He wasn't *that* guy. He wouldn't become that thing she was so afraid of. He wouldn't become one of *them* outside this room. He'd spent years fighting to stay human inside a cage and wouldn't turn into an animal now that he was on the outside. For however long he had until he was caught—and he fully expected that to happen eventually—he would cling to his code.

The smell of sizzling meat drifted to his nose, mingling with her floral scent. Apparently they were cooking. Just like it was an ordinary day with the president's daughter captive in the next room. His eyes adjusted to the darkness, fixing on Grace's features as she lay beside him.

He had to admit there was something about First Daughter Grace Reeves. Her big brown eyes appeared soft and intelligent. Even with fear lurking in the honeyed depths, those eyes were sharp, quick. Fear didn't slow down the wheels turning in her head. She saw too much. She saw he was different from the rest of them. Granted, maybe he wanted her to see that. Maybe he needed her to. And not for her sake, but for his. He had to believe he was not like them. If prison hadn't made him into one of them, it wouldn't happen now. One female wasn't going to snap his self-control and break loose a part of him that he had spent his whole life battling.

He wasn't like his addict mother. He wasn't like his deadbeat dad, who had floated in and out of his life, showing up to sleep with his mom, steal her drug money, and then take off again—only to repeat the cycle six months later. He wasn't weak like Zane either.

Grace shifted. Her soft sigh filled up the small space between them.

Thankfully, it was dark. Thankfully, he hadn't seen her naked. Not that it stopped him from imagining the small curvy body he had earlier assessed at a glance.

He jammed his eyes shut against the darkness as if that would rid of him of the thoughts. It was a struggle. She had a body that reminded him of a pinup girl from the forties. His grandfather had one of those vintage posters in his shed. Reid spent hours gazing at it as his grandfather worked on his old truck. His adolescent self had been mesmerized by the girl in the tiny sailor suit, her juicy, gartered thighs on display, all that creamy skin as tempting as a ripe peach in the summer, begging for the bite of his teeth. She shifted again, the mattress squeaking slightly. "You should try to sleep," he said, his voice coming out much too thick.

"What's going to happen to me?"

"I'll try to get you out of this."

"You said you would keep me safe," she accused.

He sighed and dropped his arm over his forehead, cutting off his vision, reducing his world to darkness. Yeah, he'd made that promise. Stupid. It was a promise he had no right to make. Sullivan was behind this, and he knew firsthand the power that SOB wielded. Not to mention he wanted his pound of flesh and intended to take it out of Grace Reeves. Sullivan was a sociopath. He wouldn't back down. "You're in a fine mess here, Grace Reeves."

"So you lied to me?" She scooted another half inch away, as if repelled by the possibility.

"I'll do my best, but I don't have any pull here. I'm not really one of them. Not anymore . . ."

"What does that even mean? You're here with them."

She would look at it that way. After all, the others had trusted him enough to let him "have" her. He'd told her that himself. Distrust crept back into the set of her shoulders. She thought he was lying. Or just blowing smoke. Either way, it was probably good for her overall chances of survival. As long as she was afraid of him, she wouldn't drop her guard.

He lifted his arm from his forehead as she rolled onto her back and turned her face toward him. "Can you help me?" she asked, her voice stronger, imploring him. "Can you get me out of here? Maybe when they all fall asleep we can sneak out?"

Of course she would ask him that. She wasn't

stupid. He'd promised to keep her safe. But if he did that for her, his credibility would be shot to shit with these guys. He'd never get close enough to Sullivan then, and doing that—getting to the bastard, making him pay—was the only thing driving him. It was the only thing that mattered.

Her voice softened into something that reminded him of the whipped cream his grandmother used to dollop on top of pie. It was one of those rare sweet memories. "I . . . I can make it worth your while."

"That so?"

"Yes. Get me out of here, and I'll see that you're rewarded."

His mind took a dive into the gutter, imagining a reward he was positive she hadn't intended when she made the offer. No, she was probably thinking money or a pass from prosecution. She didn't know that he was serving a life sentence. There was no pass from that.

"Get some sleep," he said gruffly.

It wasn't what she wanted to hear. She wanted him to guarantee her freedom. He felt her rattled sigh as much as he heard it. He'd disappointed her, and that made something twist inside him. He hated that she was here. He hated that she was afraid and that he couldn't help her.

But that was just the way it had to be.

He settled his weight into the bed and closed his eyes. He would think better after a night's sleep. Maybe then he could wade through the complicated web of saving her while simultaneously bringing down Sullivan. Moments ticked by. He was exhausted, but he couldn't sleep. For eleven years he had slept alone, and now there was a woman next to him in a bed. A warm-bodied woman with curves and breasts that would overflow in his hands. A groan built up in his chest. This was going to be a very long night.

Suddenly, the door burst open and light flooded the room. *Christ.* He jackhammered upright, yanking her partially beneath him and glaring at the unwanted arrivals. He was half expecting it. It was the reason, after all, that he'd told her to strip off her clothes. But it didn't curtail the rage flooding his veins.

His brother entered, bearing a plate of steaming food. Rowdy propped a shoulder on the doorjamb, munching on an ice cream sandwich, his feral gaze landing on them in the bed. She trembled underneath Reid. Convenient, he supposed. Not that he enjoyed her trembling in fear, but she needed to look traumatized.

"Get the fuck out," Reid growled, his arms braced around Grace, shielding her while also trying to make it look like Zane and Rowdy had interrupted them. Again he was glad that he'd made her get undressed and into bed with him. If Zane didn't think he was fucking her, he'd give her to Rowdy, no question about it.

Zane lifted the plate a bit. "Thought you might be hungry."

"Out," he repeated.

"Told you he wouldn't be interested in food right now," Rowdy chimed in, stepping closer and peering at Grace. "How was she?" he asked mildly. "Looks like she's got a decent rack."

Grace whimpered and burrowed deeper into the bed, still shaking. What's worse, Rowdy's words only made Reid all too aware of her naked breasts mashed into his chest. The twin points of her nipples burned into him. Heat clawed through him.

Zane shrugged. "Figured you might be done and ready to eat something."

Rowdy chuckled. "After all that time in the joint, he might be more than a two-pump-chump like you, man."

Grace shuddered violently beneath him, and he glanced down at her, hoping to reassure her somehow with a look. Then the sight of her hit him like a Mack Truck. He was seeing her close up now, with the lights on. Her dark hair fanned out all around her. Even his propped arms were resting in the silken nest.

The olive skin. Liquid brown eyes and curling lashes. The tiny mole at the corner of her left eye. She wasn't beautiful, but there was something about her. Something as fresh and untouched and delicate as a rose after a storm. It was something that made his stomach twist into knots. She was innocent. She clearly didn't belong in this place, with these men, with *him*.

He shook his head and blinked, killing the weak thoughts and letting in far more destructive ideas. "I'm not done," he muttered to the intruders, and then all he could think about was how a girl like this would require a lot of time and attention. He'd devote long hours to her, starting with that lush mouth. The things he would do to that mouth . . .

Her eyes flared wide at his voice, his words. Apparently, he sounded convincing.

"'Course not." Rowdy laughed roughly. "After all those years in prison, we probably won't see you for a week. C'mon, Zane."

He couldn't tear his gaze off her. She stiffened under him, and he couldn't help himself. He conducted a slow perusal, looking down her throat and shoulders. She had a smooth, unblemished complexion. His gaze feasted on all of it, watching as red splotches broke out across her olive skin. He wanted to see more.

He continued looking, taking in the top swells of her breasts pressing into his bare chest. His breath quickened, lifting his chest away for half a second before coming back down against her breasts. Again and again. He reveled in it—in the sensation of nipples he couldn't see pebbling hard against his skin.

"Here you go, bro." Something hit the end of the bed with a small thud, reminding him that they weren't alone. "Don't go making any babies. Suit up."

The pulse in his ears rushed to a roar at the thought of that. Not about making babies . . . but sinking into the warm body under him.

Christ.

This wasn't some willing female. He needed to get that sick thought out of his head. This wasn't what he was. He hadn't escaped prison to scratch an eleven-year itch with a willing woman, much less an unwilling one.

His pulse beat a tempo inside his ears. He heard the door shut as though from someplace far away. Still, he could not move. He was strung so tight, a wire on the verge of snapping, everything twisting.

Beads of sweat broke out on his forehead as he battled for control.

"They're gone," she whispered. Her tongue darted out to wet her lips. He tracked the movement of that tongue, something molten-hot curling through him at the sight of it. The last time he'd held a female in his arms, he hadn't known anything. He was just a kid, barely out of high school. He took fucking for granted. At twenty, he certainly hadn't thought to absorb the fact that Monica and Gaby, the sisters who lived in his trailer park—or the occasional party hookups—would be his last taste of intimacy.

"They didn't turn the lights off," she added into the stretch of hovering silence.

He found his voice, shoving thoughts of how, if he had the chance, he would take his time and savor every moment of having a woman in his arms. *A woman like her.* "I know."

Her eyes were russet, a brown several shades lighter than the long blue-black hair twisting all around her.

The lights were still on, and that was the problem. He could see her. Feel her. He exhaled thinly through his nose, commanding himself to roll off her. Disengage.

"Reid?"

The sound of his name jolted him. Maybe it was the gentle sound of her voice, so cultured and well-enunciated.

Or maybe it was just *her* saying his name.

He couldn't do this. He *shouldn't* be doing this . . . shouldn't enjoy the feel of her so much that hot need started to gather and pull at the base of his spine. He just came from a place that demanded he feed those needs. Take. *Claim.* That was the order of things in prison. He couldn't do that, though. Not with her. Not like this.

He launched himself off her, sending the box of condoms his brother left him tumbling to the floor. With a curse, he crossed the room.

Her gasp told him she was watching him walk away and not missing the fact that he wasn't wearing a stitch of clothing.

He flipped off the light, instantly drowning them in darkness again. For a moment he stood motionless, bowing his head, his fingers still on the switch. His cock jutted out hard and aching, hungry for action and not in agreement with his thoughts. He resisted the urge to take hold of his dick in the dark and give it a deep stroke. That wouldn't help. It would only increase his torment, because there would be no release.

Lifting his head, he inhaled and forced nonsexy thoughts into his head, He imagined roadkill and what flesh-eating bacteria could do to a body.

"They won't bother us again tonight," he murmured, his voice thick.

He said the words to reassure her, but they rang almost ominously on the air. When he made his way to the bed and settled on the mattress, it was to find that she had scooted to the edge, as far away from him as possible. Smart girl. With her scent tangled around him and the memory of her skin against his, his erection showed no signs of waning.

It was going to be a long night.

SIX

Grace woke to darkness.

Everything felt wrong. The feel of the bed; the quiet sounds and smells. The air felt different on her skin, heavy and vaporous as fog. She felt disconnected. Almost like she was inside someone else's body. As though it wasn't her lying there, but another person.

There was a prolonged moment of confusion as her mind floundered, trying to grasp where she was.

She was chest down, her cheek pressed flat into a mattress, her breath a persistent scratch against a wall of cotton. She flexed her fingers, feathering the tips, verifying the bed under her. She shifted, stretching her torso, a little startled at the sensation of sheets against her bare skin, rasping her breasts and pebbling her nipples awake.

A warm weight covered her hip. She shifted again, testing its pressure, too uncertain to reach out and touch it for herself.

Then it moved. Fingers. A hand. She wasn't alone in the bed.

Everything flooded back in a blazing rush. Her stomach bottomed out.

She'd been abducted and was in bed with one of her kidnappers. *Reid*. The good-looking one who claimed he would keep her safe. Good-looking. *Ha*. That was a tame description for him. He looked like he'd stepped right out of *Sons of Anarchy*. She watched the television series in hotel rooms and on the plane, escaping the grinding routine of events and functions Holly dragged her to one after another.

It was dangerous thinking. Comparing him to a hot actor on a television show. He was real. And dangerous. She didn't need to confuse him with some fictional character. He might be sexy, but he didn't possess some hidden code of honor. If he were truly good, he would get her out of this awful place—or at least promise that he would help her escape. None of those reassurances were forthcoming. He'd rather vaguely said he would keep her safe, but she was still here. How safe could she be?

His voice rolled across the space between them

and hit the back of her neck like tendrils of hot smoke. "How long are you going to pretend to be asleep?"

She exhaled and rolled flat on her back, accepting that she couldn't feign unconsciousness. He could probably hear the pounding drum of her heart.

He didn't move his hand. It stayed on her hip.

"What time is it?" she whispered.

"Close to dawn." His hand felt like a searing brand even without exerting any pressure.

"What's going to happen now?" Her voice was a scratchy whisper in the darkness. It sounded like another woman speaking . . . someone afraid and broken. That wasn't her. She wasn't beaten.

"I'll come up with something."

"That doesn't sound very . . . heartening." It would be daylight soon and then she would have to face those other men again. Nothing good could come of that. The promise of pain twisted their lips and lighted their eyes. She needed to get out of here.

"Heartening," he echoed.

"Yes, it means—"

"I know what it means," he replied flatly. "I love the way you talk, college girl." Only he didn't sound like he *loved* it.

She shivered slightly. His hand started to pull away and before she knew what she was doing she leaned in, closer, as though chasing that touch. A moth hunting flame. She stopped, catching herself. Her mind worked, trying to rationalize her actions. It had to be natural. This seeking of comfort when she was in such an unsafe, tenuous situation.

He paused. She realized then that it might appear that she wanted his touch.

And then it occurred to her that maybe she did. Or maybe she *should*.

If she was trying to win him over and make certain she lived through this, maybe being nice and allowing him certain liberties in order to survive wouldn't be the worst thing in the world? Bottom line, this was about survival. Sometimes dire actions needed to happen in order to guarantee that. Sometimes sacrifices had to be made for survival.

After a moment's hesitation, he inched back in again, splaying his hand over her hip, his blunt-tipped fingers spreading wide, pressing into a stomach she had long bemoaned as not nearly flat enough. She forgot about that, though. His touch sparked her skin. All self-consciousness fled as a warm fire licked though her.

Her breath hitched. *This was okay.* If she experienced a little pleasure in submitting to him, that was better than flinching in revulsion or terror. At least that's what she told herself. Those were the desperate words that wove like a serpent through her mind as her stomach heaved with nausea at his closeness, at his breath against her neck, his touch on her bare skin . . .

The mattress creaked slightly as he propped up on an elbow over her. Her chest squeezed. Even in the darkness she felt the size of him, the muscled breadth hovering over her like a great shadow.

His fingers flexed against her skin, the pads of his fingers rough, palms callused. They felt nothing like Charles's smooth hands, which she had held innumerable times for the well-calculated photo op.

"This okay?" His deep voice rumbled on the air, as dark as the ink of night all around them. Those two simple words were a gravelly utterance. Only two words and yet she could hardly make sense of them in her spinning head.

Now was the time. If she didn't want to go through with this, she needed to speak up. She needed to find her voice and say: *No, stop, don't.*

A whisper scudded across her mind. *It's the only way. He's the only way.*

She needed to play nice. "Yes," she breathed.

His hand shifted, fingers sliding over her panties, arrowing down the V of her crotch with honed precision.

Her breath quickened. She flung her hands up by her ears and grabbed fistfuls of sheet. They weren't even skin-to-skin, but his hand brushing against her panties burned her up.

He cupped her then, his hand molded to her sex, fingers pressing into her seam.

"I can feel your heartbeat," he murmured, his voice like smoke near her ear. "Your pulse. It's racing."

Oh God. Her legs parted slightly, the muscles too lax to support their weight. His hand dipped deeper between her legs, never slipping under the cotton fabric but exerting enough pressure to make her traitor sex clench and throb.

He started rubbing, creating friction that heated her core and spread outward, singeing every nerve. Her face burned at the sudden moisture rushing between her legs, dampening the crotch of her panties. He must feel that. He must know. Hot humiliation lashed her face. *OhGodOhGodOhGod*.

She shouldn't enjoy this so much. She was awful. Wanton and depraved.

She whimpered, her hips moving of their own accord, pumping in rhythm to his stroking. She bit her lip and arched, forgetting everything except how good he was making her feel between her legs.

He brought his face close to hers, his jaw scratching her cheek as his lips moved against her ear. "Is that for me, princess?"

She stilled. His voice . . . those words, washed through her in a bitter trail. *No.* This was wrong. She was *not* actually turned on. She was just faking it, pretending to go along for her survival. She wouldn't enjoy this. She. Would. *Not.*

His hand stilled and she blinked up at those eyes glowing down at her. "You want this, Grace?" There was something in his voice, a strange heavy quality to the question, but she was too far gone to make sense of it.

"Y-Yes," she answered, still telling herself she wanted this because it was the smart thing. Not because she wanted *wanted* it. She wasn't *that* depraved. In all her fantasies (yes, she had her share), getting kidnapped and seduced by her abductor was not one of them.

He didn't speak. Didn't move. Just continued to stare down at her with his hand covering her throbbing sex. She felt him like a brand there, hot and possessive, and she resisted the urge to writhe against him.

He gently squeezed her sex, brushing a finger along her seam, so close but not quite hitting that spot. "You offering me this?" Again there was a strange gruffness to his voice.

She tried to speak but choked out a strangled sound. She nodded as much as she could manage.

"You think you need to use this as a bargaining chip, Grace?" The question was biting. He didn't wait for her answer. "Well, you can keep it." He pulled his hand away and clambered off her. "I told you I'd keep you safe. You don't need to bribe me with a fuck."

She flinched. He shrugged into his clothes, leaving her gasping on the bed, her body humming and aching, unfulfilled. Shame washed over her. She'd watched plenty of Lifetime movies in a lonely hotel room. It was too soon for Stockholm syndrome to kick in, so there was no excuse for her reaction. There should only be terror. She shouldn't feel this aroused.

She sat up on the bed and buried her face in her hands, pretty certain this was what rock bottom looked like.

SHE WAS HOTTER than fire.

He never would have thought such a thing possible. He never thought anything about her exceptional the few times he'd seen her on the TV. She'd just been . . . wallpaper.

But he'd seen the fire tonight. He *felt* it.

And he wanted to dive straight into those flames and finish where he left off. He blamed it on his years in prison. Eleven years in a cage. Eleven years without a woman. That would cloud any man's judgment.

He snatched up his clothes. With a muttered curse, he struggled into them, less than graceful. He turned for the door, but halfway there her soft voice stopped him.

"Reid?"

She said his name as though testing it . . . testing herself maybe.

With a sigh, he peered through the gloom of the room. He could see she was sitting up in bed now. He inhaled a ragged breath. He had no doubt he could do every filthy thing his long-denied body craved. She'd let him. As though she had no choice. A sick little feeling wormed through him.

Maybe she would even enjoy it, but she would still count it as a necessary sacrifice. She'd still hate that it happened . . . and later hate him for it.

Silence stretched between them until he finally

answered. "Stay in the room if you know what's good for you."

He wasn't sure that she did know what was good for her. She let him put his hands on her, after all. Somehow, in her mind, she had thought that was a good idea. That such a thing might work out to her benefit.

She didn't know who . . . *what* she was dealing with. She had no clue.

With another foul curse, he yanked open the door and stepped out into the hall. Shutting the door behind him, he stood there for a moment, breathing in and out of his nose until he felt a measure of calm. Until his raging erection subsided.

Satisfied, he advanced into the kitchen and living room area. Bodies were strewn everywhere, passed out in positions that didn't look comfortable. One guy near the door was sleeping beside a pool of vomit that was already stinking up the room. They would all be hurting when they woke up. That is, until they drowned their aches in booze and drugs again.

Not everyone was asleep, however. His brother sat at the kitchen table nursing a longneck, with Rowdy sitting across from him. Dirty dishes littered the table, and Rowdy picked at the scraps, stabbing at various bits of food with the end of his knife.

Zane's eyes lighted on him. "Up early, bro."

Rowdy leered. "Have you even slept? Figure you put her to good use. Still not up for sharing?"

Everything inside him tensed, but he trained his face into a neutral expression. "Sorry. Not quite done with her."

Zane grinned, momentarily looking like the boy Reid remembered. "Well, you might want to go back in there and get her out of your system. We got plans for her."

"What would those be?" he asked, trying to sound casual. The food they had cooked earlier sat out on the counter. Rather than eat anything that had spoiled hours ago, he reached for a bag of potato chips.

"Sullivan wants us to keep her alive for a while and make her suffer. Really stick it to Reeves, you know?"

Reid bit into a chip, struggling to show no reaction to this information.

"I think we need to move her," Zane said. "Too many people know about this place and come in and out of here for business." He gestured around them. Business as in drug deals. "FBI, local law enforcement . . . Texas Rangers. They're crawling everywhere."

"We should just hurry it up and get rid of her," Rowdy supplied. "Been saying it from the start. Sullivan wants her dead in the end. We should just do it and be done with her."

Reid stopped chewing for a moment. It was the only outward sign he gave that Rowdy's words affected him. He knew his brother. He knew these men. At least he thought he did. He'd known them eleven years ago. Granted, a lot could change over the years—he certainly had—but he never thought they were killers. He never thought his brother could become that.

"I told you," Zane grumbled, as though he could read Reid's mind, "I ain't a woman killer."

That was good to hear. He knew what kind of man Sullivan was. He was without a code. Nothing was off-limits for him. But Reid had thought his brother was better than that. Their grandfather had been a good man. Reid had thought they spent enough time with him for some of his goodness to rub off on Zane.

Rowdy kicked his boots up on the seat of a neighboring chair. "Man, you need to grow up. What did you think was going to happen? You were standing right next to me when Sullivan said what he wanted done to her. Besides, she's seen all of our faces. We just gonna hand her back at the end of this and call it good?"

Reid already had that same thought. They weren't acting like men who were trying to protect their identities around her.

Zane gave a reluctant nod and scratched his scraggly attempt at a beard.

Rowdy cracked open a jar of queso and swirled his finger inside the orange goop. Sucking his finger clean, he looked at Reid. "If you want another go at her, you better hurry up, man. Looks like I'll have to do it. Zane has never had the stomach for this."

Reid knew Rowdy wouldn't blink over ending her life, especially if that's what Sullivan wanted. That guy always followed Sullivan's dictates. For all that, it felt like he had swallowed a box of rocks. Reid kept munching on chips, clinging to his poker face and acting like this didn't touch him.

His mind raced, groping, searching for something to say to knock Rowdy off this path. "She's the president's daughter. You really want to off her? That'll get you the chair."

Rowdy's lips curled. "I'm not scared."

His brother went pale. "I don't know. I'm having second thoughts, man."

"There ain't no going back now. Might as well go rough her up like Sullivan wanted." Rowdy started forward.

Reid's hand shot out to push on his chest, stopping him. "He wanted her abused for days. If her body turns up later today, he'll know you didn't listen to him."

"What do you suggest?" Rowdy demanded, thrusting his chin out at a belligerent angle.

"Take her someplace else . . . go to ground with her. Head west." Reid nodded at his brother. "Our grandfather had that house in the mountains. Use it," he suggested, still trying to act like he didn't care that much. Right now his goal was simple: delay them from killing her.

Rowdy glanced around the house, his gaze pausing on the guy near the door snoring beside his own vomit. "Guess we could send Mike off with her."

Thankfully, his brother snorted at that proposition. "Mike? He can hardly take care of himself. Even with a map he probably couldn't find the place."

The two of them started debating who should go, who should take the First Daughter out west. To the middle of nowhere. Isolated from the world. Which dangerous, drugged-out criminal among them would be alone with her and have her totally at his mercy?

A bitter taste coated his mouth. The promise he'd made to Grace ran over and over in his head as he stood there holding a bag of chips in his hands. Before he could even think about what he was saying, he heard himself speak. "I'll do it. I'll take her."

SEVEN

GRACE DIDN'T WAIT for daylight to get dressed again in her badly wrinkled clothes. Dressed, she sat on the edge of the bed, hands clutching her knees as she stared at the closed door, and tried not to jump at every sound that came close to the door barring her from a room full of criminals. Her knees bounced anxiously until darkness faded. She wondered what was going to happen to her. Wondered if the Secret Service were closing in even now. Wondered what her parents thought had happened to her. Holly must be out of her mind. Even Charles had to be concerned. Their relationship might lack sparks, but she knew he cared about her.

By the time daylight arrived, her nerves were drawn tight, imagining every worst-case scenario that might happen. The worst was Reid leaving, abandoning her among these men.

Tired of sitting, she paced the small space, stopping several times to attempt to open the wedged-tight window. Each time she failed and she cursed the lack of hours she'd spent in the gym, pumping weights so she could be stronger.

She examined every corner of the room, opening the closet and exploring every drawer, thinking she might find something she could use as a weapon. She listened at the door and walls as voices rumbled from somewhere in the house. The words were impossible to identify. She was near the door when she heard footsteps, and she scurried backwards, fortifying herself with a deep breath for whatever was about to happen.

The door opened and Reid stepped across the threshold, shutting the door behind him. As much as the sight of him discomfited her it relieved her, too. He was the lesser evil.

With the morning light streaming through the window, she was forced to confront his good looks again. Not that she had forgotten. Nor had she forgotten her shameful reaction to him in that bed. Two facts that only made her more uncomfortable.

She stood in the center of the room, well away from that bed. Humiliation washed over her as his hazel eyes raked her. His expression revealed nothing but she knew he had to be thinking about what they did, what she let him do, what she had *encouraged* him to do. She'd told herself to submit so she could win his favor. She'd told herself that was the only reason. And then he had touched her and she came out of her skin and forgot everything logical and right and *sane*.

In that moment, she forgot why she'd told herself it was okay to fool around with one of her abductors. She forgot because the only thing that mattered were his hands on her and the throb between her thighs. *God*. She was all kinds of messed up.

Thankfully, that was behind her now. Sanity had returned.

She hugged herself, chafing her hands up and down her arms. Lifting her chin, she asked, "Are you getting me out of here?"

A corner of his mouth kicked up for the barest moment before disappearing and flattening into a hard line again. "That's not what I promised you."

"That's exactly what you promised," she said in affront—as though his lying somehow shocked her and was the final indignity. "You promised to keep me safe."

"I did. You're safe for the moment."

"For the moment?" she flung back at him, the volume of her voice climbing. Again, not super heartening. "The best way to *keep* me safe would be to get me out of here. Like you promised!"

He glanced over his shoulder as though expecting someone to be standing there. Seeing nothing (or no one), he stepped closer, his voice a sandpaper growl. "Do me a favor, princess. Do us both a favor. Quit saying I promised to keep you safe if in fact you want that to be a reality." He let those words hang between them.

As his meaning sank in, she looked over his shoulder to the shut door. Understanding dawned. He was concerned with the men outside this room, too. He couldn't control them. For the time being, they were tethered animals. If they should become free—if they decided to direct their savagery on her—there was nothing he could do.

It was a grim, sobering thought.

They definitely didn't need to hear her shouting that he had promised to keep her safe.

Pressing her lips together, she nodded jerkily. "I understand," she said, her voice much more subdued.

"Here's what we're going to do," he said as he moved to one of the dressers she had examined earlier and started rifling through it. She braced herself, trying to control the sudden surge of satisfaction at his use of "we." She couldn't help it. It lessened her fear. Made her feel not quite so alone in this nightmare. It made her feel like she had a friend. An ally.

He pulled out some T-shirts and jeans, holding them up as though verifying whether they would fit him well enough. He was a big guy. She didn't imagine he could wear the clothes of the guys in the other room. He was apparently satisfied with what he found, however. He moved to the closet, pulled out a duffel bag and dropped it on the bed.

"I'm getting you out of here," he announced as he started stuffing clothing into the bag. "We're going to leave—" At her relieved expression, he stopped and held up a finger in warning. "Try not to look so excited. You're supposed to be afraid of me, remember? When I haul you out of this room, you better look terrified."

She nodded. "Who says I'm not?"

He smiled then, slowly, mocking. To her mortification, she knew he was remembering last night and just how very unafraid of him she had been in that bed. "Sure you are." He slung the bag over his shoulder and snatched up the cord from yesterday. "Hold out your hands."

She hesitated, shaking her head slowly from side

to side as he approached her. She didn't want to be restrained again. Her wrists were still sore from the last time. "I don't want—"

"Come on. Thought you were going to trust me. I can't have you skipping behind me like we're suddenly friends. You need to be tied up again."

He made sense, but that didn't make her feel any better. In fact, it made her feel sick.

His stare fixed on her face, unwavering in its intensity.

"All right," she agreed, holding herself still as he looped the cord around her neck and then her outstretched hands. He wrapped the cord several times around her wrists in a figure eight until it was so snug she couldn't freely move her hands. He left a long stretch of cord dangling. She had to know what he was going to do with it before he even picked up the end, but that didn't stop her flush of shame as he took that end in his hand and led her like a dog.

He opened the door, but before walking out, cast her a look full of silent warning, and something else. Something that made the back of her nape prickle, something that made her wonder if he really was the lesser evil.

Turning back around, he stepped into the hall. She sucked in a deep breath and followed him out.

MORE GUYS WERE awake and stirring when he emerged from the back of the house with Grace Reeves. He schooled his features into that mask he always wore. The hard look that warned no one to fuck with him. That was more important than ever here. Now. His ability to walk out with her was at stake. *She* was at stake.

He sent her a quick glance. The stench in the room was so foul that she brought her bound hands up to cover her nose. Yeah, her nose probably only ever smelled roses and fancy soaps. This place wasn't for her. These men shouldn't even be in her radius. He shouldn't be either, and yet here he was, leading her around by a leash. He felt like the biggest bastard, which in all the years of his life was saying something.

"Lookee there." A guy he didn't know stepped alongside her and picked up a thick lock of her flowing hair, rubbing the dark, matted strands between his grimy fingers. A growl rumbled up from his chest.

It took everything in him not to lunge at the jackhole. Break him. He resisted, knowing that would raise more than a few eyebrows. He shouldn't care so much about one female.

"She looks well-used."

The words lit something feral inside him.

Grace's mouth curled in a grimace and she knocked the guy's hand away with her bound hands, those brown eyes sparking fire. The guy scowled and made a move toward her, his hand raised as though he was going to strike her.

Reid snapped. He moved quickly, yanking her behind him with a sharp tug. He didn't care how it looked. Then he grabbed the guy's hand and brought it down with a severe twist. The guy howled.

Reid kept twisting, placing his mouth close to his ear. "I don't know who the fuck you are, but you don't touch what doesn't belong to you."

"What? You tapped her and now she's yours?" he blustered, his face flushed with pain.

"Pete!" Zane shoved him in the shoulder, freeing him from Reid. "Go sit down. This don't concern you."

Pete staggered away, clutching his injured hand close to his chest, his gaze shooting daggers.

Zane looked at Reid, glanced at Grace, and then looked back at Reid. It was a familiar look. His face might have hardened and matured beyond boyhood, but with his brows drawn tight with concern, he was achingly familiar, even if Reid hadn't seen him or the worried expression in years. He remembered his brother's young face as he crouched in the corner, watching wide-eyed as Reid took a beating he thought would kill him for sure. Reid used to think he would die. He used to wonder if maybe he didn't want to. One more blow, one more of his father's raised fists, and he'd break, shatter in half. Thankfully, his father only blew in and out of his life sporadically. If that had been their lives day after day, he might not have made it.

"You got this?" Zane asked.

"Yeah. I'm taking care of it. Taking care of her. Like I said." Reid shook his head with what he hoped sounded like a casual huff of breath. "Some of your boys need to learn a little respect."

"Man, they don't know you, bro, that's all. You been gone a long time."

Yeah, and he didn't *want* to know them. His brother's crew had taken a hard nosedive since he'd last seen them, years ago. They'd always been rough, but this was a new low.

He felt another stare on him. Deep and scouring. He looked up and his gaze collided with Rowdy's, from where he sat at the kitchen table. The guy jerked his chin upward in a single nod of acknowledgment.

Zane slapped a phone and wad of cash into Reid's hand. "Here's a burner and some money. I'll be in touch after I talk to Sullivan again."

Reid tore his gaze away from Rowdy. "You do that. I want to talk to Sullivan. Get me a meeting." The man kept himself as guarded as the pope. Reid knew he couldn't just go after him. Surrounded by bodyguards, they'd stop him before he could even get within fifty yards. Reid wanted—*needed*—to look the man in the eyes. He'd only have one chance, and he couldn't mess it up.

"Yeah yeah. I'll tell him." His brother clapped him on the back. "I'll let him know. What you're doing now will go a long way with the ol' man." Zane hesitated, looking concerned. "You up for this?" He nodded toward Grace. "You were never one to rough up the girls."

Reid ignored the stab of guilt at deceiving his brother. Zane was lost to him. He wasn't his same kid brother anymore. He served Sullivan now. Reid held Zane's gaze. "Prison changes a man. I'm back. Sullivan wants this done, then I'll get it done."

"Yeah?" Rowdy released a harsh bark. "For how long? You're a wanted man. An escaped convict. How long you expect to be around? You can't just slide back in here and be one of Sullivan's top men again."

"Why not? Afraid I'll make you look bad, Rowdy?"

Rowdy's smile slipped. Even Zane looked uneasy.

Rowdy uncrossed his booted feet from where they rested atop the table and dropped them heavily to the floor. He propped his elbows on his knees, his deep accent more pronounced as he said, "I ain't afraid of shit. Least of all you."

Reid shrugged and moved to the door, still holding onto Grace Reeves by a fucking leash and hating himself for it. But then that was just more reason to hate himself. The list was long.

He opened the door and guided her through it. Pausing, he looked back into the house. "I'm here now. Getting things done. Tying up your loose strings." That jab hit the mark.

He jerked his head toward Grace, waiting on the porch. "Get me in with Sullivan." He looked back and forth between Rowdy and his brother, hoping he conveyed his seriousness—a seriousness that would be expressed to Sullivan.

He needed that meeting. He needed to get face-to-face with the man. After that, he didn't care what happened. It would be over. It would finally be over after all these years.

Reid stepped out onto the porch and his brother followed.

"No worries," Zane said. "We'll have you back on top like you used to be." At the edge of the porch, his brother clapped him on the back. "It's good to have you with us again. I know it didn't end well . . ." His voice faded and he looked decidedly uncomfortable. Yeah, talking about how Sullivan fucked him over wasn't an easy topic, especially considering Zane now worked for the asshole like none of that mattered.

"Yeah. It didn't end well." Reid nodded and tried to keep the bite out of his voice. He had to appear different. Like one of them. "I went to prison."

"Well, this was how it was supposed to be." Zane forced a smile and clarified, "How it was always meant to be."

Reid only hoped Sullivan felt the same way and forgot how pissed off he'd been when he went to prison. At his sentence hearing, he might have flipped a table, cursed Sullivan and accused the judge of being in his pocket. Hopefully, Sullivan thought he had put that anger behind him for good and would see him.

His brother gave him a quick hug, hanging on just a little too long. Pulling back, he motioned to the yard. "Keys in the ignition. I put some things in the back for you, too. Place should have some canned food, a few jugs of water and dried goods, but I filled an ice chest up with things you might need."

"Thanks," he said.

Reid descended the porch. Grace stayed one step ahead of him. She looked smaller somehow on the outside. He hastened until they were walking abreast of each other. He sent her a quick glance. She looked up at him with that damned cord around her neck, a faint quiver in her lip.

"Sorry 'bout that," he said as he they advanced to the vehicle. *Sorry about abducting you. Terrifying you. Feeling you up.*

She shook her head and shot a glance over her shoulder as if verifying it was okay to talk now. He followed her gaze. The porch was empty. Zane had gone back inside. 'Course, that didn't mean they weren't being watched from the window.

He guided her to the waiting van, some relic from the nineties that smacked of "I have a kidnapped woman in the back. "It would have to do. The thing that most worked to his benefit was that Grace had been taken several hundred miles east of her abduction site. And they were only going farther west. While the state was on an overall high alert, no one had seen the van. No one was specifically looking for *this* vehicle in relationship to Grace Reeves or him. Especially not way out in the badlands of Texas.

He yanked open the back doors, satisfied to at least see a blanket spread out on the hard metal floor.

"I can't believe they are letting me go like this," she whispered beside him, as though still afraid they could hear her. "I'm actually getting out of here."

His chest tightened. He knew what she thought. Maybe he had let her think that by promising to keep her safe. She believed she was going home right now. He could tell her, explain it to her, but that would just be borrowing trouble before he needed to. It could wait.

He reached for her throat. Loosening the cord, he ignored the softness of her skin and nodded toward her wrists. "You can take those off once we get on our way. Climb in." Right now they needed to put this place behind them.

With a grateful look at him, she turned and clambered up into the back of the van. There was that guilty feeling again.

He shut the heavy door with a slam, walked around the van and climbed up behind the wheel. He adjusted the rearview mayor so he could see her, then drove out of the yard. The van bounced along the unpaved the road.

"How far is it to the nearest police station?"

He flitted a look to the mirror before training his gaze on the dirt road stretching in front of them. "We're pretty far from anything." Not exactly an answer. Definitely not the truth. But it was enough for now. All he was going to explain.

She inferred what he intended, and he bought himself a little time. She worked her wrists free and tossed the cord aside.

Eventually he would have to explain the way things worked. She wouldn't like it, but it wasn't as though she had a choice. He didn't break out of jail to play hero. He had saved her life. That was good enough for now. She would go home eventually and have an adventure to tell her future grandchildren. Maybe they'd even make a movie about her life.

He'd keep her safe. That was the only promise he'd made her.

He had to honor the promise he made to himself first.

He had to kill Sullivan.

EIGHT

THE BLANKET OFFERED little comfort beneath Grace. She felt every bump as she bounced against the van's steel floor. By the time they reached the smooth ride of paved road, she was sore and knew she would bear the bruises for it. Still, she felt only relief to be leaving that house with all its scary, dead-eyed men behind. She had only one man to contend with now.

And he was an escaped convict.

She'd heard that as clear as day back in the house. Her life was in the hands of a man who had escaped from prison. She clung to the memory of *Shawshank Redemption*. Plenty of those convicts had hearts of gold . . . and honor. Great. She was holding him up to Hollywood fiction and Morgan Freeman. That was realistic.

She scooted forward and peered at him between

the two front bucket seats, wondering how long until he stopped. How far could the nearest police station be? There had to be some type of law out here. A sheriff's department or something. Obviously, he might not feel comfortable walking her inside himself, but he could drop her off a block away. Even a mile. He didn't have to turn himself in because of her. She could assure him of that. Hell, she didn't even have to say anything about him at all.

She waited as long as she could stand it and then asked, "How long will it take to get there?"

He shot her a quick glance and then looked back at the road, one hand draped idly over the steering wheel as though this were just a Sunday afternoon drive. She stared at that hand for a moment, briefly recalling the feel of it on her skin before she gave herself a hard mental shake and banished the image.

"Few hours."

"Hours?" She frowned. "There has to be some sort of law enforcement closer than that."

Again he glanced at her in the rearview mirror. It was a moment before he answered, "We're not going to the authorities."

She processed that as the van rumbled beneath and around her, vibrating up her bones to her very teeth. "I don't understand." Her voice was getting shrill, and she swallowed, fighting for a normal tone. "Where are we going?"

"You'll be safe," he said. Again.

He'd said it to her when they were in that bed together, and she'd believed him. She believed him then because he could have hurt her a thousand different ways and he hadn't. Nor had he let the others hurt her. That had been enough then, but now she wasn't so sure. An uneasy feeling started in the pit of her belly. For all she knew, he was taking her to a grave out in the desert.

She wet her lips. "Where?" she repeated.

He stared straight ahead, not looking at her. "It's best you don't know where we're going."

Silence so tense it crackled filled the interior of the van. Understanding sank in, followed by dread. "You're not letting me go," she whispered, her skin flushing cold.

His hands flexed over the steering wheel, knuckles whitening. "I can't do that. Not yet."

"You mean you won't."

"Same difference, in this case."

Her chest grew tight, the air sliding thickly past her lips. "You're a liar. And a criminal."

His deep voice crawled toward her in the tight space of the van, slithering like a serpent. "I didn't lie to you. You heard what you wanted to hear. But you're right. I am a criminal. You shouldn't forget that."

For a moment the sight of those strong, broad hands clasping the steering wheel filled her vision. They were all she could see. She'd let those hands touch her. She shuddered with the knowledge, feeling sick. She had made a mistake trusting him.

There was no fear. Only rage growing by the second inside her. Only a desperate need for self-preservation. She surged forward, pushing up off the heels of her shoes. She clawed at his face with her manicured nails. A jarring cry bounced off the inside of the van and she dimly realized it was coming from her.

He cursed, his body banging against the driver side door. The van swerved wildly, running off the road. He slammed on the brakes. Dirt and gravel roared outside their fishtailing vehicle. She pitched forward, landing on her knees between the bucket seats. Pain radiated up her thighs. The van bumped and bounced before finally coming to a hard stop.

She didn't wait. She pushed up to her feet and turned, lunging for the side door. Lifting the lock, she slid it open and was out and running over the uneven terrain as though she had a plan. As though she knew where she was going.

She ran like she never had before, strange gasps and funny sounds escaping her that didn't even sound human. She twisted her neck, searching for a road, hoping to see another car.

But there was nothing. Just the bleak landscape of desert terrain. A horizon that went on forever, and she was lost in it. All alone. With him.

The hard, swift beat of his feet sounded behind her, and she knew he was coming. Hunting her. Her pulse hammered violently, and her panting turned into ragged sobs as she felt him closing in.

Her foot hit a rut and she staggered. She caught herself, stopping just shy of eating dirt, but it cost her. His hand snared her hair, tangling in the long strands.

He gave a yank and she tumbled backward into him with a cry. He turned her over in his arms as they simultaneously hit the ground. Hard. It would have been worse if he had not twisted around in the last second and took the brunt of their fall, leaving her sprawled atop him.

"Let go of me!" She pounded on his chest.

He was indifferent to her blows. The steel bands of his arms wrapped around her waist and squeezed, pushing the air out of her lungs.

"What are you doing?" he growled. "Trying to get us killed?"

"I'm already dead. Aren't I?" She thrust her face close to his. "Just say it! Tell me the truth for once. For the first time."

He glared up at her, his green and amber marbled eyes sharp as glass. Their breaths crashed between them, mingling hotly. He shook his head once, slowly from side to side. "The truth is, you're my prisoner for as long as you need to be."

She held his gaze, trying to read him. For once, she suspected he was telling the truth. He wasn't going to let her go until he was good and ready. Keeping her safe, in his mind, did not equate to letting her go. She understood that now.

She should be better at reading between the lines, having lived among people who said one thing and meant another. Or they outright lied. She had been watching her father do it for years.

Grace inhaled thinly, trying to dislodge herself from the top of him, but he held her fast, locked tight against him.

"You good?" he asked.

The question alone infuriated her, which was unusual in itself. She rarely lost her temper. She'd have to feel strongly in order to do that, and for so long she had been living in a state of numbness. As though someone had pressed the mute button on all her emotions, dulling everything.

"No. I'm not *good*." His mouth kicked up at the corner as though she amused him, and the urge to scratch that smile off his face seized her. She curled her fingers into her palms, nails cutting into her flesh as she held the impulse in check. Barely. "I've been abducted. Hit. Manhandled. And the one guy I thought was going to get me out of this just proved himself as bad as the rest of them."

His smile slipped. Her heart skipped a beat. Instantly, she knew. He resented being lumped into the same category as the others.

"If I was as bad as the rest of them . . ." His deep voice scratched the air between them. " . . . I would not have left you alone last night." He took her hand and dragged it between them, forcing it over the sizable bulge of his erection. Her breath caught at the hard shape of him under her fingers. "You would be well-acquainted with this."

Their gazes clashed, his hazel eyes turning more green than gold in that moment. He released her hand and she pulled it back as though burned. "Make no mistake. I'm nothing like them. Be glad for that."

Be glad. She ground her teeth, hot indignation pumping through her veins. She would not thank him for *not* abusing her. As though common decency was something one shouldn't expect.

He clambered to his feet, taking her with him. She glanced to the idling van and shook her head fiercely. She couldn't get back in that van. Not with him. Not with this criminal. He wrapped one hand around her arm and started pulling her in the direction of the vehicle. She dug in her heels.

With an impatient grunt, he bent down and flung her over his shoulder. The force knocked the wind out of her. The earth pitched and swayed as he carried her. She recovered her breath and started struggling, feeling herself tilt sideways on his shoulder.

"Stop wiggling." She squeaked as he smacked one big hand on her bottom, pinning her in place.

The side door to the van still yawned open. He dropped her inside. She scrambled to her knees, shoving her hair out of her face to glare at him. "They're going to catch you! You're going to jail."

His face was its usual stony mask. He gripped the edge of the door and scanned her slowly with those changeable eyes, acutely reminding her of the hot mess she must appear. He shrugged one big shoulder indifferently. "Before this is all over that's exactly where I expect I'll be."

His gaze turned from her then, landing on the discarded cord. His mouth formed a grim line and she knew his intention. Her pulse jackknifed against her throat as he snatched the cord. She tried to crawl away but he grabbed her ankle and dragged her back. "Sorry. Gotta do this. Can't have you causing me to run off the road again." He bound her wrists and ankles, not too tight but snug. She wouldn't be mobile. He looked back at her. "Sorry," he repeated, his voice flat and void of emotion.

"I'm the one tied up," she spat. "Don't act like this is hard for you."

Tied up and scared, she silently added. Her parents must be out of their mind with worry. Even as she thought that, an uncomfortable knot formed in her throat. Would they really? Would her father be worried about her? Or more worried about how this impacted his campaign?

Reid held her gaze as if he was going to deny the accusation, but then he nodded. "You're right." That said, flatly and without remorse, he slammed the sliding door shut, the force of which reverberated on the air for several moments.

She sat on the hard floor, the knuckles of her bound hands curled against the steel bottom of the van, her heart racing, her breaths escaping in angry pants. Her gaze darted, wildly searching for something. Some way out of this nightmare. She was at his mercy. She hadn't let herself think that way before, but she was no better off than when she was first grabbed outside her hotel.

He opened the driver-side door and reclaimed his seat. She stared bleakly at the back of his seat as he turned the ignition.

Had she thought him her savior? Her head was throbbing. She curled herself into a small ball, laying on her side, nestling her cheek against the blanket and marveling that she could be so stupid. There was no savior. No help coming. Everything was up to her.

Tears stung the backs of her eyes. She refused to let them fall. She refused to cry in proximity to him. She wouldn't dare show that weakness. When she was home and free and this was all a bad memory, then she would allow herself tears.

The van rolled a steady rhythm underneath her, lulling her. Soon she was asleep.

SHE SLEPT FOR hours. Long after he turned off the highway and onto rural roads that formed a labyrinth in the desert mountains. Thankfully, she didn't even stir when he stopped for gas.

He glanced at her several times through the rearview mirror. She must be exhausted. He grimaced.

Or the stress of her ordeal put her into a coma. She bumped along with the movements of the van, her face relaxed and at ease.

It was a relief. No more attacks that ran them off the road. No sound of her voice talking to him, begging, pleading. No tears. God, that would have undone him. Only her gentle snores. She was emotionally and physically beat. Her body had shut down and claimed the rest it needed.

It was dark by the time he pulled up in front of his grandfather's old hunting retreat. The kind of dark you only found in the country. The night sky stretched overhead, deep and studded with infinite stars.

He hadn't been to the cottage in a long time. Even before he went to prison. Not since his grandfather's death. But he remembered the place well. Sometimes, falling asleep in his cell, he would think about it. It was one of the few places where he felt safe . . . where any happy memories could be found. Hunting. Fishing in the creek. Roasting marshmallows over the outside pit.

His grandfather had built the place after he returned from the war. As though living in a remote West Texas town wasn't remote enough for him. The old man installed a well so there was running water. A generator provided the needed electricity.

The ice chest full of food that Zane packed would last them until he hunted some game or caught fish from the creek. Assuming they were even here that long. He grimaced. He hoped not.

Reid pulled up in front of the hunting cabin and killed the lights and engine. He sat behind the steering wheel for a moment, staring at the dark shape of the house. He and Zane were normal boys here. Until Grandpa died, and then everything changed.

When Grandpa lived he would keep them for days, sometimes weeks at a time. After the old man died, there was no break, no saving them from their home life. Their mother only cared about her next fix, and their father, when he decided to make an appearance, liked to use them for punching bags. It made him feel better. Like a big man.

The old, weathered wood swing on the front porch moved in the breeze, the chains clinking softly. For a moment he could imagine Grandpa sitting there, whittling a piece of wood into something Reid and his brother would later marvel over. Happy times happened here, and it felt wrong bringing her here, as though doing so would taint all those memories.

No one knew about the place. It wasn't on any map. With Zane and the others running drugs and guns so close to the border, a place this far west was convenient. When things got too hot, they could duck in here and wait things out.

Sighing, he stepped out into the humming night and rounded the car to the blaring song of cicadas. He opened the sliding door, quieter than he had before, not eager to wake her. He stared down at her for a long moment and dragged a hand through his hair. *Christ.* Nothing was going the way he planned.

Surveying the encroaching darkness, he moved to the house and unlocked the front door, pushing it open. He hovered there for a moment, staring into the shadowy interior.

Shooting a quick glance back at the van to assure himself that she hadn't emerged, he strode to an outside shed and turned on the generator. Its loud purr soon filled the air. Reid moved back into the cabin and flipped on a lamp sitting on a side table beside the couch. Gold light suffused the cabin.

He returned to the van for her. Leaning forward, he slipped his hands under her body and lifted her up, tucking her close to his chest. She still didn't wake, turning her face into his chest as though he were her pillow.

She was heavier than she looked, but he still carried her with ease. One thing you had in prison was time. A lot of which he had spent working out, either playing basketball or using the rudimentary gym equipment in the yard, building his body into a weapon. The only weapon you had in prison.

She stirred a little as his shoes thudded over the wood porch. He entered the living area, kicking the door shut behind him and muting the sound of the generator. He'd go back for the supplies in a little while.

Even musty-smelling, the cabin was better than the place they had just left. For one thing, it wasn't filthy, which told him his brother couldn't have used it that often. It was sparsely furnished. Just a couch and recliner, kitchen table and four mismatched chairs.

Reid carried her to one of the two bedrooms. He knew it was probably a good idea if they slept in separate rooms. Last time they'd shared a bed had not gone well. He still harbored all kinds of dirty thoughts . . . the things he could have done to her . . .

Except leaving her in a room to herself probably wasn't a good idea either. The memory of chasing her through a field was still fresh. He wasn't keen on keeping her tied up, though.

Reid lowered her down on the colorful quilt in his grandfather's old bedroom. The brass bed was big and cozy. He and Zane had bounced on it so much that it was a miracle the mattress didn't sag.

Faint gold light crept into the room from the living area, allowing him visibility. Grace rolled to her side and snuggled into the well-worn quilt, her dark hair a wild tangle around her. He untied the cord from her wrists and ankles. Risky or not, he wasn't going to keep her tied up all night. He was a light sleeper. He'd hear her if she roused from the room.

She sighed in her sleep, bringing her hands up and tucking them under her cheek. She looked peaceful, as innocent as a child. Not fit for his world, but she was here, dragged into it kicking and screaming. He rubbed a hand over his jaw, backing up several steps, as though needing distance, needing space from her.

Leaving her room, he went outside and carried in the ice chest and duffel bag. It only took a few minutes to unpack the ice chest and toss his duffel on the bottom bunk bed in the second bedroom.

Checking on her one more time, he satisfied himself that she hadn't budged from where he'd left her on the bed. She was as still as death, and he had to resist the urge to check her for a pulse. Touching her was to be avoided.

Hiding the keys inside a bowl in a cabinet just

in case she woke, he stepped into the small bathroom and stripped off his clothes. He turned on the shower and adjusted the dial to the desired temperature, remembering from years ago to set it just at two o'clock.

Waiting for the water to warm up, he propped his hands on the edge of the sink and stared at his reflection, studying the man he had become. There were mirrors in prison, but he never bothered to take much time to look at himself. He was too busy watching everyone else . . . watching his back and the backs of his crew. *Except North.*

Reid hadn't looked out for North. Not well enough. Not as he had promised Knox. He had staged a fight in order to get sent to the local hospital. It was supposed to be simple. It wasn't supposed to involve others. Just him and some skinhead from another crew who got sent to prison for rape and murder. Reid hadn't meant to start a riot. He hadn't meant for North to get hurt. His shoulders bore the brunt of that, the weight threatening to cripple him.

He had failed, and now here he stood, free. At least until he was back in there—which was an eventuality. Hopefully North and the rest of the boys would be fine without him until he returned.

The mirror started to fog up, obscuring the reflection of the hard-eyed stranger looking back at him. He didn't bother wiping it clear. He didn't particularly care to look at himself. He'd gotten his friend hurt. And there was Grace Reeves to consider. He winced. Hopefully, she wouldn't bear any lasting injuries. No more than she already had. Hopefully, within the week he could let her go. He'd already saved her, he reasoned. Keeping her for a few more days wouldn't harm anyone . . . and if it brought down Sullivan, it would serve the greater good. Right?

As bad as the rest of them . . .

Her words had hit their mark. Maybe she was right. He thought himself so different than Zane and the others, but what had he done with his life? Maybe he hadn't killed the man that he was sent to prison for killing, but his hands weren't clean. You couldn't spend a decade at the Rock and come out clean. He'd seen things . . . done things. And he would continue to do things. Things like killing Otis Sullivan. Just because he felt justified didn't mean it wouldn't be murder. The way he looked at it, he was already in jail for that particular crime. He might as well make it a reality. And killing Sullivan would be worth it.

Reid stepped into the minuscule shower. Warm

water was fleeting so he made quick work of washing himself. Bowing his head, he let the last of the warm spray rush over him. Now he only had to stop thinking about what Grace Reeves felt like, all those curves and sweet skin and how long it had been since he had sunk deep between a woman's thighs. With a groan, he slid his hand down to grip his dick, giving himself several hard strokes.

This wasn't exactly how he had imagined spending his precious days of freedom. He had imagined he would eat a good burger. Find a quick, anonymous fuck. Then he would top everything off by killing Sullivan. The icing on the cake of his brief bout of freedom.

He rested his forehead against the wall of the shower and pumped his dick, working it almost savagely, desperate for release, something to take the edge off. Thinking about her wasn't hurting anything. Remembering how hot her sex had felt, how wet her panties, how easy it would have been to slip the fabric aside and find her slick heat with his fingers. He closed his eyes, his breathing growing ragged as his balls drew up tight. His fantasies took a turn and it wasn't just his hand anymore. In his mind he was spreading her thighs wide and driving his swollen length into her. She'd arch, her body swallowing him, fitting him like a glove, milking his hungry cock.

He came, blowing his load with a head-tossing groan. He stood beneath the spray of water, rattled in the aftermath. He was certifiable. Just the thought of her had him jacking off to the best orgasm he'd had in years. And that was still saying something, since all his orgasms in recent—and not so recent—years had been self-service. This one shouldn't have shattered him so much.

Water crashed over him, kneading the lingering tension from his muscles. No question about it, she had a hot little body under the sexless clothes she wore, and those big brown eyes did things to his head. He cursed and reminded himself that he'd always liked blondes, the occasional redhead, and mile-long legs. That was his type. He should be able to keep it together around her. He was all about control. In prison. Out of prison. It made no difference. He hadn't fallen so low that he would take a woman against her will. Prison hadn't ruined him that much.

But what if it wasn't against her will?

The question slid insidiously through him, a tempting little whisper. She had responded to him on that bed last night. Even if she was attempting to manipulate him then, she had not been unaffected by his touch. He could make her want it . . . want *him*. He was good at reading people, and he knew one thing for certain about Grace Reeves. The woman had never been well fucked.

He shook his head, shoving the idea out of his head. He wouldn't do it. He wouldn't seduce a woman his brother had abducted for Sullivan. Even if she wasn't the president's daughter, it was wrong on every level.

It would only be a little longer and then he'd be rid of her. Zane had promised that he would know something in a few days. Then he would get what he wanted.

The sudden image of Grace Reeves asleep in the bedroom next door appeared in his mind. Funny how she popped into his head when he thought about what it was he wanted.

NINE

GRACE WOKE TO stinging wrists and the sound of running water. Blinking, she lifted her head and looked around the unfamiliar bedroom. The motion reminded her of the soreness on the side of her face. Her hand drifted up to cup her cheek. She shuddered as everything rushed over her. Darkness pushed at the glass of the room's single window, letting her know she'd somehow slept the day away in the back of the van.

It felt as though a lifetime had passed since she was grabbed outside her hotel. Since she was hit and thrown in the back of a van by a gang of thugs. A lifetime since she shared a strange bed with a man she had thought she could trust. A man she had let put his hand between her legs. Shaming heat rushed through her. Not because she had thought to use her body to manipulate him. This was about survival. She did what she thought she had to. She still would do that. Whatever it took to get out of this. Whatever it took to get home.

No, her shame was because she had felt something. She'd grown wet as he palmed her sex. She inhaled sharply at the sudden clench in her belly, an echo of the want he had roused in her. Still mortifying. She was pathetic. *Crazy.* Clearly her dormant sex life was catching up with her. When she got home, she was going to have to correct that. She would finally sleep with Charles. For all intents and purposes, he was her boyfriend. Might as well cash in on the perks. Maybe surviving this nightmare would bring them a greater appreciation for each other.

The quilt was soft and smooth underneath her. Her fingers flexed against the yielding, well-worn fabric, clinging to it for something solid. She inhaled again. There was none of the stench of the last place. The air smelled faintly stale, but not foul or rotting as before. She sat up fully, wincing at her aching muscles.

Her brain started functioning, putting together the fact that the sound of running water was a shower. Everything clicked into place. Reid was in the shower. He wasn't in the room, watching her.

And her hands and feet weren't bound. Now was her chance.

She vaulted off the bed, ignoring the twinge of discomfort in her muscles and wrists. She lunged out of the bedroom, rotating in a swift circle in the living room, her heart galloping sixty miles a minute. Her environment distracted her for a moment, confused her. It was nothing like the last place. This house, even as sparsely furnished as it was, felt like a home. Yellow-orange lamplight flickered over the wood floors and paneled walls, casting dancing shadows over an Aztec-patterned blanket draped over the couch. The place smelled of cedar and pine. All deceptively comforting.

Time was fading. She could still hear the water running, but she knew it could stop at any moment. Reid could walk out of the bathroom and see her.

Heart still thumping madly, she scanned all the surfaces, searching for the keys to the van. Nothing. No sight of them. He must have them with him in the bathroom.

Suddenly, the water shut off. She squeaked and danced on her feet for a moment before making a split decision.

She bolted. Flung open the front door, taking a moment to shut it behind her, hoping that bought her a little more time. Maybe he would search inside the house before looking outside.

She had no clue where they were. Presumably still in Texas. She didn't know how long she had slept while he drove them here, but it was a big state. She knew you could drive forever without leaving it. Squinting, she peered into the darkness. She stood in a small patch of open yard. Just beyond it, trees and shrubs crowded together beneath a horizon of distant mountains several shades darker than the night sky.

A narrow road peeped out between the thick foliage. That ribbon of dirt looked like the only way in or out. She took off down it, hoping desperately that another car would appear or that she would reach another house, people, someone . . . *something*. Fervent, frantic, wishful thoughts. Prayers, really. Prayers that she knew would go unheeded. As she ran, her shoes beating into the dirt road, she faced the likely truth. There would be no cars, no people, no other houses.

No, Reid would have made sure there was no one close to them. She knew that much about him. He was a criminal, but he was no idiot. Wherever they were, it would be isolated. That realization led to another. She couldn't continue running down the road—he would eventually catch up with her.

All he had to do was hop in the van and track her down.

Pumping her arms faster, she swerved off the road and dove into the thick undergrowth. Thick was an understatement. It was like wading through sludge. Her breath came faster, vapor-thick and wet with panicked sobs. God, she really should have taken Holly up on her unsubtle offers to run with her in the mornings. Or join her for cross-fit. Then her lungs wouldn't feel like they needed a hyperbaric chamber.

Her chest tightened and constricted, pushing and pulling air in and out. In and out. It was slow going. Too many trees, too much brush clawing and grabbing and tearing at her. A sharp branch sliced her cheek. She whimpered but kept going, not worried about where she was headed as long as it was away. Far away from the cabin and the man inside it. Anywhere else was better. Safer than here. Safer than with *him*.

THE FIRST THING he noticed when he shut off the shower and stepped out was the silence. Thick as fog. He wasn't used to that. In prison there were always sounds. Solitude was an illusion.

He rubbed himself dry with a towel, scrubbing at his face and head, and then he paused, relishing this moment. Outside he could hear the cicadas and a faint mountain breeze rustling the leaves on the trees. If not for the fact that there was an abducted woman asleep in the next room, he could almost imagine himself free. At peace.

At the Rock, even at night, asleep in his cell, there were voices. Coughing, sniffing, a distant guard laughing or playing a radio. Sometimes, on certain nights, you could hear someone crying. Nothing like prison to turn grown men into babies, weeping for their mothers.

He exhaled and glanced at the tiny square window above the toilet. The night was ink dark out there, the position of the window too low to grant him a view of the stars. Too bad. He would have to go out on the porch and admire the view later. He wouldn't have that when he went back to the Rock. He wouldn't have a lot of things when he went back.

Against his will, his mind drifted, latched onto the image of her in the next room, curled up on the bed asleep, all soft female, waiting to be touched. Christ. No, she wasn't. If he walked in there and touched her, she would wake up screaming.

He knotted the towel at his waist and stepped in front of the mirror, wiping the glass clean of fog. He stared at his reflection, considering what he saw for a moment . . . considering what Grace Reeves saw when she looked at him.

He was nothing like the fine men in suits she was accustomed to. Scarred and tatted, muscled and rangy, he wasn't gentle or refined. His wet, close-cut hair looked almost dark against his scalp. When he was a kid he had worn it long, well past his neck. He learned quickly in prison that long hair was not a good idea. It gave the guy jumping you something to grip as he was trying to kick your ass.

Stepping out of the bathroom, he started to head for the second bedroom, where he had dropped his bag.

The moment he stepped out, however, he froze. Something wasn't right. Something was different. He scanned the room, searching for anything out of the ordinary. All was still and silent, just as it had been before he entered the shower, but the wary feeling was there, deep in his gut. The same wariness that had kept him alive for so long at the Rock.

He moved suddenly toward the bedroom where Grace slept and peered in. The bed was empty. She wasn't where he had left her.

Shit. He spun around and lurched for the front door. It wasn't locked, and he knew he'd locked it automatically behind him. Stepping out onto the porch, he scanned the yard. The van sat there, staring back at him, mocking him in the dark night. A slight movement or sound had him lifting his head and looking farther down the road.

There was a flash of something pale against the darkness, and he realized it must be her—that cream-colored blouse. She was already quite far down the road. He didn't expect any cars coming up this way, but if she slipped off the road and went into the woods, he could lose her. It was a vast wilderness out here. She could lose herself in it. She had no idea what she was doing.

With another curse, he dropped down off the porch and started running, his bare feet smacking the ground hard. He didn't even care or look back when his towel dropped. He kept running, bare-ass naked, arms pumping swiftly.

His gaze fixed on the cream-colored blouse . . . even when she dove off the road and into the woods—the precise thing he was hoping she wouldn't do. He ran harder, not wanting to lose her in the dense foliage, and dove into it behind her.

"Grace!" He swerved between trees, slowing down for moment and trying to glimpse her. She couldn't be that far ahead. He couldn't have lost her that suddenly.

He heard a snap and whirled around, glimpsing a flash of her blouse through the darkness. He plunged ahead. She must have heard him, too. He caught a flash of her face as she looked over her shoulder, her eyes wide in alarm.

"Grace!" he cried again, but the sound of her name just seemed to ignite her, pushing her faster.

Finished playing chase and not about to lose her in the woods, he dove, stretching his hand out to grab her. She screamed as he locked onto her shoulder, twisting her around to face him. Her hands balled into fists and she pummeled his chest and shoulders. Suddenly she stopped. Her fists opened. She flattened her palms against his chest.

He couldn't see her face in the dark but he felt her shudder. "You're not wearing a shirt!" By the motion of her head he could tell she was glancing down. "You're not wearing *anything*!"

He chuckled, pulling her flush to him, enjoying her outrage more than he should. "Sorry about that, but when I saw that the little bird had flown the coop, I didn't have time to get dressed."

She sucked in a deep breath and resumed struggling. "You're an animal!"

Turning, he started dragging her back toward the road. With her resistance, it wasn't an easy feat, so he just wrapped an arm around her waist and picked her up, holding her against his side.

"If I was an animal, you would be naked, too," he muttered.

And under me.

She gasped again, her warm breath fanning the side of his throat, raising his skin to gooseflesh. That's not all she was raising. He stopped himself from glancing down. He didn't need to look to know. He was rock-hard and pulsing. Fuck, he ached. There was no maybe about it—he was enjoying this too much.

And he could be enjoying it far more. An insidious little voice tracked through his mind. *You could make it good for her.*

Even if he took her here in the dirt, he could make her come first so that when he sank deep inside her she would be writhing and begging for it.

Sweat beaded his brow. His breath fell hard, crashing on the air, and it had nothing to do with exertion. It had everything to do with long years of denial.

He kicked that callous voice to the curb. It wasn't him. He wouldn't do that. He couldn't.

Her fingers clawed at his hand where it clenched around her waist, trying to peel them off. It was as though she sensed the pheromones on the air . . . how close he was to breaking. "I—I'm sorry. I won't try to run again, just please put me down."

Her soft, breathless plea undid him. As did her body pressed against him. Time to put space between her and his cock and his rapidly melting self-control.

"Fine," he grunted. He lowered her feet to the ground. She took a hasty step back, clearly wanting space between them.

He pointed straight ahead. "House is this way—"

She kicked him hard in the shin and bolted.

"Shit!" He hopped for a moment, grabbing his shin as pain radiated through his leg. *That little liar.*

Grunting, he dropped his leg and spun on the balls of his feet, sprinting after her. "No, you don't," he growled, launching himself and tackling her to the ground.

She shrieked as they rolled, tussling.

"Damn it! Stop! You're going to get hurt!" A rush of breath escaped him as she landed a sharp blow to his ribs.

They rolled to a stop with him on top. He naturally settled in the shelter between her legs, sparing her from the bulk of his weight. One of her fists struck him in the side of the face. "Right! Because you care about me getting hurt!"

He tried to catch her flailing hands. The nails of one hand latched onto his jaw and raked down his neck. He hissed and grabbed it, slamming the hand on the ground near her head.

"You might decide to care about your safety and stop attacking me," he snarled into her face, still trying to seize her other wild hand.

"Oh, what's wrong? You don't like getting your ass kicked by a girl?" she taunted up into his face.

He grabbed her other hand, pinning it above her head. The move stretched her beneath him—all ripe, quivering female splayed under him, her breasts a lush pillow against his chest.

And he was naked, dammit.

He dropped his face into her shoulder with a shudder, inhaling her vanilla-sweet hair as he resisted the urge to bury his face in those tits.

She stilled, like a creature of prey coming into full awareness, caught in the sights of a predator.

"You really need to stop fighting me," he groaned, thrusting his dick right against that sweet spot between her legs.

Another one of those satisfying gasps ripped from her throat, and he rocked himself against her again. Harder. Deeper. "You're making it harder than it has to be. For both of us, Grace." He laughed roughly, not missing the innuendo.

She panted as he rolled his hips, grinding into her. God, he was about to come like some inexperienced fifteen-year-old with his first girlfriend.

"All right," she blurted. "I won't fight you."

He forced himself to still, lifting his face up from her hair. Her wide eyes glimmered in the dark. She wanted him off her. He was just a dirty felon scaring the shit out of her. "Right," he got out between clenched teeth. He was going to need another cold shower.

Standing, he yanked her to her feet in one deft move and started dragging her through the woods.

"What would your mother say if she could see you now?" she asked in a shaky voice full of contempt.

He laughed. "My mother would probably ask to borrow money for her next fix." That silenced her. "I know what you're thinking. You're thinking that explains a lot about me. Right?" His voice had gone cold. He heard it. Felt it, too. Just like he felt her gaze, as searing and judgy as one of those fine church ladies who used to drop off boxes of used clothes for him and Zane so they could go back to their nice houses and pat themselves on the back as they recounted their good deeds to all their friends.

She probably felt dirty because he put hands on her.

He closed his eyes in one hard blink. Bad memory. It did nothing to alleviate his hard-on.

She stumbled, and he wrapped one arm around her waist. Slipping his other arm under her thighs, he lifted her up again and cradled her against his chest. She yelped, her hand going around his neck.

He felt her glare on his face as his long strides ate through the woods. He didn't even need to look at her to know those dark eyes of hers were staring daggers at him. She released a heavy huff of breath and crossed her arms tightly in front of her.

"Now you're going to pout? Give it up. You're not going to escape me."

"I'm the victim here," she reminded hotly. "It's my right to be angry. To try to escape." With that said, she resumed struggling and tried to break free as if she possessed no true fear of him. That thought did something to Reid. Made him feel funny on the inside. The perpetual tightness in his chest loosened a fraction, just enough to make breathing not such a fucking struggle. It was always a struggle. Always a fight being him.

He tightened his hold and fought a smile. Maybe

he was sadistic after all. He was actually enjoying having her around . . . captive and all.

"Escaping is only going to make me mad. Make me catch you and pin you down. And trust me, you don't want me to do that again. Every time I pin you down I have to fight the urge to fuck you." Might as well be honest. Maybe that would scare her into behaving.

She went still in his arms. "You're cruel."

Her accusation sank sharp little teeth into him.

"You don't know cruelty," he snapped. "You haven't been raped. Or beaten. Haven't even missed a meal. I saved your ass back there in that house, princess. Not that I expect gratitude from you for it but—"

"You'll get my gratitude when you release me."

"Well, that ain't happening yet."

She was quiet for a few moments. "I can walk," she said after a bit.

"Then walk." He set her back down on the ground, still keeping a firm grip on her arm. They had reached the road by now and were halfway back to the cabin.

"You can let go of me. I won't run."

He smiled humorlessly. She blinked up at him so innocently, as though she thought he might actually believe her. "I don't think so."

They fell into silence as they finished walking back to the cabin. It was just the song of cicadas, wind, and their footsteps.

As they entered the house and stepped inside the warmly lit living room, her gaze dropped, looking him up and down. Hot color flamed her cheeks and her stare darted away.

He didn't care. He resisted the urge to seize her chin and force her stare back on him. Let her look her fill. Let her see what she did to him. His fingers flexed on the smooth flesh of her arm. Whenever he was with her, it became all about her. What she did to him. What he would like to do to her. Everything else seemed to drop away.

That was dangerous. He'd already let her sway him off his course. For God's sake, he was in this cabin with her and nowhere near Sullivan.

She twisted her arm, trying to break his grip. "Can you release me now?"

"I don't know. It doesn't appear that I can trust you. Maybe I need to tether you to me."

Her chocolate eyes widened, sparking dark fire at him. "Please, no."

He shook his head and let go of her. For his own good if nothing else. Stepping back outside the cabin and onto the porch, he turned to face her. He held up one finger in warning. "Don't run again."

Her expression turned mulish. She held her chin at a defiant angle but said nothing. He studied her for a moment. Strangely enough, there was dignity to her—with her bruised cheek, wrecked clothes, and tangled hair sporting bits of leaves and twigs. A woman like Grace wasn't accustomed to abuse. She should look fragile, but he knew that was the furthest thing from the truth. His shin still throbbed, and it reminded him of one universal truth: never underestimate anyone. Even the smallest inmate could surprise you with a reserve of strength or hidden skills. Skills like plunging a shiv into your spine when you least expect it.

Marching out into the night, Reid snatched his towel from where he had dropped it and wrapped it back around his waist. Returning, he closed the door behind him and faced her, wondering what he was going to do with her. He couldn't keep her tied up, but he didn't trust her not to try and run again. Or clobber him over the head the first time he turned his back.

Crossing his arms over his chest, he announced, "I imagine you would like a shower."

Her eyes widened. "Are you serious?"

He didn't like it. The sense that he was doing something nice for her. He didn't need her to think he was *nice*. He stared her down. "Do you want a shower or not?"

"Yes," she blurted, nodding rapidly, as though afraid he might retract the offer.

"Your clothes are finished." He looked her up and down. "Mine are too large, but maybe we can scrounge something up in one of the drawers." He nodded toward the master bedroom.

"Yes, that'd be great."

He moved to the master bedroom, sensing her following him. He opened drawers, searching for something that might work. He found some clean T-shirts that probably belonged to his grandfather, size medium. He tossed one at her. In another drawer he found some boxers and a pair of sweatpants with a drawstring waist. Straightening, he propped a hand on the tucked edge of his towel and tossed her a pair of boxers. "Sorry. No underwear. You'll have to go commando. It's actually quite liberating. You might find you enjoy it, princess."

He didn't need to scandalize her. It was just that a perverse part of him wanted to remind her that he was a *not*-nice guy. He wanted to remind himself of that, too. Maybe he *needed* to remind himself of that.

She stood there frozen for a long moment, hands fisting the clothes, red suffusing her face like someone had just slapped both cheeks.

He arched an eyebrow. "Shower?"

She blinked. "Y-Yes." Turning, she fled from the bedroom.

Reid followed at a slower pace. Upon entering the bathroom behind her, she turned and gasped, clearly startled.

She inhaled, nostrils flaring. "Am I not to expect any privacy?"

His gaze moved away from her, scouring the small space, making certain he wasn't overlooking some obvious means of escape. She wouldn't be able to fit through the tiny window above the toilet. His gaze returned to her. "Be quick. I know you had a nice long nap, but I'm beat."

"I'm not stopping you from sleeping."

Her quick rebuttal irritated the hell out of him. Didn't she know how to behave like a proper hostage? "You're stopping me from a lot of things."

"What's that supposed to mean?" Her molten brown eyes flashed.

"If it wasn't for you, I wouldn't even be here." He would be doing what he broke out of prison to do . . . what he put North and other members of his crew in danger to do. None of which she would understand.

"Oh, it's my fault your gang kidnapped me? It's my fault you won't let me go free?"

Valid points, and that irritated him even more. He advanced a step. "You asked me to get you out of there. I did."

"And you brought me here!" She flung her hands up. "I should thank you?"

"For getting you out of there? Away from them? Damn straight." They were standing so close he could feel the warmth of her body radiating into him. Her lashes, a deep fringe of dark ink, lifted up in a slow, sweeping blink. There was no fear. They pulled him in. It was a dangerous thing. He took a slow step back.

Her gaze trained on his face, accusing, sharp and probing. It disturbed him. *She* disturbed him. She should look terrified. Instead she was this argumentative, fierce female with barbed words.

He retreated another step, and that's what it felt like. A retreat. Necessary, though. He wasn't fool enough to think himself immune. He might have jacked off in the shower, but he was hardly sated. Not after eleven years. That race through the woods and unsatisfying grind into her softness only got his blood pumping harder. He was haunted by the sensation of her, the warmth of her sex pulsing against his hand. He should have never touched her. *Christ*. He shouldn't even be here with her now. Not that there had been any choice.

"Twenty minutes," he said, grabbing hold of the doorknob. "Then I'm coming in for you."

Her eyes flared, but he closed the door, desperate for the barrier. He only needed to hang on for a few days. Be strong. He'd spent a lifetime behind bars and managed to keep himself together. How could this be any harder than that?

There might not have been a choice in bringing her here, but he had a choice when it came to whether he was going to lose control around her. He would stand firm. He would not let her get under his skin.

TEN

THE SHOWER FELT better-than-sex-good. She winced beneath the spray, certain it was no coincidence that she had sex on the brain. Probably had something to do with the living and breathing female fantasy one room over. Well, minus the whole escaped felon thing. That didn't figure into most fantasies. At least not hers. Dangerous men that held her against her will were not the fodder of dreams.

Even so, she could imagine all the inappropriate things Holly would say about Reid if she clapped eyes on him. *I'd like to lick his lollipop. He could tie me up any time.* If Holly were here, he wouldn't be able to keep his hands off her, and she doubted if Holly would mind. The two of them would be going at it like beasts.

Jealousy flared inside Grace. *God.* She was

mental. Was she actually jealous of a fictitious scenario her overactive imagination had cooked up?

She rested her forehead against the wall of the shower. Her libido had turned into a full-fledged chorus in her head.

The water pounded over her battered and sore muscles. The temperature was lukewarm, but she didn't care. Pushing the clamoring chorus of her libido to the back of her mind, she closed the door on them.

She shampooed with a generic shampoo that smelled decidedly unfloral. Definitely a brand for men, but she didn't care about that either. She was blessedly clean, and after this she would sleep on a bed and not the steel floor of a van.

She dropped her head and moaned as the sudsy water sluiced down her spine. It was a struggle to hurry through her shower. She just wanted to stay under the water forever, but she knew twenty minutes would fly by, and the last thing she wanted to do was take him up on his threat.

Her face burned at the prospect of him walking in on her. She'd seen him naked. God. That image of him was singed to her eyeballs. She wasn't experienced enough to say with one hundred percent conviction, but Reid was endowed. *Well* endowed.

God. Why was she even noticing that? It had to be the stress talking. Or shock. Or trauma.

They'd shared a bed together. He'd touched her intimately. She'd been stripped down to her underwear, but there had always been darkness between them. He hadn't *seen* her naked and she intended to keep it that way.

Reluctantly, she shut off the water and wrung out her hair, flipping the heavy rope over her shoulder. Stepping from the small shower, she wrapped her body in a towel and faced herself in the mirror. She was pale underneath her olive complexion, the bruise on her cheek a bluish-yellow tinge that only made her eyes look bigger, darker, like some wounded animal staring fearfully out at the world. No one would probably even recognize her if she were to turn up looking this way.

She was a far cry from the well-packaged First Daughter paraded about the country—not that she was any Grace Kelly by any stretch of the imagination. No, not even on her best day. There'd been enough skits on *Saturday Night Live* featuring her awkwardness for her to know precisely how she was perceived.

But this woman staring back at her didn't possess even a fraction of her usual polish. She was a hot mess. Gone was the tightly contained hair. She normally wore it pulled up or blown out into smooth sleekness. Also missing was the power suit and heels that her stylist insisted slimmed her down, giving her body length and her girlish features an aura of maturity. Whatever the hell that meant.

She angled her face from side to side, studying herself. She could use some makeup. She looked defenseless without the armor of cosmetics. Her fear and uncertainty were too readily visible.

She sucked in a deep breath and schooled her features, attempting to deaden her face. To not look so nervous. Her father lived by that mantra. Never let them see you sweat. No matter what he confronted, he never showed fear. The only emotion that leaked out of the man was carefully planned and orchestrated. He expected the same level of control from her. He drilled that into her often enough, even if nine times out of ten she came up short and disappointed him.

Sometimes it baffled her why her father didn't simply let her go live her life somewhere away from the spotlight. She could come around during the holidays and on important occasions. He'd refused her request to attend graduate school, claiming he needed her on his "team" even if she wasn't a sparkling First Daughter. Her mother brought the sparkle. She was beautiful, if not the cleverest. She looked good on his arm. Grace simply completed the picture of family man.

Her father insisted the excitement of a wedding would give his campaign additional life. He imagined that the buzz could escalate along the lines of Prince William and Kate Middleton's wedding mania. He was delusional.

Shaking her head, she wished she had just given her father a flat out no instead of ditching her detail and making a run for it. She didn't have to do what he said. In the past it was just easier to give in rather than fight him. She was an adult. Everything she was going through now was decidedly harder than a confrontation. Facing down her father after all of this would be easy enough.

Another thought trickled in, clouding her features as she gazed at her reflection. She wondered if he was disappointed in her now. If he blamed her for this. He must know she had slipped her Secret Service detail by now. Those guys would not hesitate to reveal the truth. They never wanted to be assigned to her. She'd picked up on that vibe often enough. They thought it was a joke. A powder puff detail. They would be looking to protect their own butts. Not that the truth would save them. They were probably fired anyway for letting her slip out undetected.

Her father had to know this was her fault. The granddaddy of all lectures probably awaited her if she got home—and not just from him, but from various members of his staff, Charles included. Charles especially. He would not understand how she could have bailed on her security detail. He would deem it the height of recklessness and irresponsibility. Not that he would be wrong. Especially in hindsight.

She blinked at her reflection, just then catching her previous slip. *When* she got home. Not *if*. Reid wouldn't hurt her. Sure, he hadn't released her yet, but he wasn't like the others. Truly. And yet there was still that intensity to him, a look in his eyes that made her stomach knot. She didn't understand it. It wasn't fear precisely. It was something else. Something uncomfortable. He might not be like the others, but the man was dangerous.

Shaking off the tangled thoughts, she dropped the towel and slipped on the well-worn cotton T-shirt. The boxers were too big and she had to fold them at the waist several times, which only hiked them up.

Closing her fingers around the doorknob, she stepped out of the bathroom in her indecently short boxers and plain cotton T-shirt. She half expected him to be standing there, waiting for her with that hard expression of his, but he was nowhere to be seen.

The house was silent. A lamp beside the couch radiated a low glow that saved the place from total darkness. It was something out of a Norman Rockwell painting. She almost expected to see a pair of little girls in old-fashioned nightgowns scampering across the wood floors, dragging rag dolls behind them.

Blinking, she shook off the fanciful image. There was nothing sweet about this scenario. Her bare feet padded quietly across the wood plank floor. She moved tentatively, stealthily. She slid a longing glance to the front door, wondering if she should dare try again. She might use up the last of his goodwill if she attempted another escape tonight. No, the next time—and there would be a next time—would be better planned so she wouldn't fail. This whole nightmare was her fault. The least she could do was get it right by escaping.

She moved to the door of the room where she had earlier slept and peered inside. He was there (thankfully no longer naked), pulling back the covers. Her lungs tightened, air seizing for a moment at the way his back worked and rippled with his movements. *Whose back looked like that?* Two possibilities popped into her mind. *A Calvin Klein model or a felon who had a lot of time to work out.* Obviously, she knew which one he was.

He looked up at her from where he was leaning over the bed and slowly straightened, putting that big body of his on even further display. He wore a pair of sweatpants that sat low on his hips. It was sinful, the way his skin looked both soft and hard at the same time, stretching over ridges of sinew and cut muscle.

She wasn't the only one staring. He took his time looking her up and down in her ensemble of T-shirt and ill-fitting boxers. "Feel better?"

She nodded jerkily, tucking the hair behind her ears self-consciously and glancing from him to the bed. With the covers pulled back, it looked inviting . . . big enough to sleep two. She lifted her chin. "What are you doing?"

"Getting ready for bed. I know you took a nap, but I'm beat."

Nap or not, she didn't feel rested.

"You're sleeping in here?" She pointed to the wall in the direction of the neighboring room. "But there's another bedroom."

"Yeah. After your little sprint through the woods, that idea gets a fat no."

"You're sleeping with me?" she asked, needing the clarification, needing to hear him say it before she could even start to panic.

He nodded, a grim twist to his mouth. "You don't trust me. I don't trust you. So this is where we're at."

She didn't want to be *at* this place at all. Not with him. Not again.

Her gaze flicked to him and the bed, the panic in her heart alive and real. "No."

He angled his head as though not trusting his hearing. "No?"

She nodded.

He sighed, and she heard the weariness in that sound. "I'm not up for another battle with you, Grace. Just give me a night to sleep and I promise we can keep playing this cat and mouse game tomorrow."

She pulled back in affront. "This isn't a game to me. It's my life."

"And I promise you'll get back your life. Just a few more days." His steely gaze held her stare for a long moment, as though hoping to let that sink in, hoping to convince her. "But right now I'm getting in this bed and so are you."

She inhaled and took a step away, letting that be her answer.

His glittering eyes narrowed and he crossed his arms over his nicely formed chest. It galled her that she couldn't help noticing that. Those nice arms only seemed to draw attention to that chest. "Is this because of the last time?"

Last time. He meant last night. It already felt a lifetime ago.

"I promise there won't be any of that going on," he added. *That* being his hand fondling her between her legs and making her almost orgasm on the spot. *That* being the most shameful and mortifying thing to ever happen to her. "Even if I was interested, I'm exhausted."

"Oh. That's right. I'm not your 'type.'" The words burst forth before she could stop herself. And she hated them. Hated herself for saying it. She sounded wounded when really it was skepticism she felt. Was she so undesirable? He was a felon fresh out of prison. He couldn't be that picky.

He hesitated. "Yes, that's true."

"Forgive me if I have my doubts. You're an escaped felon. I doubt me not being some leggy blonde matters."

His features hardened. "I might have escaped from prison, but that doesn't mean I don't have a code. I'm not a rapist. If I was going to attack you,

I already would have." His top lip lifted in a slight sneer. "Your virtue is safe."

He was right. And that was when she had to face the truth . . . when she confronted what it was that truly frightened her. *Herself.*

Then she knew exactly how much trouble she was in . . . isolated in this cabin with this man.

Oh, no, she wasn't worried about him raping her. Grace knew he wouldn't do that. She was worried that he wouldn't have to—that he could have her if he wanted her. With a look, a word from him, she would give him everything. Permission granted, he could take her. That had become her worst fear.

She was afraid she would respond to his touch. Welcome it, even. Maybe invite it if she got into that bed with him. In the darkness the temptation to forget herself—forget the world—could overtake her when she was pressed against a man whose body was made for tangling in sheets and taking a woman hard, using her in a way that would unravel her.

A part of her wanted to shatter the proper and controlled veneer of her life. To finally be touched. For someone to see her and peel back all the layers and tap into something that was real. To uncover that part of her that was locked away, neglected. Never felt. Never touched. Never seen.

If he made any overture, she could crumble.

It was strange. You never knew where you were going to be when self-realization decided to Taser your ass.

She inhaled a shaky breath. He stabbed a finger toward the bed and she almost flinched at the ferocity in the gesture. He had reached his end for the day. "Now get in this bed, Grace."

She didn't know what did it for her—if it was his tone of voice or the shock of her self-realization—but she stepped forward and slid beneath the sheets. Now that she knew her vulnerability, she could resist. She was armed with the knowledge of her weakness. She would not fall prey to him—or herself.

The bedside lamp clicked off and he slid in beside her. A small measure of light spilled into the room from the lamp in the living room.

She curled on her side and her mind immediately turned to escape. She couldn't count on him letting her go and she definitely needed to get as far from him as soon as possible. She began turning over the possibilities. Once he fell asleep she could ease out of the bed, grab the keys, take the van and go. It was doable. Except she didn't know where he stashed the keys.

Then his voice rolled over her in the semidarkness. "And just in case you're thinking of running again . . ." He sat up and flipped the covers off them. Cool air wafted over her bare legs. She yelped as he picked up her foot and looped something around her ankle.

"What are you doing?" she demanded, sitting up in the bed and watching him as he leaned over her feet.

She felt a tug on her ankle. He turned slightly then and seemed to be working on his own ankle. "Just tying our ankles together. There." Reid settled back down beside her, propping himself up on one elbow. He lifted his foot. The motion pulled her ankle up, and she could see the plaid scarf connecting them.

Her gaze flew back to his. "You've got to be kidding!"

"I'm a light sleeper. I will feel it if you try to untie that knot." He didn't wait for her to respond. He simply rolled onto his side. Even with a good amount of slack on the scarf between them, her ankle felt the pull.

"Ass," she muttered beneath her breath. His light chuckle told her he must have heard her.

With a huff, she rolled onto her side, indifferent to the sudden move that yanked the scarf taut between them.

Fuming, she lay there, convinced she would never find sleep, but eventually her lids grew heavy. She closed her eyes, thinking about how glad she was going to be when she got out of here . . . and how she was going to make certain her life changed for the better. She would tell her father she was finished living her life campaigning for him. She would break things off with Charles for good. And she would never again be a woman longing for the touch of an unsavory criminal.

ELEVEN

*R*EID WOKE WITH a raging hard-on. It wasn't so unusual. It happened. Especially in prison where the yearning for a woman could be so acute that wet dreams occurred with high frequency. He blinked a few times, chasing away the cobwebs of what had been a deep sleep.

The only unusual component to the situation was the woman sprawled on top of him. Her hair was all over him like some kind of damn silken web. An accurate description He felt ensnared.

Her head was cushioned on his shoulder, one of her legs wrapped around him like he was a giant pillow. The fullness of her breast nestled into his chest. She was braless. He felt the bead of her nipple through the fabric of her T-shirt. He wanted to roll her onto her back and pull that breast into his mouth so badly he ached. And there was his dick at full mast . . . wanting to do other things to her, too.

He faced the ugly truth. It didn't matter what good faith words he spouted. His body wanted what it hadn't had in years. It wanted Grace Reeves.

He could profess that he wouldn't touch her all he liked, but putting himself in this kind of proximity with her was just misery.

He sat up abruptly with a curse and reached for his ankle, ready to put an end to the torture. She stirred, coming awake slowly. "Wh-What's happening . . . ?"

His fingers fumbled, but he eventually got the knot undone. "Go back to sleep," he said tersely.

He strode from the room, careful to keep his back to her so she didn't see his traitor cock. He marched into the second bedroom and yanked the bedding and pillow off the bed. Positioning the pillow in front of him, he returned to the master bedroom.

She was sitting up in the bed now, blinking those deep, endless eyes of hers at him as he flung everything down on the floor in front of the door. He didn't even bother to hide his temper. He was pissed. At her, at himself . . . at how easily she got to him. He should tie her up tomorrow and drive into town and get his itch scratched by someone else, then he would put an end to this thing between them and put things in correct perspective. He was the captor. She was the captive. He wasn't some sick fuck that got his rocks off abusing women. He wasn't like Rowdy or half the guys in prison.

"You're sleeping on the floor?" she asked in a soft voice. Even that voice got him hard. Well, *harder.*

He settled himself down on his makeshift pallet. Even with the bedding, it was uncomfortable. His prison mattress was better than this.

"Yeah, I'm still in the room, so don't think about making another run for it. It won't go well for you." He knew he sounded like a surly bastard, and from the way her brow furrowed she didn't like it. Which was for the best. She didn't need to like it. She didn't need to know that he was cock-hard for her either.

He didn't want her to think he was totally soft and without threat. A little bit of fear was a good thing. For both of them. She'd keep her distance that way, and God knew he needed that.

"Is something wrong with the bed?" she asked.

Yeah, you're in it.

"Just go to sleep," he growled.

It was a while before she lowered herself back down. He listened as she rustled around on the bed before finding a position she liked and going still. He listened, counting the minutes until her breath evened and she went to sleep. It was torment. He didn't relish spending the next few days sleeping on the floor, but he would do what he had to do. Just like he always had. His life had been a series of unpleasant events, one after the other. Why should that change now?

Reid never expected life to be easy. He didn't know what easy was, so it was natural that he shouldn't look for something he didn't know existed. Even so, he saw that other kids had it different. Better. Kids whose moms packed their lunches. Kids who got new shoes and talked about the vacations they took.

His mother worshipped at the altar of whatever drug was available. Crack, molly, heroin, meth. Whatever she could get her hands on. She was an equal opportunity addict. Whatever flavor the current man in her life provided, she gladly embraced. It enslaved her, made her weak, made her forget about her children living under the same roof with her.

She forgot about food. That fell to Reid. He'd scrounge for loose change under the car seats and couch cushions. He'd use that and whatever Grandpa gave him between visits. Not trusting to keep it in the house with Mom and her burnout friends coming and going, Reid would bury the money in the woods behind the trailer park in an old mason jar.

Once a week he'd dig up his money, take what he needed, and walk to the corner store with his brother. He bought the essentials, carefully tracking the cost. Peanut butter, a loaf of bread, some juice, a couple cans of soup. Just enough to keep them from starving.

Reid would feed his brother first, then venture into his mother's bedroom, wade through the stale air that reeked of sweat and cigarettes. He'd force some water and peanut butter sandwich down her. Peanut butter sandwiches she never made him but he was an expert at preparing.

As shitty a mom as she was, he loved her. He held on to vague memories of being tucked in, her cool fingers brushing through his hair as she hummed him to sleep. There was that. She wasn't all bad. Not as long as he had those memories.

The best thing she ever did was give her father unlimited access to him and Zane. They'd stay weekends with their grandfather. In the summer he would take them for weeks at a time.

Once, when Reid was eleven, his grandfather asked if he and Zane wanted to move in permanently with him. Things were pretty bad then. Mom less and less sober. The boyfriends not even that anymore. Simply men. Strangers that drifted in and out. Different but the same. They ignored Reid and Zane for the most part, which made them tolerable. They were actually easier to handle than the old man.

Whenever Tommy Allister decided to put in an appearance, Reid walked a tight rope. Tommy equated parenting to beating the shit out of Reid. He called it discipline. Teaching Reid to be a man. Punishing him because the trash was overflowing and he hadn't seen fit to take it out. Or because the kitchen faucet had an annoying drip and somehow that was Reid's fault.

The reason never mattered just as long as there was a reason . . . an excuse for Tommy Allister to beat the shit out of his oldest son. Mom never made a protest. She was usually passed out anyway . . . or too high to pay much attention to reality.

"I can't petition to be your full-time guardian legally," Grandpa explained when he offered to take Reid and Zane full-time. "I've made a few inquiries already. I'm old, and with my heart condition I'd likely be declined . . ." Grandpa's voice faded as he stared out at the pond where they fished. Zane stomped along the bank, probably scaring the fish away. "Even so, your ma would let you boys move in. If'n you want to. You'd have to tell her it's what you want, though. She'd need to hear it from you. Your dad might kick a fuss when he blows through town and decides to play at being a daddy, but he won't follow through with anything. Never has."

Reid thought about it hard.

Leaving his mom. Moving in with Grandpa. *Leaving Mom.* That was the part that stuck.

She needed him.

"If it's just the same, sir. I'll stay with Mom."

So he had stayed. Taking care of Zane and his mom. It should have been the other way around. She should have been looking out for him. He probably should have gotten over it. Left her. And not just for him, but for Zane.

She was just too weak, though. He'd always been the strong one.

In any case, Grandpa died six years later. He was seventeen then. A year later and he could have left, but he couldn't leave Zane behind.

Then he got sucked into Otis Sullivan's web. The money. The sense of belonging. Stupid kid that he'd been, it had lured him. He'd been missing his grandfather and at the time believed Sullivan like the grizzly old man. Rough around the edges, but with honor. Someone who might break a few rules but was essentially good. A man with a code who looked out for his own.

Reid couldn't have been more wrong.

He'd paid for that mistake. Eleven years he paid. He knew about consequences. And suffering.

A few days with Grace Reeves wasn't going to break him.

He could stay away from her for a few days. He could handle a little self-denial. He was accustomed to that.

Taking advantage of her, using her, hurting her . . . he wasn't accustomed to doing that to a woman. He never had before. He wasn't about to start now.

TWELVE

GRACE WOKE TO the smell of frying bacon. There were worse ways to greet the day. As a captive, she guessed this was especially true. She was awake after all—alive and unharmed and, presumably, about to be fed.

She stretched sore muscles in the empty bed, her gaze straying to the door. Not only was he gone, but his makeshift pallet was missing, too. It was as though he had never slept in the room. But she knew better, of course. He wouldn't have left her unsupervised through the night. Not after her bolt for freedom.

She rose from the bed and hurried out into the bathroom, her feet padding quietly over the wood floor.

She slipped on her bra and once again donned the big cotton T-shirt she'd borrowed. It was in better shape than her silk blouse. She pressed a hand against the window above the toilet, feeling the frosty glass. It was chilly inside, but even colder outside.

She slipped the too big boxers back on and returned to the bedroom to search for something warmer. She hit pay dirt. The drawers held quite a few garments. All for men, but she wasn't picky.

She slipped on a pair of baggy sweatpants, knotting the drawstring as tightly as she could before emerging into the kitchen.

He looked up from the stove, lifting bacon onto a waiting plate. "Morning."

"Morning," she returned, easing carefully into a chair at the table as she took in the domestic scene.

"Sorry. No eggs. But we have bacon and toast." He set a plate in front of her.

"That's fine. Thanks." She picked up a piece of toast, convinced she couldn't eat beneath his watchful gaze, but the moment she took her first bite, she didn't stop until the last scrap of food was gone. Swallowing the last bite, she looked back up at him. "Aren't you eating?"

"Already did. C'mon," he announced, turning away from the sink and moving to the door. She watched warily as he put on his boots.

"Where are we going?" She edged to the door and her shoes waiting there. He arched an eyebrow that seemed to say: *Does it matter? You have to do what I say.*

He opened the door and gestured for her to precede him, like he was any gentleman she might have met out on the streets back home. Except he wasn't. He was a far cry from that world. In all her years of private school education, including four years at an all-girls college, she had never encountered an individual like Reid. He represented a world she was never supposed to touch. Unsavory, twisted, and of the criminal variety.

She stepped out on the porch before him, still keeping a careful distance. Everything looked much different in the light of day. Awash in browns and greens, her surroundings hummed and crackled as wind moved through branches and leaves. There was no grass to speak of—trees and shrubs offered the only green. It was raw and compelling and beautiful. In many ways synonymous to him.

The morning was cold, a faint mist clinging to the air. His boots thudded across the porch and then dropped down, hitting the dirt-packed ground. She followed him, her gaze scanning the line of brush, recalling her mad, desperate dash for freedom that had failed so miserably. Really, she was a little embarrassed by it now. If she was going to escape, she needed to be smarter.

"C'mon," he called, looking over his shoulder.

She hurried ahead obediently, telling herself that for now this was how she would play it. She would follow his instructions, play the beaten little puppy and gain back his trust until a moment presented itself for escape. No more impulsive, ill-planned attempts to break away. The next time she made a break for it, she would succeed. If there was one thing she had learned from watching her father and his staff all these years, it was that strategy was everything.

"Where are we going?" she asked, catching up and following one step behind him as he rounded the back of the cabin.

He didn't answer, and she wondered if he was still angry at her for yesterday. Would he treat her to perpetual silence now?

He stopped at a shed and opened the door. Ducking inside, he emerged moments later with a fishing pole, tackle box, and net. He extended the net to her. "Carry this."

Bristling at his bossy tone, she accepted the net and followed him through thick shrubs that snagged and grabbed at her legs.

She addressed his back. "We're going fishing?"

"You ever fish for your dinner before, princess?"

She bristled at the nickname. "No."

"First time for everything, then."

She stared at his broad back, her eyes following the play of muscles working under the thin cotton of his shirt. She couldn't see his face but she could hear the smirk in his voice. He thought he knew her. He thought he had her pegged. Her determination to beat him, to escape him, only intensified.

She heard the water before they reached the edge of a midnight blue pond. Her lips parted on a tiny gasp. It was the kind of thing photographed in nature magazines.

He squatted in front of the tackle box, flipping it open. She took the time to study him, scanning corded-tight muscles moving like fluid beneath his clothes. This guy had escaped from prison. That meant he was more than some ripped meathead. There were dimensions to him. He was intelligent. Cunning.

The mist had melted away and sunlight gilded his hair into dark gold as he baited the hook with a colorful bit of plastic tackle that reminded her of something her mother teased the cat with.

Satisfied, he stood and walked out on a ridge of rocks, sure-footed, his gait even. Balanced perfectly, he tossed out his line.

Unsure what to do but pretty certain it wasn't stare at the way the denim hugged his amazing backside, she sank down onto the ground, still holding onto the net.

She drew her knees up to her chest and sat there for several minutes, intermittently watching him (not his backside) and scanning their surroundings.

He moved with quiet stealth as he fished. Even as strong and deadly looking as he was, there was a natural grace to him—a patience she hadn't expected. Weren't criminals supposed to be an impulsive sort? But then, he was a criminal who had successfully escaped prison. That probably put him outside the box of everyday criminals.

As the minutes slid by, the morning mist evaporated. The day was no longer so cold. Still chilly, though . . . a fact he was apparently indifferent to when he reached one hand behind his neck and pulled his gray T-shirt over his head in that move guys always did. Well, no guy she knew, but she watched plenty of guys do it on TV. Her mouth dried and she quickly looked away, her gaze resting on the discarded T-shirt he'd flung onto the bank, anywhere but at him—at the sight of his ripped up, tattooed body.

It was several moments before she looked back at him, and it was as though he felt her gaze. He looked sideways at her. Heat punched her chest and flared outward, but she didn't look away. She held his ice gaze.

He finally spoke. "Bet you've never had fish as fresh as you're going to get tonight." Was he trying to make small talk?

She pulled a dried-up bit of root from the parched ground. "You know this place well," she stated.

He nodded affirmation.

Her mind groped on some memory, some bit of knowledge about captives making a connection with their captor. It was to her benefit if they could forge a connection, a relationship. Ostensibly, it would be harder to harm a person you actually knew . . . you actually liked.

She winced. Time had proven that she was not very likable. The last poll had established that America was not a fan of First Daughter Grace Reeves.

Deciding she needed to try, she cleared her throat and asked, "So you came here a lot . . . before you were incarcerated?"

His lips pressed into a firm line and his hazel gaze hardened as he gazed out at the glasslike water. Well, that didn't take long. She'd gone too far. Asked something that brought his walls crashing down.

Then, suddenly, he shrugged. "Guess it doesn't matter. This place won't be a secret for long. Not after you're free."

The breath eased out of her. *Free.* Just hearing him say that as a foregone conclusion made her shoulders relax and the air flow easier past her lips. "You think I'll tell people about this place?"

"You won't have to," he said as though unaffected. "You'll tell them about me. With the resources available to the FBI and Secret Service, it won't take them long to close in on this place."

After she told them about him: Reid. Escaped convict. That's all she would need to say. They would figure out the rest. And of course, she would tell them. Why wouldn't she? He was a dangerous criminal. Just because he wasn't as dangerous as the rest of the men who took her didn't mean he should get off scot-free. If he was really heroic, he would have taken her straight to the authorities. He needed to be brought to justice for his crimes.

"You know I can help you . . . put in a good word for you with the authorities."

He smirked as he reeled in his line. "That so, princess?"

"If you let me go, sure. I would do that, of course."

"Still angling for me to let you go?" He threw out his line again. It plopped cleanly in the water. "Already told you. I can't do that just yet."

"Should I stop trying, then?" she snapped.

"By all means, keep trying. No one likes a quitter." His smirk was a full-fledged smile now and it did stupid things to her insides. She fought it, trying to quell the flip-flopping of her stomach.

"Don't you want to help yourself at all?"

"There's no helping me, princess. It's cute you think I'm redeemable, but I'm a lost cause. So it doesn't really matter if you tell them my name." He waved out at the water. "Or about this place."

He ceased smiling. He simply stared out at the water, and despite the day's growing warmth, she shivered. It really was pointless trying to reach someone who had nothing to lose.

She propped her chin on her knees. "I wish you would stop calling me princess."

"Isn't that what you are? Closest thing to royalty we got in this country."

She snorted. That would seem true, except for the fact that the media has dubbed her "Graceless Reeves." She was no princess, to be sure.

"I'm not . . ." Her voice faded. Maybe he hadn't heard about her in prison—or seen any footage of her fumbling awkwardness. None of the *Saturday*

Night Live skits. For a moment, that perked her up, but then he filled in the gap of silence.

"You're the closest thing to a princess I've ever met."

"And what's your definition?" she asked, still feeling that prickle of annoyance and knowing she wasn't going to like the rest of what he had to say.

"Pampered, spoiled . . . you probably have servants—"

Of course he would think that. "I don't have servants. This isn't the eighteenth century. I have . . . employees . . ." Her voice faded under his sharp scrutiny.

"Yeah? And what is it you do, 'princess,' to have these 'employees'? Besides being your father's daughter?"

She stared at him, hating how, in that moment, he suddenly made her feel guilty for being born into a life of privilege. Her life wasn't all roses, but this man who had only ever experienced the harshness of the world and led a life of crime would never understand that. "I was a student," she began, hating how lame she sounded, trying to give her life value and purpose. She shouldn't feel compelled to make this argument to him, but she was doing just that.

"Was?" he cut in. "But not anymore? So what is it you do, then, to have these serv—oh, sorry, 'employees'? And your nice clothes? Do you work to earn the clothes on your back? I bet that nice blouse of yours cost more than most people make in a week."

Her blood simmered. He did *not* know her. He didn't know anything about her at all. Who was he to judge her? God only knew all the awful things he had done in his life.

He continued, "You haven't got a clue. And that, 'princess,' is why I call you princess. You don't know what it's like to have to work your fingers to the bone for something, to take orders, to have absolutely no freedom, no say over when you get to come and go. Where and when you eat, when you can take a piss."

She snorted. Was he for real? It was like he was describing her life to the letter. She snapped. "You suck."

He blinked. "What?"

"You heard me. You suck!" She shook her head. "You think I don't know what it's like to have my every move monitored . . . my every word planned out for me? Those clothes I wear that you seem so interested in? I don't even get to pick them out." She grabbed a hunk of her hair. "I don't even get to say how I want my hair cut. I don't know the last time I styled it any way I wanted." She flattened a hand over her chest. "Maybe we have more in common than you think, huh?"

He stared at her, his cat-gold stare inscrutable. "Maybe," he finally allowed, his eyes skimming her where she sat on the bank, warming her. She felt a sudden uneasiness under that appraisal. Was she really holding herself up to him and finding similarities? Did she want him to see them as alike? It was dangerous ground.

Grace inhaled a shaky breath, suddenly determined to insert a little distance between them. "Except that you had a choice. Right?" She nodded once, jumping from one cliff to another, this one dangerous in a different way, maybe even more precarious, but she couldn't help herself. "You got yourself put behind bars. No one did that but you."

A ripple of something passed over his face and his eyes sparked green-gold. Even across the distance, she could see his scarred knuckles turn white as his hand tightened around the fishing rod. "Oh, and *you* don't have a choice then, princess?" He laughed harshly. "I call bullshit. You're in control of your fate. You don't like being a princess, then don't be."

He made her want to scream. She never remembered a time when her father wasn't an important man. A senator. Governor. Vice president, and finally, president. She'd been in the spotlight all her life. Short of getting herself legally emancipated (yeah, fat chance), she never had much of a choice in anything. "Go to hell," she got out before she could reconsider the wisdom of insulting him.

He chuckled. "How do you work in politics with that temper?"

She inhaled, battling the temper he accused her of having. Which was crazy because she never lost her temper. He was the only one that made her feel like stomping her foot.

"First of all, *I* don't work in politics." Even though it often felt like she did. Okay, it felt like that *all* of the time. "Secondly, I don't normally talk like that . . . I don't act like that. It's you making me crazy." She picked up a smooth rock near her shoe and tossed it into the water. "You bring it out of me."

"Interesting. I make you lose control?" He nodded slowly, thinking God knew what.

"Don't look so flattered." She reached for another rock. "It's not such a leap that I would act out of character around my kidnapper."

"Maybe you act like the real you with me."

She froze at that suggestion, clutching the rock in her hand. Could there be some truth to that? Had this scenario forced her to drop all her walls and just be who she truly was? Who even was that? It had been a long time since she did any self-examination. She had simply been living on auto-pilot. Her gaze narrowed on him, resenting that he was prompting such thoughts. It was tempting to fling that rock at him.

"And last time I checked, I'm not your kidnapper," he added. "I didn't abduct you."

"Maybe not initially, but you can't claim innocence. You're holding me captive right now. You're not letting me go."

His lips flattened, and she knew he didn't like the reminder. "I told you. You'll get home, and I think you can give me a little bit of your trust since I was the one who protected your pretty little neck back there."

Pretty little neck? A flush of heat washed over her. It was probably just an expression. Still, it felt intimate. She shifted where she sat, glancing around her.

A number of things had been said about Grace in recent (and not so recent) years. Her father had been in the public eye a long time. Even before the presidency. No one had ever described her as pretty. Even her grandmother had bemoaned that she lacked the Artigas beauty. The beauty that her mother possessed had come in very handy to catch her father. She had been a beauty queen. There wasn't a pageant in South Florida she hadn't won. The media still loved to flash pictures of the First Lady in a bikini with Miss Miami emblazoned across her chest. When your mother resembled Sofía Vergara it was enough to give you a complex.

She gave herself a swift mental kick. *Hey, Stockholm-syndrome-freak-girl, stop getting off on his unlikely and unwanted interest in you.* Her appearance didn't matter. He'd established that she wasn't his type. And he certainly wasn't her type.

A sudden splash pulled her attention to the water.

"I got one!"

She jumped to her feet and pranced up and down along the bank excitedly. "What do I do? What do I do?"

"The net!" His biceps bulged as he worked to reel in the fish. For someone who knew nothing about fishing, she thought whatever was on the end of that line was big.

She hopped across the pond, haphazardly using the rocks he had used as a path, but not nearly as skillfully. She slipped several times, sinking to her knees in the freezing water. By the time she reached him, he was reeling in a gorgeous fish, shiny red on the back with a white belly.

"What kind is it?" she asked, as if that would hold any significance to her.

"Red drum, I think."

It was big, bowing half of his rod. She anxiously stretched out the net. He lowered it inside with a triumphant shout, grinning in a way she had never seen from him. It was a grin of victory. He looked . . . happy, and she couldn't tear her gaze from him. The grooves along the sides of his face actually looked like dimples.

"Eleven years," he declared, "but I haven't forgotten how it's done."

"Must be like riding a bike," she laughed in turn, her cheeks starting to ache from the stretch of her smile as she adjusted her grip on the now heavy net.

He chuckled. "Or fucking."

And just like that it got awkward.

Her smile melted. Nervous, she met his stare. He had stopped laughing. His eyes—sweet God, his eyes actually changed color—went from gold to green as they locked on her with laser-hot focus.

"Guess that's true," she hedged, floundering. *Fucking.* She bet with him that's what it was. Sex wasn't sex. It was fucking. Hot and messy and rough. She wouldn't know anything about that.

They stood close together, but she didn't take a

step back. It would be like calling uncle—or being the first to blink in a staring contest. She didn't want to be the one to capitulate.

"It's the kind of thing you never forget how to do," he added, his voice deep and thick, like the drag of soft fur against her skin.

She fought to swallow the boulder-size lump in her throat, nodding dumbly, still trying to act like everything was normal, like her pulse wasn't racing and her breasts didn't feel heavy and achy, straining inside her bra.

"Yeah," she agreed nervously. As though she did in fact know. As though her relationship with Charles or her college boyfriends had taught her anything about fucking. She was ignorant when it came to that kind of thing. None of those guys had taught her anything about orgasms either. That remained the stuff of fairy tales.

They remained where they were, connected by the net she was holding with the fish in it that was still hooked to his line. She told herself that was the only thing linking them, the reason she couldn't break away. The reason she couldn't stop looking at him . . . stop her heart from pounding in her chest.

"Sometimes it's even better than you remember," he uttered, not looking at the fish. Looking only at her.

It didn't feel like he was talking about the fish at all. Staring at her, she felt stripped naked. His gaze dropped. Was he looking at her mouth now? No, she had to be projecting. Imagining his gaze on her mouth. Imagining he was on the verge of stepping closer and kissing her like this was some old romantic comedy that would end with the two of them together. Nothing about this was funny. It was life and death and she was sitting here acting like she was Meg Ryan.

She broke eye contact and looked down at the fish flopping inside the net. "What do we do now?" She squeezed her eyes tight in a long blink. That, too, sounded like she could be talking about something else besides fishing. "With the fish, I mean. What do we do with the fish?"

He took his time answering, but when he did, his voice was carefully modulated and unaffected. "I clean it." He took the net from her and moved to the bank. Bending, he grabbed a knife from the tackle box. She followed him and stood silently as he worked.

At least he didn't require her help. There was no further conversation as he quickly gutted the fish and cut it into clean fillets. He worked so quickly and efficiently, like he did this every weekend and hadn't been locked up for years.

"Where'd you learn to do that?"

"Clean a fish? My grandfather taught me, among other things." A smile played around his mouth. "This was his place. He used to bring my brother and me here before he died. He was a good man. He tried to be there for us, you know . . . but my parents . . . Well, you're stuck with the hand you're dealt. You can't do much about who your parents are, can you?"

Something about the way he said that made her chest ache. It was more what he didn't say, what he left out about his parents that convinced her his childhood was not something out of a Norman Rockwell painting—no matter how quaint the cabin.

"No," she agreed. "You can't."

He paused, not looking at her, but she felt as though her simple acknowledgment was telling him something about her, too. It reinforced her early point that they weren't so totally unalike.

"When did he die?" she asked, before she could reconsider the wisdom of having a personal conversation with him.

"I was seventeen. He had a stroke. He went fast, which was good, I guess. His life wasn't left for my mother to decide." He snorted. "She couldn't even take care of herself or her kids. My grandfather wouldn't have wanted his fate left to her." He chuckled, and the sound was lacking all humor. "She would have made a mess of that for damn sure." He sent Grace a quick glance before looking back down at what he was doing. "I've only been back here a few times since then." Another pause fell, in which she watched him. The afternoon sun glinted off his hair, casting it dark gold. "The place has a lot of good memories."

"And now it has new memories. Of me. Your hostage." She angled her head and sent him an arch look.

"Funny."

Her mind worked, calculating. His grandfather died when he was seventeen. He had to have gone to prison soon after that. "How old are you?"

"Thirty-one."

He went to prison when he was just twenty. So young. What had happened in the years between seventeen and twenty that charted him a course straight to prison?

Finished, he stood. "Come on."

He stepped past her, his manner brusque again. Gone was the laughing guy who'd reeled in a fish. That brief flare of chemistry between them had vanished, too. If it had even existed at all. Maybe it was all one-sided. Just in her head . . . or long-ignored libido. Or something that was the result of their isolation together. Either way, it was a good thing that it was gone.

She followed him, trekking back to the house, water squishing out from her wet shoes. He stopped at the shed near the cabin, depositing his tackle box. She left the net there, too, and kept moving. At the porch, she stopped and looked back at him. Who was this guy who liked to fish and share stories of his grandfather?

He'd broken out of prison for a reason, and she wasn't certain it was to rejoin his old criminal network. Nor did she think he was trying to forge a life of freedom for himself. If that were his goal, he wouldn't be holding her hostage. He'd be headed to Mexico. He was this close to the border, after all. He'd told her he was going to end up back in prison. That didn't sound like a guy trying to start over clean.

He wanted to meet with this Sullivan person. She'd heard him insist on that with the others when they were leaving yesterday. That was his goal . . . she just didn't know why. He was an enigma.

Shaking her head, Grace turned and stepped inside the house, putting him out of her sight. For the time being at least. She knew she couldn't avoid him forever. Still, she shouldn't be spending so much time trying to figure him out. He didn't matter. Not his hotness or how dimples had appeared when he smiled and made him look younger. More approachable. Not how fun it was to learn to fish with him. Not his background or his motivations. She didn't *want* to know him.

She needed, instead, to figure out how to land herself out of this mess. One thing was for certain. His goal was this Sullivan guy. Not her well-being. Not getting her home. No, that was entirely up to her.

THIRTEEN

GRACE HAD THE cabin to herself for most of the day. Reid started a fire in the fireplace. It crackled enticingly, but she didn't want to position herself in the main room where she would risk further interaction with him.

Instead, she sequestered herself in the bedroom where she found an old beat up copy of *The Hobbit* on the nightstand. She burrowed on the bed beneath the heavy Aztec-patterned blanket, appreciating the warmth and telling herself the book would distract her. She smiled, thinking of Reid's grandfather reading from the epic fantasy. A good man, Reid had called him. A man with depths, she also suspected.

Cold seeped in from outside, penetrating the skin and bones of the house. Winter was coming. She pulled the blanket to her chin, looking up from the well-read book to the frosted windowpanes, gazing out at the distant mountaintops, a few already capped in snow.

Reid stayed outside most of the day, only coming in once or twice, the thud of his boots alerting her and making her heart stop hard before picking up again.

She emerged to eat a lunch of peanut butter crackers and orange juice—something she could grab quickly and then dive back into her bedroom to (hopefully) avoid Reid.

Once before ducking back into the room she crept cautiously toward the front window. The fire popped and a log crumbled in the fireplace as she munched a cracker and peered outside.

He was there. She watched for some moments. He didn't drift from the front of the house. She was certain that was deliberate. Not so she could spy on him, as it were, but so he could keep an eye on the front door. He did not trust her to stay put.

Grace leaned against the doorjamb, watching him secretly from her vantage point. He buried himself under the hood of the van for a short while, his strong arms flexing as he worked, using tools whose names she didn't know. He was seemingly indifferent to the cold, not even bothering to don a jacket, leaving her to observe the way the muscles in his broad back played beneath the thin fabric of his shirt.

Slamming the hood shut, he moved into the shed, pulling out an old motorcycle that looked like it hadn't seen action in years. After several failed attempts to get it started, he set to work on it. Like he was just any guy spending an afternoon working on his bike. Like he wasn't a wanted man with a hostage that every law enforcement agency in the country was hunting.

Turning away, she picked up her plate and disappeared inside the bedroom, where she spent the next few hours reading and rereading the same pages, trying not to think about Reid and reflect too much on the idea that a boy with a *good* grandfather who taught him to fish couldn't be *all* bad.

Later, she returned to the kitchen with her plate and took another look outside. He was still at work on that motorcycle. She watched him for a while, marveling at what kind of escaped-con/kidnapper/career criminal he was before shuffling back into her bedroom.

Inside the deceptive safety of her room, she gave up on reading and explored, searching all the drawers, looking into the closet and finding only more clothes. The nightstand beside the bed had a single drawer containing a Bible and a few papers. She opened the Bible and saw a name written inside. Jeremiah Hollister. Reid's grandfather? Of course, he read the Bible. And Tolkien.

Grace closed the book and started to put it back in the drawer when a sheet of paper fluttered out. She bent to pick up the folded page from the floor. There was a child's drawing on the slightly yellowed page. Though rudimentary, she could see that it was an illustration of this very cabin. A bright sun overhead, the orb yellow with happy orange rays. A gray, bearded man with a slashing red curve for his lips stood on the porch. It was sweet in its simplicity. Large blocky letters scrawled across the top. *I love you, Grandpa.* At the bottom was a single name. *Reid.*

He had drawn this picture and his grandfather had thought to keep it . . . slipped inside the pages of his Bible. Jeremiah Hollister had clearly treasured it.

Reid had called his grandfather a good person. Well, he wasn't the only one. Reid had been good, too. An innocent boy. He could have led a different life. Maybe if his grandfather had lived he wouldn't have ended up in prison.

For some reason, her eyes burned as she thought

about the little boy who drew this picture growing into a man who lived in a cell.

Grace blinked her stinging eyes, refolded the page and stuck it back inside the Bible, then slammed it inside the drawer. Out of sight. There was definitely something wrong with her if she was starting to feel sorry for him.

Dusk tinged the air outside the windowpanes. She grabbed fresh clothes and ducked back into the bathroom, suddenly restless and eager to take a shower.

In the tiny bathroom, she stood under the spray of water and used the shampoo that smelled faintly astringent. The water started to run cold and she shut it off. Instantly the cold air hit her and she grabbed for a towel, shivering as she rubbed her chilled skin and sopping wet hair. Dressed again, she wrapped her head in the towel, sniffing at the air. Something delicious and buttery wove its way around her. She unwrapped the towel from around her head and attacked the wet snarls with a brush, longing for her conditioner. She slid on a pair of thick men's stocks to combat the chill and stepped out from the bathroom.

Reid stood before the stove in the kitchen, his back to her. She watched him for a moment, noting that he seemed to consume all the space in the tiny kitchen. She edged closer, enjoying the heat flowing from the crackling fireplace. He'd added more logs and it burned with gusto.

He glanced over his shoulder at her. "Hungry?"

"Starving," she admitted. And she was. It had been several hours since those crackers and juice.

"It'll be ready soon."

She stood on her tiptoes, eyeing the fish in a large black skillet. "You get to cook much in prison?"

"No. Never had kitchen duty."

"One of the many things your grandfather taught you, then?"

He grunted. "We cooked whatever we caught the very same day. Doubt you ever had fish this fresh, princess. Even in your fancy restaurants."

It was always there—that gulf separating them. As there should be.

"Take a seat." He nodded to the table.

Grace sank down in one of the four chairs at the small square table, tucking her hands between her thighs and the chair. She watched as he scooped the fish from the pan onto waiting plates.

He set a fork on each plate and carried them to the table, tendrils of steam floating above them. "Want a drink?" He moved back to the fridge and pulled a beer out. He waved a second bottle at her.

"Water, please."

Shrugging, he grabbed a glass from a cabinet, moved to the faucet and poured her water from the tap. She wrinkled his nose as he sat it in front of her. It was decidedly *not* transparent. There was a hue of rustiness to the liquid.

"It's well water," he volunteered. "Might not taste like what you're used to but it's okay to drink."

"Guessing you don't have any coconut water in the refrigerator?"

She was only partially kidding. He stared at her and she registered that he had never even heard of coconut water. Of course. There were probably a lot of things that were part of her everyday world that he had never heard of.

"Maybe I'll have that beer," she murmured, trying not to feel foolish. "I'll get it." Rising, she grabbed a bottle out of the fridge.

He was sitting before his plate when she slid back into her chair. He picked up his fork and started eating. She followed suit, forking up a flaky bit of fish.

It was good. Simple. Pepper and salt with a hint of lemon. Pan-fried in butter. He'd served it with some canned peas on the side.

"This is good."

"You sound surprised."

She lifted one shoulder in an awkward shrug. It was fair to say he was surprising her. He'd cooked a nice meal and was treating her like a dinner companion and not a hostage. She wasn't tied up. He hadn't abused her—for the most part. It was bewildering. They ate in silence. She was even hungrier than she realized. She ate quickly, beating even him.

He lifted an eyebrow as he took a pull on his beer. "I wish I could offer you more but we ate it all."

She took a sip of beer and managed not to wince at the bitter taste. She'd never developed an affinity for the stuff.

"Sorry," she muttered. "It really was good."

One corner of his mouth kicked up and for a moment she thought he might smile. Wrong. "Thanks." Standing, he took both their plates.

"Can I help you—"

"No. I got this," he said abruptly.

Probably for the best. The kitchen was a tight space and she didn't relish being in such close quarters with him. They might have to touch.

Dishes clacked in the sink as he started washing. He cooked *and* did the dishes. That was more than Charles had ever done for her. Most nights they went to whatever trendy new restaurant he wanted to try. Wherever they could get their photo taken and eat something that looked like tiny little spheres topped with edible flowers.

She quickly stifled the thought. She was not in a relationship with Reid. Hardly. She should not be comparing the two men. Or if she did, the comparison should be along the lines of: escaped con versus Harvard grad touted on the Hill as the Hottest Under Forty. Charles was kind. If he could cook, she was sure he would and he'd do it for her.

Crossing her arms, she moved into the living room. Hugging herself to the sound of him washing dishes, she strolled over to an old television propped up on an old trunk. It was square like a box. She couldn't remember the last time she had seen one like it. "Does the TV work?" she called.

"It should," he replied.

She glanced back at him as he dried dishes. She smoothed her hands down her sides nervously, over the fabric of her too big sweatpants. "You mind if I turn it on?"

He stared at her for a long moment, and she knew he was considering the pros and cons of what she would see. Undoubtedly, if she found a news channel there would be coverage about her. Clearly, he was considering how that could play out . . . if there were any negative scenarios that he could stop from happening by preventing her from watching.

He came to a decision and shrugged. "Sure. Go ahead."

She flipped on the TV. The reception wasn't the best. The picture was fuzzy and she could only pick up a few channels.

"Don't suppose you have a laptop? Wi-Fi?"

He looked at her blankly.

"'Course not," she muttered beneath her breath and went back to fiddling with the TV. His laptop was probably right next to where he kept the coconut water. "What I wouldn't give for Netflix right now."

"What's Netflix?" he asked, leaning a hip against the counter.

She looked away from the old television set and met his gaze. Again with the impassive stare. He wasn't joking.

Shaking her head, she turned her attention back to the dial. He'd been imprisoned eleven years. Of course he didn't know about Netflix. She'd bet money that he never even heard of *Sons of Anarchy, Daredevil, Broadchurch*—all her favorites. The shows she watched alone in her bedroom or in hotel suites. She and Charles watched *Doctor Who* faithfully. It gave them something to talk about.

But Reid probably wouldn't need the common ground of a television series to talk to a woman. No, she could imagine how he would spend his time when he was with a woman he liked.

Her cheeks burned as she fiddled with the knob.

One channel finally came through. It happened to be the evening news.

Her heart locked in her chest at the sudden image on the screen. It was the White House, only not as she had ever seen it before. Hundreds, maybe thousands of flowers lined the front gate. Teddy bears with notes pinned to their chests. A banner fluttered with the words: BRING GRACE HOME.

A dull roaring filled her ears as a voice spoke over the scene in a crisp monotone: ". . . concerned citizens continue to leave flowers in front of the White House in support of First Daughter Grace Reeves. The White House has officially issued a statement putting to rest speculation that Grace left of her own accord. There is no doubt that the First Daughter was taken, but where this leaves the Secret Service and FBI on locating the missing woman still remains to be seen. Earlier today, upon returning from a private mass with the First Lady at St. Matthew's, President Reeves made the following statement."

The panorama of the flower-riddled White

House disappeared, and it was suddenly her father standing behind the podium in the press room, handsome as ever in his impeccable suit, gray hair perfectly coiffed. Mom stood one step to the side of him, her exotic beauty not marred in the least by her red-rimmed eyes.

Her father cleared his throat several times before speaking. It was the first time she ever heard hesitation from him. Her heart gave a little pang. He was always perfect in speech and manner. Never hesitation. Business, in this case the running of the country, came first. Everything else came before her. Maybe now, for the first time, she came first. Her fingers drifted to her lips as she sucked in a breath. Maybe she mattered.

When he lifted his gaze, he looked tired. "The outpouring of support my wife and I have received from all around the world has been humbling and a great comfort to us in our time of distress."

Grace gave a little start and released her breath. He was still the politician—seizing this opportunity to his political advantage. She heard it in his choice of words, in the careful tenor of his voice, in the steady way he stared at everyone in the room. She was missing—*abducted!*—and however much he worried for her, he still worried about his office. About winning.

Giving her head a small shake, she tried to clear the rushing sound of blood in her ears and to focus. She tuned back in to the rest of the speech. ". . . right now, I am addressing this country, the world . . . as a father." Here he paused, and she knew that moment was calculated. "A father who wants his daughter back . . ."

Studying him closely, she didn't blink, too afraid she would miss something. She knew this man so well, his tics, his moods. She'd seen him rehearse in front of the mirror. She knew all the behind-the-scenes details that went into every speech her father ever gave. He never spoke in front of the camera without a thorough prepping. This time was no different. Even with her abduction hanging over him, even distraught, this was rehearsed. At the moment, he wasn't speaking from a place of fear or loss or panic. He was being a politician.

She stood up and flicked the TV off, unable to watch him. She knew who her father was. She knew she did not rank at the top of his priorities, but she thought this would have been different. This would have caused a shifting of priorities. Anything could have happened to her . . . anything *could* be happening to her right now. Even with that fear running through his head he was still campaigning.

She was breathing hard, her chest lifting like she'd just run a great distance. She dragged a hand over her face as though that would somehow help her pull herself together.

A floorboard creaked and she recalled that she wasn't alone. She dropped her hand and looked up.

Her gaze flickered over Reid, an unwanted audience witnessing her little meltdown.

"You okay?" he asked.

She nodded once, hard, and then swiftly shook her head from side to side. "No. No, I'm not," she admitted, her hands trembling.

"I promise you'll get back to your family. I know what I say doesn't amount to much to you, but I promise you that."

He thought she was emotional because of her father's plea? "Ha," she got out, the sound strangled. She swallowed to clear her throat. "Don't tell me you bought into that little drama."

He angled his head, clearly unsure what to say.

She continued, her words flying out in a rush. "That's what he does, you know. He lies." She rounded the couch and grabbed the beer Reid had opened and left on the counter. She took a deep swig, forgetting that she hated the taste of the stuff. She was letting her emotions get the best of her. Her father wasn't lying precisely. She knew that. But she wished, for once, he would just be a parent and not that polished public servant.

Reid watched her uncertainly. "I'm sure he's worried and wants you home safely. He's your father—"

She laughed hoarsely. "Oh, I suppose he's worried about me. I know he wants me to be okay. But it's a toss-up whether he's worried about the polls more. About his re-election more." She sobered and drummed her fingers against her lips. "He's spinning this in his favor. Maybe I should show up dead. That's sure to get him reelected—" Her voice broke. It was a terrible thing to say . . . and even more terrible to think.

Reid was in front of her now. His hands closed around her arms, warmly clasping her as he gave her a small shake. "Don't talk like that. You're upset—"

"You have no idea." She wrenched her arms free and took another pull from his beer. "Why did your friends kidnap me?" she demanded, leveling her gaze on him.

His look turned wary at the sudden change in subject. "They're not my friends."

She snorted before taking another drink. "Whatever." She waved a hand dismissively. "I'm guessing they took me because they want to get to my father, hurt him in some way? I would have thought they wanted ransom money, but since they've made no efforts there—at least I think they haven't." She sent him a questioning look, took his blank stare as confirmation. "Didn't think so. So clearly my father pissed off the wrong person . . ." She let her voice fade deliberately, waiting for him to fill in the silence with an explanation.

Nothing. That was telling enough as he stared at her, his expression even more wary than moments before. That muscle ticking in his jaw showed he wasn't unaffected.

She finished the bottle and then moved to the refrigerator. Grabbing another beer, she faced him again. "No comment?"

He watched her like she had sprouted a second head or was simply crazy—and maybe she was. She just declared to her abductor that he could kill her and no one would care. Well, *much*. Probably not the smartest thing to tell the guy holding you hostage. "Hey, I'm worthless and it doesn't really matter what you do to me" probably wasn't the best thing to say.

Still. She couldn't stop vomiting words. Tears burned the backs of her eyes and it was either this or break down and cry. She'd never been big into letting people see her cry, so there was only this over sharing.

She leaned forward as though about to impart something confidential, dropping her voice to a conspiratorial pitch. "I'll let you in on a little secret. My father is not the perfect man that forty-seven percent of the country think he is."

Reid angled his head. "Only forty-seven percent?"

She nodded. "Last polling. Horrible, right? Especially heading into re-election. Although I'm guessing he's rating higher right now. Personal tragedy wins empathy." She waved her bottle in a little circle. "This is probably doing wonders for his campaign. Bet there is a lot of back-clapping the moment he gets behind closed doors."

"Stop it, Grace. Your mother looked wrecked."

Grace looked away as she took another drink, shrugging. Her mother loved her but not as much as she loved her husband. No, her mother would love no one more than she loved him. Secretly, Grace had always thought that's why she never had more children. She suspected her mother never felt enough of a connection to her to have another child.

The reminder of her relationship with her mother only fueled her self-pity. "Suffice to say, you don't know shit about me or my life." She tilted her head and took another drink, gulping in an unladylike way that would have horrified her mother.

Something passed over Reid's features before a wall slammed down on his face, killing any sympathy that might have been there for her. "I can see what's in front of me well enough."

"Yes? And what do you see, Yoda?"

His nostrils flared. "A spoiled little princess who didn't like what she just saw. Daddy wasn't crying enough for you and now you need petting." He waved an arm at the TV. "The whole fucking country is leaving roses for you, but that's not enough—"

She hissed a deep breath. Her eyes stung at his razor-sharp words and the kernel of truth they held. "Shut up—"

"You still want more. Being the center of the universe isn't enough? Your ego needs more—"

"You don't get it . . ." He didn't. Ego was the last thing she possessed. She didn't need or want to be the center of the universe. Every time Charles dragged them out to dinner, she wished they could have just stayed in and ordered pizza. Reid was wrong. She wasn't that vain creature he was describing. The only thing she wanted was acceptance from her parents. Love. She'd done everything they ever wanted, shelved her own dreams, hoping to have that from them.

The world couldn't mourn her? They didn't

know her. This was the same world that voted her unlikable in the polls last month. So what if they were leaving flowers for her now? They weren't her family. Her father was supposed to love her. Above anyone else, a girl's father should want to tear the earth apart to get her back safely. He should care about her life above all else, right? She was his daughter. He shouldn't expect her to marry someone for the sake of his campaign. And he should be wrecked that she was missing.

Staring at Reid, she imagined that felon or not, he would care if someone close to him was in trouble. If someone belonged to him, he wouldn't quit until that person was safe. The idea was faintly compelling. And dangerous. Her gaze skimmed the strong line of his shoulders, the way his biceps pushed against his snug thermal shirt. She remembered the strength in those arms. The power. This guy would move heaven and earth for—

She crushed the thought. She would never be that person to him.

"That's right, princess. I don't know you. You know who would leave flowers for me? Fucking no one."

She stifled a flinch. *No.* She would not feel sorry for him. "Big shock there," she flung out instead, reaching for the memory of him chasing her down and slinging her over his shoulder like a sack of potatoes. No hugs for him.

"Oh, that's right." He advanced a step, his lips moving, spitting out words like arrows. Doubtlessly trying to use his size to intimidate her. She wouldn't let him. She stood her ground. "I'm just a dirty felon."

"That's right. An escaped convict that belongs behind bars."

"Yeah, well sorry, sweetheart, but this dirty con isn't buying into your little pity party—"

"Stop it!"

"If Daddy doesn't love you enough, maybe you need to take a hard look in the mirror and figure some things out about yourself."

Her fist rocketed out and struck him in the jaw. Hard. Hard enough to hurt her hand. Hard enough to force him back a step.

She stared, shocked at herself. She had struck him. No measly girly slap either. She full-fledged hit him with her fist, and her knuckles throbbed for it. She'd never done that before.

Her chest lifted with savage breaths. His words echoed through her, accusing her of the very thing that had hidden in her heart ever since childhood. There was something inherently unlovable about her.

She couldn't blink, couldn't look away from his

face. That muscle was alive and kicking in his jaw again. He looked fierce—like some Viking walking into battle . . . or emerging from battle. All that was missing was his battle-axe.

Too late she realized her mistake.

She'd forgotten herself. She forgot who she was. Simply a captive. And more importantly, she forgot who he was. A merciless criminal who would stop at nothing to get what he wanted. So what if he wounded her with some ugly words? He could hurt her in far worse ways.

There was no sound save the crash of their breaths filling the space between them. She started sliding back a step, but his hand shot out. She squeaked and lifted her fists, prepared to fight him, however hopeless it would be against his greater strength.

His hand closed around the back of her neck, hauling her closer until all of her pushed against the lean length of him. It was like being pressed up against a living, breathing wall. A wall that radiated heat. Their angry breaths collided, mingled. Their gazes devoured each other. His cheek burned an angry red from her fist.

She realized his intent the moment before his head swooped down. His mouth crashed over her own.

Her hands were lost, crushed between their

bodies. She couldn't move. His other arm stole around her, pulling her in tight, wrapping her up in him. It was impossible to break his iron hold.

Of course, there was the question of whether she wanted to.

His kiss was firm and demanding, punishing and yet seductive. Her head swam as his mouth softened slightly against her lips. His fingers curled into her hair, fisting the heavy mass and pulling her head back, forcing her chin up.

Her lips parted on a gasp, and his tongue slid along her bottom lip in a sinuous move. Her blood sang, everything in her melting. She opened her mouth wider, inviting him in. Their tongues touched and it felt like a bolt of electricity shot through her.

The sparks they talked about in movies and books, but she never felt? What she hoped to find with Charles? This was it. She'd found it at last, and it was with a criminal. Her mother would be outraged.

That single thought gave her the final push. The idea of her mother's disapproval, her horror, broke any fleeting resistance.

All tentativeness fled. She leaned forward, diving into the kiss, into him like she was dehydrated and he her last chance for water.

He growled, deepening the kiss, gripping her hair harder, angling her head so that her mouth was in a position to his liking. He took. He claimed, and that only made the need pulse harder inside her.

She struggled to free her hands, but it wasn't because she wanted to push him away or fight him. No, not anymore. She wanted to wrap her arms around his neck and climb inside him. There was no such thing as too close. No such thing as too much or too far.

He growled as if sensing her surrender. It was the longest kiss of her life. She didn't know that a kiss could last until her lips went numb and bolts of sensation flooded to every nerve in her body.

Her entire being ended and began where his mouth fused with hers. The heady taste of him, rich and deep and faintly meady from the beer—or maybe she was tasting herself on him. She didn't know. She only knew that minutes ago she had been hurting and now there was this. Desire and want and sex. Sex with mouths alone. She never wanted it to end. She could climax through this alone. She knew it. This kiss could keep going and it would happen. She already felt the twisting ache starting at her core.

He broke away, still holding onto her with that fist in her hair and his arm locked around her waist. He looked down at her with blazing eyes. "What the fuck was that?"

She moistened her tingling lips. His eyes tracked the movement of her tongue, the flecks of gold standing out within the green of his eyes. And glowing. Glowing like candlelight. "You kissed me," she returned, her voice a whispered hush.

"You needed kissing."

She thought about that for a second, recognizing the truth, terrible or not, of that statement. She needed kissing. *Yes. Yes, I did.*

And I needed more.

"So what's the problem, then?" she asked.

He frowned. "You weren't supposed to like it. You weren't supposed to kiss me back like . . ." Words failed him.

Like what? She searched his face.

Her body burned. She felt dizzy, drugged, words elusive as she struggled for speech. Stringing words together felt like too much of a challenge when all she wanted to do was kiss him again. And again. And maybe they could follow that with more kissing. "Maybe you should do it again, then. This time, I'll try not to like it so much."

A hissed breath escaped him. "You shouldn't say things like that."

"Why not?" Even as she asked the question, she

knew. She knew why not. He was who he was. She was who she was. Everything was wrong about this. Except her body thought it felt right. Her long-denied libido thought it felt pretty perfect.

"Because I might take you up on your offer." She felt him then—the hard erection digging into her. Her mouth parted on a gasp.

He pushed his hips forward, and that succeeded in making her moan. She felt her own eyes widen. Felt her muscles quiver and clench between her legs.

"Would that be so bad?" she whispered, even though she didn't need to talk in such low tones. Even though it was just the two of them all alone out here in the middle of nowhere. No witnesses. The outside world forgotten, this great big thing that didn't matter or exist. That's how it felt in this moment. That was how she wanted it to be.

His fingers flexed in her hair, pulling her forward so he could fan the words across her lips. "Careful, little girl. This is a game you don't want to start with me."

It was her turn to frown. "I'm not a little girl."

"Then you know that kissing leads to other things."

"Sure. And it's not anything I haven't done before." God, was she actually saying such things to him? Was she actually baiting him into sleeping with her?

She had clearly crossed a threshold. He should terrify her, but she couldn't dredge up a shred of regret. There was no impulse to flee or go back. Only forward.

Something passed over his features and his pale eyes darkened, the flecks of amber bright inside the deep green. "I can assure you . . . you haven't done it with me before."

She studied his face, admiring its brutal beauty. No, her list of lovers was short, totaling two, and neither one of them were anything like this man. Really, they were boys in comparison. Nor would any man in her future be like him. She knew that without a doubt. She didn't cross paths with warrior Viking types. This might be her only chance to have this, to be with someone who was so . . . raw. Someone who didn't have sex. Her gaze skimmed him, wholly convinced. He didn't have sex. He fucked.

He stepped back, dropping his arms from around her.

She stood there, feeling bereft and trying to hide it as she recovered from the kiss to end all kisses.

Without a word he turned and marched out of the kitchen into the bedroom, leaving her alone.

Left to herself, mortification slowly slipped in, settling alongside his rejection.

He'd told her she wasn't his type. Apparently he meant it. He might have kissed her in some fit of temper, but he didn't want more. He didn't want her even though she had flung herself at him like some dog in heat. *God*. She closed her eyes in a long, pained blink, rubbing one palm against her overheated cheek.

She had definitely crossed a threshold. She was ready to bump uglies with an escaped felon, her kidnapper. It was so messed up. *She* was messed up.

She inhaled deeply. It was the stress of the situation. If they'd actually done it, she would have been riddled with regret afterward. It wouldn't have been real. It couldn't ever be real.

It was a sign. When she made it back to the real world, she would make some changes and get her life in order. No more living for her father. It was overdue, but her life would finally be her own.

FOURTEEN

*G*RACE DISAPPEARED INTO the bathroom. She wished she could just disappear altogether and didn't have to face him ever again, but since she was still his captive, the bathroom was the only place she could truly hide.

First order of business after she got out of here? Get laid.

Okay, maybe not first order. She'd have to break the news to her parents that she was leaving DC and taking back her life.

Deciding that a cold shower always worked in books and movies, she stripped off her clothes and stepped inside. She gasped at the shock of cold. She felt like she deserved a little punishment after that kiss. Her behavior had been unforgivable. Responding . . . embracing it.

She endured the icy water for as long as she

could. She didn't need to wash her hair again, so she angled the showerhead so the water didn't make contact with her body. In no rush to face him, she pressed her palms flat against the shower wall and dropped her head, stretching her too-tight neck. Her mind backtracked over the events of the last couple days, landing on one all-important, definitive fact. She was still alive. That was the everything of it. The most important fact. Reid had promised he would keep her safe. He'd promised that there was an end date to this, even if he didn't tell her when. Eventually, he would return her back to her life.

Her life. She mulled over that for a moment. After the terror of her abduction and near brush with rape back at that house with all those horrible men, after witnessing her father's exaggerated display of grief over her abduction, she suddenly viewed her life with intense dissatisfaction. She viewed it with fresh determination. It needed to change. She was twenty-six years old. She was finished living according to her father's dictates. When she got out of this mess, she would no longer be playing the part of puppet for her father, and she was most definitely *not* announcing an engagement to Charles.

If their relationship didn't improve, if chemistry

didn't actually arise between them, she was finished with dating him. If it could even be called that. They dined out for the benefit of cameras. Shared chaste pecks, again for the benefit of cameras. They watched *Doctor Who* together. The rest of the time he talked about work. Politics. Her father. Mood killer, that. He talked about the future. *His* future.

She was finished with everything in her life that wasn't real. Maybe she would start dating someone who actually wanted *her* for her. Just because Reid had rejected her didn't mean there wasn't someone out there for her. Her ex, Nathan, always told her she was a good kisser. She had something to offer in the sex department. Granted, kissing was just a part of it, but she wasn't totally inept. Now that she knew her libido wasn't dead—thanks to a certain muscle-bound escaped convict—she felt certain she could find someone who got her blood pumping. More than Charles did anyway.

Wincing, she shut off the water and opened the wobbly fake-glass door.

She owned the inappropriate thought. She'd done enough lying. Publicly, she had been lying for years, pretending that she had the perfect life, the perfect family, perfect boyfriend. Pretending to care about things she didn't care about. The least she could do was be honest with herself. Even if it was messed up to admit it, her captor was hot, and her long neglected girl parts had noticed.

She reached for the scratchy cotton towel on the hook. Not nearly big enough to wrap around her body. An unwanted image of naked Reid rose in her mind. It must be like a washcloth against his big frame. Instead of striking her as ridiculous, the visual only burned her face.

By the time she emerged, he'd shut off most of the lights in the house. Only the lamp in the living room glowed.

She stopped at the threshold to the master bedroom that she'd spent so much time in today. He'd arranged his pallet near the door again, leaving room for her to pass. The sight of him there brought home the reminder that he still did not trust her.

She stepped around him. He didn't stir. Pulling back the covers, she slipped into bed, turning on her side. She stared unseeingly at the opposite wall, watching flickering shadows chase the darkness. She tried valiantly not to think back to that footage of her father, but she couldn't help herself. She saw him standing there in the press room. Saw his lips move, heard those words that she knew were meaningless to him.

Then she heard Reid's voice in her head. *If Daddy doesn't love you enough, maybe you need to take a hard look in the mirror and figure some things out.*

It was cruel, but she wondered if he was right. Lying there in the darkness, old insecurities found her and bit deep. She felt like a little girl again, forced to play the piano in front of her father's guests. Every time her fingers stumbled or hit the wrong key, she could feel her parents cringe.

Maybe there was something fundamentally wrong with her in that she couldn't inspire love and devotion from her parents. From anyone.

Bullshit. For the first time, she felt the stirrings of anger deep in her belly. She didn't blame herself for that anymore. People cared about her. She had friends. Granted, the list was short, but it was hard to make friends she could call her own when everyone had to be vetted by her father.

Still, she had Holly. She might be on her father's payroll, but no one forced Holly to like her. And there was her college roommate, Abby. Not a week went by when they didn't talk. They texted almost every day. Especially since Abby got engaged. And Charles. They were friends, just not lovers. They spent too much time together to fake friendship.

When Charles first asked her out, she thought

it was actually because he wanted to go out with her. But after a few dates she knew the score. Her father had put him up to it. There was probably no chance for sparks once she knew that. Maybe it was her fault. Maybe she'd never given him—them—a chance.

She sniffed and rubbed at her nose, blinking burning eyes. She'd wasted all these years, hoping she might eventually earn her parents' love and approval. No more. She wasn't going to try any longer. She was taking back control.

Tonight, with Reid, she had been bold and stepped outside her boundaries. As crazy as it had been, she had learned something from it. She was going to seize life. She would live boldly—just no more making out with escaped convicts.

The bed dipped and she grabbed the edge to stop from rolling to the center. She craned her head to look around at Reid sliding in beside her.

"What do you want?" she snapped, blinking burning eyes that brimmed with tears, rubbing them with the heel of her hands.

"Why are you crying?"

Damn it. She was crying. She hadn't even realized it.

"I'm not—"

"Liar."

She snorted. "Why do you care?"

"Because I can hear you sniffling from across the room."

"I have a cold. Don't concern yourself."

He was quiet for a long moment, staring at her in the dark, his disbelief palpable between them, which only made her feel more wretched. The urge to cry was still there, pressing on the back of her throat. But these tears were different. Not self-pitying. She was pissed.

His hand closed over her shoulder, forcing her to roll around and face him fully. Her feet brushed along his. He hissed a breath. "Damn, woman, your feet are like blocks of ice."

"I did what you suggested," she confessed, her throat tight.

"Yeah?" His deep, gravelly voice stroked her skin. "Remind me what that was."

"I took a hard look at myself, and you're right. There's something wrong with me." The last half of her words escaped in a strangled choke. "But that's going to change."

A muffled curse escaped him. "I never meant—"

"It's fine. As soon I get home I'm making some changes."

"You shouldn't listen to me. Half the time I don't know what I'm saying. I'm a dick."

She nodded against the pillow. "You are a dick. But you're right. I'm done letting others control me. Yes, that goes for you, too."

"Me, too, huh? You think I'm in control of you?" His voice sounded funny, almost like he was strangling a little. He reached out, brushing his thumb across her cheek, catching a tear she didn't even realize had escaped.

She gulped, trying to drag back the tears. One slipped loose anyway.

His hand slid alongside her cheek, his fingers wrapping around her neck. "Don't," he whispered, tugging her toward him, bringing her forehead to rest against his. "Sweetheart, don't cry."

The tenderness of his plea thawed the worst of her anger. This dangerous, rough man with all his jagged edges actually felt sorry for her. Damn it. A fucking felon felt sorry for her. The floodgates opened. She wept ugly, copious tears. Her captor felt pity for her.

Holding her by the neck, his lips moved, murmuring nonsense against her cheek. She wasn't sure when it evolved into kissing, but his lips were on her face, brushing the tracks of tears, crooning, "It's going to be okay. Hush. Don't cry. Don't cry, sweetheart."

She couldn't stop, though, and she couldn't

catch her breath between the sad little sounds tearing from her lips.

Then he kissed her. Full on the mouth. He swallowed her sobs. His mouth moved over hers, devouring. She tasted the salt of her own tears on his lips, felt his groan, took it inside herself.

Stunned, she stopped crying. It was hard to feel sad when his mouth was so very good, so very hot. His tongue worked against hers like she was some kind of dessert and he was determined to have every last morsel.

Her hands drifted to his bare shoulders, reveling in the firmness of his skin.

There were no more tears, but other sounds welled up in her throat. Hungry, needy little sounds.

She clutched his shoulders harder. "This is a mistake," she gasped against his lips.

"Definitely a mistake," he agreed, deepening the kiss and coming over her, his knees settling between her thighs, nudging them apart.

His elbows settled on either side of her, fingers diving into her hair, palms holding her head in position for his plundering lips.

Yeah. A mistake, but she couldn't stop. For the first time she was going to do something just because it felt good. She'd handle the consequences later like a big girl. Obviously this wasn't going anywhere, but she'd take it. She'd take now. Deal with later . . . later.

Widening her thighs, she invited him in and lifted her hips to meet the hardness of him through his sweatpants. She found him, hard and jutting to meet her. She gasped into his mouth and ground against him.

His mouth lifted from her with a gasp and stinging curse.

"Reid," she whimpered, but he was gone, moving, the full weight of him lifting off her.

She bit her lip both with relief and excitement when she felt him seize the rolled waistband of her boxer shorts. He pulled them off her in a move so swift it stole her breath.

Only a T-shirt and the panties were left, saving her from complete nakedness. He came back over her, crouching between her legs. She felt his gaze crawl over her like a caress. His hands settled on the outside of her thighs, his palms work-worn and rough. Her belly twisted at the sensation.

His eyes gleamed in the dark, finding her face. "Are you faking it this time?"

"Wh-What?"

"This . . . you and me? Is it real?"

Then it clicked. He was referring to their first night when she tried to manipulate him with her body. Of course that had backfired even then because she had liked it. Desperately. She had liked his hands on her even then.

"I'm not faking anything with you." And she wasn't. Terrible or not, she wanted him. She *needed* him. She wanted him to show her what it was like . . . what he had been talking about earlier today. *Fucking.* In a moment of striking clarity, she realized this might be the most genuine she had ever been with anyone. This thing between them, this heat . . . it was real.

Apparently satisfied, his hands started a slow ascent up her thighs, his thumbs turning and arrowing for the crotch of her underwear. She slid down a little on the bed, inching to meet him with a shaky sigh.

His thumbs centered on her, stroking up and down the crotch of her panties, trailing along her seam before finding and pressing down on her clit. She cried out and arched, her palms pushing down on the mattress. She wanted her panties gone, off. Incinerated to ashes. The barrier of damp fabric was torture.

"You don't get to come back from this," he growled, propping one hand beside her head and coming over her like some great beast in the dark, his hand still working between her thighs, fingers rubbing in fierce circles, bringing her to a frenzy.

She both nodded and shook her head in wild, jerky motions. Senseless. Mindless for him. She was close. The tide of an orgasm swelled up on her. So close. She bit her lip.

His fingers paused on her. "I'm sorry." His voice shook slightly. "I shouldn't take advantage of you like this, but I have to have this . . . *you*. Before I end up back in prison, I need this."

Eleven years. He'd been in prison for eleven years. For the first time, she didn't feel the usual disgust. That fact made something hot unfurl in her belly. "I know what I'm doing." She'd be his first woman in all that time. It shouldn't matter, but for some reason it did.

"I doubt that or you wouldn't let me touch you like this. Like I'm going to." He leaned down on his elbow and slid his hand into her hair, gripping hard, pulling her head back and angling her face so that they stared directly into each other's eyes. "Say this is real," he demanded. "Say you want it."

She unclenched her teeth from her lip. "I want it."

His eyes flicked back and forth between hers like he was assessing for the truth.

She inhaled a thick breath. "I want *you*."

A growl rumbled up from his chest, vibrating into her. The sound made her feel desired, beautiful. Wanted by this big, gorgeous brute with his piercing eyes and magic hands.

He did this thing with his wrist and bore down, making her gasp, moan. She couldn't help herself.

She ran her fingers into his short hair, learning the shape of his skull beneath her palm. The promise of release welled back up inside her again, bigger than anything she had ever felt before. She couldn't stop it. She didn't want to. She rode the wave arching under him.

He pushed, touched, stroked. All over the thin soaking wet fabric of her panties. She wasn't even naked. There was no penetration.

"God. You're hot for it," he grunted against her mouth before claiming her lips in another scorching, messy kiss that was full of pants and moans.

And then, suddenly, he knuckled aside her panties and pushed one finger deep inside her, curling up and touching her so deeply that she shattered, crying out loudly. Wildly. Uninhibited. Something she had never done. Never thought possible. Especially with a man like him.

It was like he wasn't going to give up until he wrung an orgasm out of her. Her grip twisted tighter in the sheets. "Give it to me. Come for me, Gracie. I need to hear it, feel it, from you."

No one had ever called her Gracie before. It was

cute. Feminine. Not nearly formal enough for her parents' tastes, and it was another hit, another attack to her overwrought system.

"I—I . . ." She tossed her head from side to side, not knowing what to do with the overwhelming sensations.

"Now, Gracie," he said, his voice hard. In control. "Come for me now."

She arched, breaking apart as his fingers worked over her, not stopping, not slowing down even through the wave of her mind-obliterating orgasm.

She gripped his skull with one hand as her other palm skated down the smoothness of his muscled back, the aftershocks of her orgasm eddying throughout her.

This wasn't her. It couldn't be her. And yet it was. It was and she didn't regret it. They were still partially clothed, his finger buried deep inside her. The hunger was still there, pulsing within her . . . unfed in him.

Even through his clothes his erection rocked solid against the inside of her thigh. She was acutely, achingly aware that there was much left to explore and a lot left unfinished between them.

And they had a long night still ahead of them.

FIFTEEN

*T*HIS HAD BAD IDEA written all over it. His entire body shook with restraint as he hovered over her. He took a gulp of air as he fought to pull himself together.

He'd forbidden himself to cross this line with her. It was wrong on so many levels. Even if she wanted him now, she would regret it tomorrow. Or the next day. Or simply when she was back in her world . . . back in her role as First Daughter.

She would look back at this time with him in horror. What he'd just done to her was bad enough . . . but if they went ahead and had sex. Well, that would be worse. He might not be forcing her, but she would feel just as traumatized later.

Still, with all of these very reasonable, very sobering thoughts tracking through his mind, he did not withdraw. His one hand remained buried in her hair while his other was still lodged between her smooth thighs, his finger deep inside her. He breathed slow breaths in and out, the pulse thudding a fast tempo in his ears as he reveled in the way she throbbed all around him. He felt awake and alive in a way he had not felt in years.

That could be you buried inside her. She wouldn't stop him. She was saying all the right things that signified consent.

If he didn't get off her, Reid didn't know if he could stop himself. He was too hard, too hungry, too desperate . . .

He withdrew, sliding off her. His body protested, wept for her, but his mind held strong. He couldn't stand the thought of her hating him later. For abducting her and holding her captive, sure. That was fair. He'd take the hit for that. But he wasn't going to fuck her when it was something she would regret later.

One of her hands grabbed his arm, her slim fingers digging into his skin. "Where are you going?"

He inhaled a deep breath. "Grace, we can't. We're done."

Her eyes widened, liquid-dark pools that could drown a man. He certainly felt like he was drowning. And not just in her eyes. In her scent. In all that night-black hair that his hands couldn't get enough of. In the taste and texture of her.

Christ. He needed out of this room.

"What?" she whispered, her voice no less demanding for its quiet.

He decided to go with honesty. "I didn't climb into this bed to do this. You were crying . . . I was concerned—"

She recoiled as though he had struck her. "That was pity?"

He shook his head, realizing that wasn't the full truth of it either. Touching her had nothing to do with pity. "No—"

She angled her head, her voice mocking as she bit out, "Here's an orgasm to make you feel better?" She let him go and scrambled for the covers, pulling them over her bare legs. "I'm such an idiot." She shook her head, tossing all that lush hair behind her. "You're just a full-service kind of criminal, aren't you? Abduction and orgasms. Do you know how to bake brownies, too?"

"Gracie—"

She shook her head harder. "No, don't call me that."

"You've been through a lot. You don't want to do this with me." He motioned between the two of them. "You're going to go back to your world soon and you don't want to regret—"

"I get it." She held up a hand, clearly hoping to stop him from saying more. "No need to explain. We've been through this already. I'm not your type. And hey, you're not mine. I already have a fiancé."

He stiffened. Somehow he had forgotten that fact. Just another reason to keep his distance. She wasn't his to have. She belonged to someone else.

"That's right." He nodded, an ugly tightness stealing over him. All reasonableness fled him. Gone was the cool logic of moments ago. His urge to fling her down on that bed and make her his, mark her forever, stamp her as his own, was over-powering. For eleven years he'd lived by a code of taking, claiming, and holding onto what's yours with your last breath if need be.

Irrational anger pumped through him. He wasn't in a position to be with her and yet that didn't stop him from resenting like hell that an-other man could be. "You have someone to fuck you just as soon as you get home."

He felt a stab of satisfaction at her sharp inhala-tion.

"That's right!" she echoed. "And he won't stop

when the job's half done. He'll have no problem finishing."

His hands curled into fists at his sides to stop from reaching for her. He felt like shaking her, but God knew what he would do if he actually touched her.

Turning, he strode toward his pallet, his feet hitting the floor hard. Bending, he snatched up his bedding. There was no way in hell he could sleep in the same room with her. He straightened and glared at her, sitting at attention on the bed, and she glared in turn at him, her dark eyes coal bright.

With one hand on the doorknob, he tossed out, "Be sure to let him know that I kept you warm and ready for him."

With a growl of indignation, she grabbed a pillow and threw it across the room. It landed several feet short of him. He glanced from the pillow on the floor to her. He knew he should walk out. He was angry. Sexually frustrated. Anything he said at this point couldn't be kind.

Still, he couldn't stop taking one more parting shot. "Try not to think of me when it's him inside you."

"Why would I?" she hissed. "I haven't a clue what that's like . . . thank God," she added with a flourish, waving her arms out on either side of her.

He tsked. "How quickly you forget you were just begging me for it."

"Bastard!"

Grinning, he shut the door. He tossed his blanket on the couch and settled in, lying flat on his back and propping his hands behind his head. His smile quickly evaporated, taking with it any smugness he had felt. He glanced toward the closed bedroom door, feeling an uncomfortable tugging in his gut.

He'd forgotten how much he sucked at the relationship thing. He'd had plenty of girls, but never loved any of them. He didn't know how to do that. He'd gone to prison at twenty years old, so maybe that would have come with time. Maybe not. It wasn't as though he'd had any stellar examples to follow.

His grandmother died when he was just a baby. His grandfather had been a quality person but had never been the model for a healthy, monogamous relationship. His parents had only shown him dissipation and general fucked-up-ness.

Christ. He scrubbed two hands over his face. Why was he even thinking about love with Grace? Or relationships? This had an expiration date. And it wasn't like anything was possible between them even without one. They were from two different worlds. Might as well be different species.

Damn. He was obsessing. He needed to get out of here and get on with it all.

Pushing up from the couch, he strode to the kitchen. He didn't care if it was late. He grabbed the phone and called his brother, pacing until Zane picked up. It sounded like he was at a party. Music and voices overlapped in the background.

"Hey, Reid. How's it going out there?" Zane said in an overly loud voice.

"Fine. What's the word, man? Heard from Sullivan?"

"Yeah, yeah. Talked to Sullivan. Honestly, he wasn't too happy. He doesn't think you've got the chops to see this thing through with the girl."

"Zane, I need you to convince him." Just like he needed all of this to end. This thing with Grace. Over. Sullivan? Yeah, he needed to finish that, too. It was the whole point. The reason he broke out— although too much of his head was wrapped up in the girl in the next room. He was starting to lose focus.

"Don't worry, man. I got your back." Voices and laughter broke out in the background. "Hey, save me some!" Zane shouted with a laugh.

"Hey! Don't forget about me," Reid warned, his voice snappy.

Zane spoke into the phone again. "You got our

hostage. No one's forgetting. How's she doing? You roughing her up?"

Emotion clogged Reid's throat. Grief for the kid brother he'd lost. Anger at the man who had taken his place.

"You come up here much, Zane?" he asked, gazing blindly into the darkened kitchen, focusing on the window above the sink, the frosted glass, the world outside of it. Brittle leaves drifted from the branches of a big oak.

"Nah. Why? Is it run-down?"

"No, just being here reminds me of the old man. Those were good times."

"Honestly, I don't remember him too much."

Reid closed his eyes in a slow pained blink. That might explain some of it. His brother didn't remember their grandfather and all he had taught them . . . shown them. How not to be like their father and men like Rowdy. How to not fall under the thumb of a man like Sullivan.

Shaking his head, he swallowed down the thickness in his throat. "All right. You keep working on getting me that meeting with Sullivan."

"Will do."

He hung up the phone and turned back to the couch. Settling down on it, he fixed his stare on the door that separated him and Grace. *Gracie.*

That's how he would always think of her. When he returned to his cold jail cell, he wouldn't think of her as Grace Reeves, the First Daughter. She was Gracie. His. Even if she wasn't.

GRACE SPENT THE next day in her room. Mostly. She came out in the morning, but only because she had to use the bathroom and eat. She managed to avoid his gaze as she made toast, grabbed an apple, and poured herself juice.

In the afternoon she wasn't so lucky. She emerged to an empty cabin and tiptoed like a teenager sneaking out. Stealth was critical. She opened the refrigerator and took out a package of cheese slices and slapped together a cheese sandwich. Under normal circumstances she would have grilled it on the stove, but she wanted to be back in her room before he returned from wherever he was. She knew he was close. He wouldn't have strayed too far. Last night had changed nothing. If anything, things were worse. More tense. He still wouldn't trust her.

She grabbed a can of soda and bag of potato chips to go with her sandwich, ready to dive back into her room when the front door suddenly opened. He walked in, carrying an armful of firewood.

His gaze locked with hers. Tension crackled and she felt her face heat, the memory of him in bed with her, his hands on her, touching her where she hadn't been touched in so long. In a way no one had *ever* touched her.

"Getting chilly," his voice rumbled. "Tonight should be downright cold." He turned his back on her and squatted, stacking logs in the firewood rack.

She shifted on her feet, her mouth drying as she gazed at him. "Didn't think it got this cold in Texas," she said inanely.

"Texas is a big state. Lots of different climates. It snows early in these mountains. Soon this place will be blanketed in white."

It would be beautiful. Something right off a Christmas card. She bit back the comment that she would like to see that. This wasn't a holiday. And he wasn't a friend . . . contrary to how the lines might have gotten blurred last night.

Turning awkwardly, she moved toward the bedroom, ready to slip inside where she didn't have to look at him anymore. Where she didn't have to reflect on everything they had done last night. Everything she had let him do. Everything she had felt.

His voice stopped her.

"Afraid to eat out here? In my company?"

She turned back around. "Why should it matter to you where I eat?"

After a moment he replied, "It doesn't matter."

She stared at the broad expanse of his back, admiring the way the muscles and sinew flexed under his thermal shirt. She headed back for the bedroom, but his voice stopped her again. "How'd you meet your boyfriend?"

"Charles?"

He rose, dusting his hands, leveling those green-gold eyes on her. Amusement lurked there, and something else. Something she couldn't name but that did funny little things to her insides. "Yeah."

"He's my fiancé," she reminded him.

His lips twisted, looking down at her hand. "No ring?"

"Not yet. It's not official." She knotted the hand that should have showcased an engagement ring. "I met him during my father's first campaign," she answered.

"So he works for Daddy."

There was no mistaking the derision in his voice. "Yes. You could say that."

His gaze flicked away, dismissing her. "Doesn't seem your type."

She straightened her spine, heat flaring in her cheeks. It wasn't the first time she'd heard someone say that about Charles and her. Not the first time some cute intern blinked her long eyelashes at her and tapped her glossy lips with some passive aggressive remark. *You two seem soooo different. I never would have pictured you two dating.*

"Oh, you know him, do you?"

He shrugged like that was a moot point. "No."

"Then you know me so very well?"

At this, he looked at her and paused again. *Really* looked at her. Almost like he did know her. Like he saw her. She couldn't remember the last time anyone had looked at her like that—as if seeing past flesh and bones to the woman who had been trapped inside for so long—and she felt an uncomfortable flush of heat.

"Well," she prodded, even though she knew she should let it go. "Why is that?" she demanded, her fingers clenching around the edge of her plate.

"He just seems so slick."

And why did it sound like he just said *sewer rat*?

"Well, he is the White House communications director. Being polished is part of his job." Defensiveness edged her voice.

"It's not just that." He advanced on her where she stood holding her plate. She held her ground.

She knew she shouldn't rise to the bait, but she heard herself asking, "Then what is it about him that doesn't seem my type?" What she was really asking was: *What is it about me?*

"Well, if you have to know . . ."

His voice faded as he closed the last few feet separating them. She backed away until she bumped the small kitchen island. His hands settled around the edge of the counter, caging her in. Her plate was wedged between them, saving them from full body contact. He idly glanced down at the dish.

She swallowed the boulder-size lump in her throat and nodded at him to continue.

"He seems a little *too* polished for you," he elaborated, his voice low and husky, reminding her of a dark room and his hands on her skin. "Not the kind of guy to bury his face between a woman's thighs because it might mess up his hair. Know what I mean?"

Actually, she did. Charles took great pains with his hair.

The heat scoring her face reached nuclear level proportions. "Oh." Suddenly that's all she could imagine. Reid's face between her legs, her hands in his hair.

"Oh," he echoed with a lazy smile.

Her girl parts stood up and did a cheer, pompoms waving. That smile really was criminal. Ha! A criminal smile for a criminal. *God.* She winced at her inside joke. She was losing it. Or was it just that smile, rendering her stupid? Making her forget things like the fact that he was an escaped felon?

"And you," he continued, "well, you're the kind of woman that revels in a guy going down on you."

I am?

Yes. Yes. She was.

Maybe not before, but suddenly that's who she was. Maybe she had been that all along and just didn't know it. He had awakened that dormant side to her. Unleashed this uninhibited, sexual creature.

He leaned close enough that his words fanned against her lips. "There's a hellcat in you. You would like it wild. You'd use your nails. Your teeth."

Her mouth dried and watered, her breath picking up. She moistened her lips. "Charles is perfect. A true gentleman."

Something flickered in his eyes. A flash of hot emotion that faded almost as soon as it appeared. "Of course he is. And that's what every woman wants. A gentleman." He smirked at her.

She lifted her chin. "It is. Something you most definitely are *not*."

"No, I'm not a gentleman. Especially in bed, princess. Actually, though, that used to win me points back in the day."

Back in the day. Because he hadn't had sex in years. *Easy there, girl parts, down.* He had a lot of pent-up sexual energy. Her breasts grew heavier just thinking about how he could put all that sexual energy to use. On her.

Damn him, he was right, though. She had to admit it if only to herself. There was something about a man that could go all Tarzan in the bedroom. Throw her down on the bed. Or the floor. Or against the wall. Up until now that had been a safe fantasy. Something she could long for because it would never happen. She would never cross paths with a man like that. Except now she had. She bit her lip, stifling a moan.

"C-Can I go to my room now please?" she managed to get out.

After a long moment he stepped aside, waving her to move past. She hurried around him and dove into her bedroom. Setting her plate on the dresser, she paced in an attempt to settle her nerves, shaking her hands out in front of her.

She needed to get it together. Remember who he was. Who she was.

When her pulse steadied she picked up her plate and sank down on the edge of the bed. She bit into her sandwich. It tasted like dust in her mouth. Tossing it back down, she left the plate on the bed and rose to her feet again. Moving to the window, she tried to open it. Again. She'd tried several times before. Still, it didn't budge.

Dropping her forehead against the cool glass, she stared outside at the frost-tinged trees.

And what would she do if she got the window open? Run into the woods? He would give chase. Like before. He'd find her. Like before. That's what men like him did. Her pulse skittered at her throat.

And why did that give her a treacherous little thrill?

SIXTEEN

*G*RACE SPENT THE next half hour pacing the room, trying to cool her flushed skin and slow her hammering pulse. At one point she heard an engine revving outside and emerged from the bedroom cautiously. She crossed the living room and peered out the window to see that Reid had managed to start the motorcycle he had been working on since yesterday. He was still wearing that long-sleeved thermal shirt that did nothing to hide his strong physique as he labored. He seemed so solid. Capable. It was hard to imagine him ever being less than this. Less than free, less than strong, less than a man among men.

She'd let him deliberately think she was engaged to Charles . . . that it was a real relationship. It was a prideful thing to do, but she didn't regret it. She knew Reid's power over her. Well, over her libido at least. He likely knew, too. She'd been his for the taking. So many times now. Much to her embarrassment. He could be smug in that knowledge.

He started heading for the cabin. She jumped with a squeak and dove into the bedroom, closing the door behind her. It had been an impulse to hide. Or instinct, rather. Following that instinct, she hopped on the bed and pulled the blanket over her. She didn't know if he would check on her, but it seemed safer to feign sleep. Less risk of interaction.

Settling on her side, she closed her eyes and lay perfectly still, tucking her hand beneath her cheek. She held motionless for several long minutes, listening to him as he moved around the house. His steps came close to the door, hesitating just on the other side. She held her breath, wondering if he would enter, hoping he would, praying he would not.

She waited as the sound of his steps faded away. Her limbs relaxed, growing as heavy as her eyelids, until it was hard to keep them open anymore. In fact, she didn't need to pretend to be asleep at all.

NIGHTMARES HAD BEEN a regular part of Grace's childhood. Her mother accused her of being overly dramatic (and eating cookies before bed—somehow the two were connected). She stopped coming to her room after the first couple of times. Daddy called it tough love and insisted Grace was in dire need of it lest she become weak spirited. Her mother, of course, agreed. Daddy was always right—and neither one wanted a weak daughter afflicted with nightmares or anything else that might mark her as *less*.

So that left Anna, their housekeeper. She was always there to comfort Grace in the middle of the night when she woke up screaming. She'd pet Grace's head and cluck sympathetically, asking about her dream and encouraging her to talk about it. The problem was, Grace didn't know what to say because she didn't remember any of it.

Grace knew children were supposed to have these great memories, when their minds were fresh and young. But that wasn't the case with her. Her dreams vanished like wisps of smoke as soon as she woke. Only the terror remained, clawing her throat and coating her mouth with the taste of metal.

Tell me, sweet pea, what is it?

And she never could tell Anna despite the housekeeper's encouragement. She wanted to. Anna seemed to think it was important. As though Grace could somehow defeat her monsters if she put a name to them. Eventually the nightmares stopped. She grew up, which was a good thing since Anna retired and she didn't have anyone to comfort her in the middle of the night anymore.

Unfortunately now, when she woke up screaming, gazing blindly ahead in the cabin bedroom, she remembered everything.

There was no haze of smoke to obscure the nightmare that had her bolting upright in bed, her scream ringing in her ears. There was no forgetting it. She could see it all too well—actually felt as though she were still trapped in its grip, the images chasing her into lucidity. Her chest heaved, aching in a way that felt unsafe—like she might actually be having a heart attack. Her hands were bound again—and she was running. Only this time it wasn't Reid chasing her. It was the other men. Rowdy and Zane and the others. Their faces contorted in a crazy blur like something out of a fun house. She was crying, choking on sobs as they caught her and tossed her between them. Tearing at her clothes. Striking her with their fists. Shoving her down beneath the crush of them.

"Grace!" Hard hands shook her, and for a moment she thought it was still part of the dream. She fought back, striking and scratching, earning a grunt from her attacker.

Her hands were seized and pinned above her head. "Grace! What's wrong?"

She blinked up at Reid's shadowed features. The room was draped in the soft purple of dusk. Blinking, she assessed the room and him. Her chest deflated with a breath. "Reid," she breathed. He wasn't Anna, but she wasn't alone. He was here.

"Gracie." He brushed the hair back from her face, his touch as gentle as his voice. Her stomach flipped at the sound of that nickname on his lips. His hand skimmed down the length of her arm and took her hand. "It's all right, Gracie. It was just a dream."

She nodded, choking back a sob, marveling that such a rough, frightening man should possess even a scrap of gentleness. "They were after me. Those men . . ." She shuddered, the image so very real she could feel their hands, smell their sweat, and still taste the fear so clearly. "I couldn't get away from them. They were animals—" She abruptly stopped, sucking in air. She was talking about his friends, after all. One of them was his brother. He could very well take offense.

"Ah, sweetheart." He folded her into his arms. She went, collapsing against him, nestling her cheek against the hard wall of his chest. "I'm sorry," he muttered into her hair.

"What are you sorry for?" He hadn't been the one hurting her in the dream.

"I think it's pretty obvious. If you're having nightmares, it's because of me."

"Not you," she managed to say, her fingers curling around the edge of his short sleeve. "Without you I would be living that nightmare right now. I'll gladly take the nightmare over the reality."

And reality was this sweetness. Right now. Being held in his arms and feeling safe.

The thought jarred her.

It wheedled into her consciousness. She felt safe. *He made her feel safe.* A surprising thought. She felt safe with him, a dangerous man that she knew she shouldn't trust.

She tried to shove it out, but the feeling persisted, a jagged rusty little nail that found its way loose to burrow under her skin.

She squeezed her eyes tight in a long blink and then opened them again to the dusk-shrouded room. It had happened then. She had devolved into full-on Stockholm syndrome. She was past the point of identifying with her abductor. With him there were . . . *feelings.* Feelings that were decidedly un-captive-like.

Except he wasn't really her abductor. At least not initially. A point not to be overlooked. It was the other guys who haunted her nightmare.

God help her, there was that rationalizing again. She was making a distinction . . . defending him.

She sniffed wetly, fighting to regain her composure. He still held her hand, his thumb rubbing the backs of her fingers in a lazy circle. She used her other hand to rub at her eyes, pressing her fingertips against her eyelids to assuage the sting.

She laughed weakly. "You must think me a little kid, crying over a bad dream. Haven't done that in years."

"They don't only happen to children, you know. There's no shame in them. I've had my share of nightmares, too. Every time I close my eyes, they're there. The things I've seen and done . . . they don't fade from memory easily." He shifted, stretching out his legs on the bed, their bodies so close, her cheek still pressed to his chest. She kept her face there, inhaling his masculine scent. It was probably safer than looking at his face again. That face did things to her insides.

"How do you deal with that?"

"I make certain that I'm too exhausted to dream when I fall into bed. That's the goal anyway. In prison, I spent a lot of time working out. Running the yard, playing ball."

That would explain his amazing body.

He continued, "The good news is that your

nightmares will only ever be that. Nightmares. Nothing bad is going to happen to you, Gracie. Wait and see. You'll be home soon and your nightmares will end."

Her chest swelled, that feeling of security suffusing her again. "Have yours, then?" she asked. "Now that you're free of Devil's Rock? Did your nightmares stop?"

His thumb paused from making that lazy little pattern on the back of her fingers. "Don't worry about me, princess. I'm a survivor."

"That's not an answer."

"I might not be in prison at the moment, but I'm not free. If I feel that way, I'm just kidding myself. It's an illusion." And that was maybe the saddest thing she'd ever heard. His hand eased away from hers and he stood up from the bed as if sensing the sentiment and not wanting it from her. "Out here or in there," he added, his voice harder. "It makes no difference. I'm still not free."

She stared at his shadowy form, wanting to say something. Give comfort . . . be like Anna for him. Had he had anyone after his grandfather died? Maybe if there had been someone for him his life would have turned out differently?

She gave her head a hard shake. His nightmares were real—something that actually existed when he woke up. She couldn't vanquish his monsters. There was nothing she could say or do for him and they both knew it. Nor should she feel compelled to.

"I'll go start dinner." Turning, he left her sitting on the bed, staring after him.

SEVENTEEN

AFTER HE LEFT, she closed the door as if that would be a barrier to him and all the confusing thoughts and feelings crashing through her in wave after wave.

Maybe her father could do something to help him? Maybe he could have a reduced sentence? He'd done nothing short of save her life by removing her from those other men. He deserved no less.

Rubbing a hand against her forehead, her mind tracked over the arguments she could present to her father.

Through the door she could hear the sound of running water as he turned on the kitchen faucet. Then another sound emerged. A steady trilling ring.

Someone was calling him on his burner phone. Her pulse kicked to life. No one had called him since they arrived here. The ringing stopped and she knew he had answered. His deep voice rumbled across the air but too far away for her to catch more than a word or two.

She pressed her ear closer to the door, her breath catching when she thought she heard her name.

It was about her. If someone were calling him, of course it was probably about her. Maybe it was this Sullivan person arranging the details of her release. Her heart jumped.

Unable to resist, she slowly turned the knob, easing the door open. She stepped out, her bare feet treading silently across the wood flooring. He stood in the kitchen in front of the sink, his broad back to her. His words were clearly audible and she froze, not wanting to alert him to her presence. He was quiet at the moment, evidently listening to the voice on the end of the line.

He sighed and ran a hand over the back of his head. She tensed, expecting him to turn around, but he didn't. Not yet.

"I have," he said after a while. Then, he added, "Yes. I am. Tell me what you want . . ."

A pause fell.

"What?" he asked. "I thought you wanted to draw this out and really torture the president. Do you think that's such a good idea?" A longer silence fell. From where she stood, she watched the set to his shoulders grow rigid. Then he replied in a voice that sounded flat and dutiful, like a soldier responding to his superior. "No. That's not what I think." A pause, then: "I'll do it. I'll kill her. Consider it done."

Her stomach bottomed out. She pressed a hand to her roiling belly, afraid she was about to be sick. She'd trusted him.

She'd been wrong. About him. About everything. So wrong.

And she would pay for it with her life.

EIGHTEEN

*H*IS BURNER PHONE started ringing in the kitchen. He raced to get it, relieved, hoping that Zane was finally calling him with some news. Only when he answered the phone, it wasn't his brother's voice greeting him.

"Well, well, if it isn't Reid Allister."

It had been years, but he hadn't forgotten Otis Sullivan's voice. His free hand immediately curled into a fist and he felt like punching something.

"In the flesh," he replied. "Well, more or less."

Sullivan chuckled. "You got some balls, I'll tell you that. Busting out of the hospital like you did. No one wants to even admit that they lost you. The state has enough bad press right now as it is." Sullivan's laugh deepened, full of smug satisfaction at his role in said bad press.

"Thanks to you," Reid returned. "I suppose I owe you for providing me with a distraction."

"Maybe it was lucky for me that you showed up when you did. Right convenient. I was coming to terms with the fact that Zane and the boys might have bit off more than they could chew taking the girl."

Reid didn't know how to respond to that. He just held silent, all of him tense, blood pumping hard through his veins. Unfortunately, he couldn't reach through the phone like he yearned to do.

Sullivan continued, "But then you always were good, weren't you?"

"Not always. Ended up in prison, didn't I?" Because he wasn't smart to know that the tide had turned and he'd fallen out of favor with Sullivan. He didn't sniff out the trap before he'd stepped into it.

"And ended out of it, I see."

"Eleven years later." Eleven years of his life gone because of Sullivan. A man dead and him to blame. Again, Sullivan's doing.

"Let's not rehash old news. You're out. Let's look ahead. You do care about the future, don't you? Zane said you've been eager to talk to me . . . to see me. I can only surmise that means you want to talk about your future in the business."

Yeah. His fist clenched tighter at his side. Something like that.

Before he could answer, Sullivan continued, "A man of your talents is an asset, of course. There's no question of that. No, when it comes to you, I have other concerns."

"Such as?" He would do anything, say anything, to get back into the fold. To get close. Sullivan was too out of reach otherwise. He didn't just want to kill the man. That would be too easy. He wanted to reveal to the world exactly who Otis Sullivan really was. In order to do that he had to get close.

"Trust is not easily given by me, Reid. Nor is forgiveness. Maybe you remember that?"

Yeah. He remembered that. He had all those years behind bars as testament to that. He'd stood up to Sullivan back then and tried walking away. He told Sullivan that he and Zane were out—as in finished and done with him. That had been a mistake. Sullivan had made sure Reid suffered for that. He'd set him up. Sent him out on one last job. Only when he got there, the security guard was dead and he didn't have a chance to get away before the police arrived.

The only advantage he had right now was that Sullivan didn't know he wanted payback. Sullivan only thought he wanted back in. He thought he'd succeeded in beating Reid.

The opposite was true, of course. Sullivan had

set him up. He had not forgotten that. He never would. He'd say and do whatever it took for Sullivan to think it was all water under the bridge between them.

"Yes," Reid finally answered. "I remember. I want back in."

"Good, good." Sullivan's voice carried through the phone, a dangerous silkiness entering his voice. "Then you'll prove your loyalty to me and do as I ask. That is if you want to be back in my graces as you claim . . ."

"I do."

"According to your brother, you've been putting your time to good use and roughing the girl up."

"I have," he lied. "Yes, I am. What do you want . . ."

"Good. Wasn't sure you could do it. You were always a little soft. Guess prison changed you for the better."

He ground his teeth at the satisfaction he heard in Sullivan's voice. "Tell me what you want—"

"Kill her."

The man was insane.

"What?" Reid asked as though he had heard him incorrectly.

"You heard me. I want her dead."

He sucked in a breath, his mind feverishly working, searching for a way out of this. "I thought you wanted to draw this out and really torture the president. Do you think that's such a good idea—"

"That's always been your problem, Reid. You think too much. You think when you should just be taking orders. Maybe you haven't changed, after all. Maybe you're still that stupid punk who thinks he's calling the shots here. Is that what you think?"

"No," he said numbly, his fingers aching where he clutched the phone to his ear. Never in his life had he so badly wanted to hurt someone. Not even in prison when he'd been at his lowest, when rage had been his closest friend and all he wanted was to lash out. He wanted to crawl through the phone and break Sullivan with his bare hands. "That's not what I think."

"Now why am I having a hard time believing you?"

"I'll do it." In that moment, he would say whatever lie he had to. "I'll kill her. Consider it done."

The sharp gasp behind him had him spinning around. His mouth dried as his gaze clashed with Grace. He shook his head at her, trying to convey that he didn't mean it, that she didn't need to be afraid of him, but she backed up a step, and just like that their tenuous truce snapped like a twig.

Sullivan kept talking in his ear, but he could hardly hear what he was saying. All he could see was Grace's face losing color. ". . . let us know when it's done. Call Zane and he'll give you instructions and tell you where we can meet."

"Understood," he said, not looking away from Grace. Even from where he stood he could see the fierce hammer of her pulse at the base of her throat. In that moment she reminded him of a frightened doe, prepared to bolt.

"Good. We'll be seeing each other soon, then."

He grunted something that must have been satisfactory, because the line went dead in his ear. He lowered the phone to the counter. "Gracie—"

"No." She held up her hand, palm face out as though that could ward him off. "Don't call me that. *You* don't *get* to call me that. Like we're friends. Like you're actually helping me. Like you don't mean to kill me."

"I was lying—"

"Oh, really? To me? Or whoever you were talking to?" She rounded the counter, her gaze darting wildly, panicked in her search for an escape. She made a dart for the door, but he cut her off, light on the balls of his feet. She turned and raced back into the kitchen, positioning herself behind the small island. As if that would keep him from her if he in fact wanted to get to her. He could easily vault the damn thing, but he didn't want to scare her any more than she was.

He flattened his hands on the island counter. "I was just saying that to appease him. You can't think after everything that I would do that to you—"

"You're a liar." She shook her head, her long braid of dark hair bouncing over her shoulder and partly unraveling. Just like he was unraveling inside. She looked at him with such terror. "Every time your lips move it's just lies . . ."

"That's not true. You don't believe that." He took a step to round the island.

She pushed that hand farther out. "Stop. Stop right there."

He hesitated before continuing, all the while talking to her in a low, coaxing voice. "Be reasonable, Grace. You know me. You know I won't—"

Her face screwed up in scorn. "I don't know you. I know you're an escaped convict and you've been playing with my head since the moment you walked into my life. I know you belong to a gang of criminals who abduct innocent people."

Frustration bubbled up inside him. All the ground he'd covered with her, gone. Just like that. And after all he'd done to try to keep her safe.

"Now listen here, Gracie—"

Her gaze performed a quick scan again, landing on the knife near the cutting board. She snatched it up and brandished it in front of her, gripping it with both hands.

He lifted his hands and waved them slowly. "Come on, Gracie . . . put the knife down."

She shook her head, wisps of dark hair escaping the loose braid. "Nuh-uh."

He lifted his arm, stretching a hand out toward her over the island. "Hand it to me, Gracie. Before someone gets hurt."

"Yeah. By someone you mean *you*."

He hesitated, studying her carefully before continuing, "What are you going to do, Gracie? Are you gonna use that knife on me?"

"Yes." She stabbed toward him as he inched another step around the island. "Maybe." She matched his step, sidling around and keeping herself directly across from him.

"You wouldn't do that. You wouldn't hurt anyone." He kept coming and she kept retreating. He took that as a good sign. She didn't *want* to use the knife. That was something at least.

"Don't be too sure of that. Self-defense is a great incentive. "

"You don't need to defend yourself against me. I'm not going to hurt you. I'm trying to help you."

She shook her head, her knife bobbing in the air. "You expect me to believe you after what I just heard?"

He lunged across the island, grabbing her arm and dragging her around, closing the distance between them. "I think I'll risk it," he growled.

She whipped the knife around, pressing the tip of the blade to the center of his throat, directly into the center of his collarbone. It wasn't the first time anyone held a knife to him. In prison, he'd stared down a shiv plenty of times. He even bore a few scars from when they made contact.

It was, however, the first time a woman pointed one at him. Especially a woman he cared about. *Christ.* With a jolt he realized he did care about her. He wanted to keep her safe, and it wasn't just because it was the right thing to do. It wasn't simply because he wasn't a killer. He wanted to keep her safe because the idea of anything happening to her filled his heart with a sick ache.

"I'll do it," she whispered, her wild-eyed gaze dropping to where the knife pricked his flesh. She flexed her fingers around the hilt, and for one moment he wondered if he was taking a gamble. Her eyes glittered with fear, but there was resolve mixed in there, too. She could easily plunge the knife into him.

She moistened her lips. "Just give me the keys to the van. I'll walk out of here."

"I can't do that." Tempting as it was to let her go, a pang punched his chest at the thought of her walking away. And it had nothing to do with failing Sullivan.

She wiggled the fingers of her free hand. "Give them to me and no one gets hurt."

He lifted his throat slightly, offering her even greater access. He felt that prick of the blade. The slight pinch as warm blood trickled down his neck. "Go ahead then. Do it."

Her eyes brightened, gleaming wetly, unnamed emotion brimming there. "You said you'd kill me . . . like it was nothing."

"You heard me lying." He held her gaze, ignoring the pressure of the knife at his throat. "Look at me. If you think I'm that man . . . if you think I would truly kill you, then do it. Use the knife."

Her hand started to shake, but she didn't move the knife away from him. Her lips trembled, and he knew she was waging a war with herself. He leaned in, moving slowly, holding his breathing, ignoring the sharpness digging at his throat. Hopefully he wasn't about to get his throat cut.

He stopped his lips a hairbreadth from hers. "Gracie," he breathed.

A whimper broke from her lips, and he dove that last inch in and kissed her quivering mouth, and then it was easy to forget the knife because there was only the softness of her lips. Her taste. The way she opened to him. Her sigh as he licked his way inside her mouth.

He reached between them and covered her hand where she gripped the knife. Her fingers loosened around it, allowing him to take it from her. He watched her silently as he held it between them. He turned the knife over in his hand, the tip grazing her T-shirt. She glanced down at the blade now fully in his control and back up at him.

She didn't blink, her wide gaze traveling over his face as though memorizing him. Those eyes of hers messed with him. Burrowed deep. And there was that tiny mole at the corner of her eye that highlighted the chocolatey depths, beckoning him.

He arched an eyebrow at her and gripped the neckline of her shirt. Using the edge of the blade, he ripped her shirt right down the middle, the renting fabric loud on the air.

She sucked in a sharp breath. He brought the knife back up, laying it flat between the deep valley of her heaving breasts. Leaning in, he claimed her mouth again. She was ready. Meeting him with open mouth. The kiss went deeper, hotter. It was tongues and teeth and gasps.

He broke away from her and traced the tip of the knife over the lacy cup of her bra, scraping the fabric and watching her nipples harden against the barrier. She ceased to breathe. Her breasts didn't so much as rise or fall.

"I'd fall on this knife myself before I let it hurt you," he vowed, holding onto her gaze.

She nodded jerkily.

He dropped the knife on the island behind them and grabbed her by the waist, lifted her up onto the surface in one move. Then they were back at it again, kissing. Savage kisses that he couldn't temper. Even as his head told him to slow down, his body urged him on. That voice that had always commanded him to stop before had gone silent. The possibility didn't even enter his head. There would be no stopping this time.

He tunneled his hands into her hair, dragging through her loose braid, unraveling the dark sections of hair. He grabbed fistfuls of the soft, fragrant mass, reveling in it. The back of his fingers brushed her bra strap and his fingers turned, diving to unclasp it. The straps slid down her shoulders, the bra falling away between them. He stepped back to examine her.

He swallowed a moan at the sight of her full breasts. "I've dreamed of these." The same flawless skin as the rest of her except the skin of her breasts looked delicate, baby-soft. Olive-hued with deep plum nipples. "The reality is so much better." His hands closed over the lush mounds, holding their weight, thrumming her nipples between his fingers.

Her head dropped back with a long gasp, exposing the arch of her throat. Another thing he couldn't resist. He nipped and kissed and tongued his way up the gentle slope, his hands still molding to her breasts, his thumbs dragging over her nipples in steady strokes.

"More," she sighed.

He squeezed and massaged the heavy swells, his fingers plucking and rubbing at her nipples until they grew pebble-hard. She pushed out her chest and made these wild little sounds that knocked him over the edge. He dropped his mouth to her chest, pulling a nipple deep into his mouth. She released a small shriek, surging up off the counter. Her hands went to his hair, gripping the short strands and pulling him in tighter, as though she couldn't get enough of him.

He laved that nipple with his tongue, tasting and

sucking and feasting on it like a starving man. She cried out again when he scored his teeth across it.

He turned his attention to her other breast and treated it to the same worship. "Please," she whimpered, writhing against him. She slid her hand between them and rubbed his dick through his pants. "Reid, please . . ."

He looked down at her, his chest clenching at her desire-clouded eyes, her puffy, kiss-swollen lips. *She should look this way all the time.*

Just as soon as the thought entered his mind he killed it. No. He didn't want her to look this way all the time. He didn't want the world to see her like this. He wanted to be the only one to see her like this. The only one to know her.

Instantly, he was reminded that there was another man. A fiancé who could see her like this anytime he wanted—who probably *had* and who would continue to in the future. The reality of that crashed over him and fury hissed through him. He should probably respect that. She belonged to someone else. Her fingers clawing through his hair, her sweet sighs and moans for more, weren't his to have.

Fuck that. Right now she wanted him and he wanted her. He wasn't going to deprive himself anymore. He'd had eleven years of deprivation. It was time to feast. He would take her and her fuck-me eyes and her warm sweet-smelling skin and have something to remember when he was back in hell.

NINETEEN

GRACE TENSED WHEN Reid paused to stare at her. She fought down the tide of lust that urged her to fling herself at him and beg him to keep doing all the crazy-hot things he was doing with his mouth and hands.

This guy's hands and mouth were nothing short of magic.

But they'd started things before that got cut short, so she held her breath and waited, watching him, ready for this to end like all the other times. She took a deep breath, hoping that it helped to cool the maelstrom raging inside her.

She lowered a hand to grip the edge of the counter, prepared to slide down and touch the floor, but his hands went to her waist again. He pulled her in close. "Wrap your legs around me," he commanded.

She blinked up at him. His bossy tone didn't invite argument, but still she hesitated. A moment ago she was holding a knife to his throat, and then he had turned it on her—proving if he wanted to hurt her he could—and now she was shirtless with breasts that were aching and raw from his mouth and the scratch of his five o'clock shadow.

He yanked her legs up, urging her to lock them around his waist. "You're thinking too much," he growled, slanting his mouth over hers, his tongue diving inside her mouth. "Stop," he hissed into her.

She locked her ankles around him, losing herself in the hot persuasion of his mouth, hardly even aware when he lifted her up and carried her to the bedroom. He followed her down on the bed.

She felt drunk, dizzy from the play of his mouth and tongue. She did exactly what he said. Easily. There was no thinking when he slid down her body, his teeth and tongue blazing a trail between her breasts, over her rib cage, and down her navel. His hands seized the waistband of her boxers and deftly slid them down her hips. This time he didn't waste time with underwear. He took those off, too, in one swift yank.

Then he was there, his big shoulders wedged between her thighs, his hands spreading her wide for him.

"I've dreamed of this, too," he breathed against her core.

She slid her fingers along his scalp. "You've been dreaming of me a lot, then. I wouldn't have guessed that."

He looked up at her, his hazel eyes gleaming hotly from where he crouched between her legs. "Since the moment I saw you I pretty much thought about a thousand dirty things I would like to do to you."

Her breath caught. A thousand? And yet he had held back. Denying himself. Denying her. "Then we've been wasting a lot of time."

He slowly grinned then, darkly and with wicked intent. She held her breath, bracing herself as he disappeared between her thighs. The first brush of his tongue against her pulled a soft sigh from her lips. Then he grew more aggressive, stroking her deep and hard with the velvet of his tongue.

She gripped his head with both hands, writhing and twisting under him. She cried out and muttered incoherent pleas. She was close. *So close.*

He lifted up, his green-gold eyes feral like a lion as he prowled up her body. "The next time you come it will be with me inside you." Her heart stammered inside her chest as he uttered this.

He hopped off the bed. She sat up, bewildered,

watching as he bounded to his bag on the chair. He returned quickly, assuring her he wasn't gone for good—in case his avowal hadn't convinced her of that already. Before rejoining her on the bed, he dropped his sweatpants.

She sat up higher, eager for another look at him. The first night she had seen him naked felt like a long time ago. Even though the image of him had imprinted itself on her retinas, the memory still did not do justice to this sight of him. He had a war-rior's body and it made everything inside her melt and turn to goo. Her sex throbbed, almost hurting in her need to be filled with him.

He slid right back in between her thighs, his own rock-solid thighs rubbing against hers. It was shocking for a moment, the sensation of a man against her. It had been too long. And never really a man. Never someone that looked like he was forged by some mythical god to fight epic wars. His hands found her everywhere, her breasts, her stomach and hips. Touching, stroking. She was bombarded with sensations, release rising up inside her again.

"I could touch you all night," he growled as his hands slid under her, cupping her cheeks, lifting her like she was weightless underwater.

"Please," she choked. "End it."

There was a crinkle of wrapper and a sharp tear of foil. He had a condom. At least one of them was still living in reality and thinking. She hadn't even thought that far. That's how lost she was.

She propped up on her elbows, hungry to touch him. "Let me."

He hesitated and then turned the condom over to her. It was purely selfish. She wanted to know him, feel him with her fingers before she took him into her body.

She positioned the condom over the tip of him and eased it down, rolling it over his length with shaking fingers. He was big and hard and it made her girl parts clench in anticipation.

Once he was fully encased, she closed her fingers over him. Wrapping him in her palm, she pumped several times, watching his face, enjoying the way the lines and hollows seemed to grow more stark, torment-ridden. The good kind of torment. The kind she knew so well at his hands and now she was able to inflict on him.

His breathing grew ragged. "Gracie," he choked.

She ignored him, pumping deeper, taking her hand all the way to the base of him. She felt in control. Powerful. Her fingers slid back up and she dragged her thumb over the engorged tip of him.

"Gracie," he said again. "Not like this . . ."

In response, she squeezed him, her own breath hitching as he pulsed and jumped in her hand.

"Enough." He grabbed her shoulders and roughly shoved her back down on the bed.

Her pulse hammered in excitement against her throat. She thought that was it. He would ram into her and she was okay with that. She wanted it so badly she burned for it. She would revel in it. She felt like she had been waiting for this forever. And maybe she had. Maybe all these years, she had been waiting for him. She wasn't burning for *it*. She burned for *him*. It could happen anywhere with anyone. This need was for him. The *it* was something only he had unlocked inside her.

He rose up into a sitting position between her legs and froze, each of his big callused hands gripping one of her thighs. He slid them down and under, lifting her slightly off the bed. He looked down at her, all of him tense, every muscle and sinew locked hard and tight, ready to go off.

"I can't promise this will last long—it's been a hell of a long time for me, but you're going to come. I promise you that." His thumb worked small, hypnotic circles inside her thighs as his gravel-deep voice pebbled over her. "And then we're going to do it again . . . slow."

Her eyes widened. Holding her up with one

hand now, he fisted his cock with his other, guiding himself to her opening.

She gasped as he started to slide inside her, a part of her wondering if that were true. Would they do it again? None of her previous partners were up for a second round in the same night. Then all thoughts fled. She panted as he filled her, gliding in slow, stretching her until he was buried in to the hilt. She felt her eyes go wide, shocked at the unfamiliar sensation. She had never felt this. So full . . . so invaded.

"You feel amazing," he whispered against her mouth.

"I feel you everywhere," she returned, talking against his lips.

And then the ability to speak was lost because he started moving, holding her hips, leveraging her for himself but angling her in a way that built the friction and made her arch and cry out.

Tears burned her eyes as something snapped. Some invisible, coiling band broke and she came undone, her muscles going limp. Reid didn't slow down. His hands slid under her and gripped her ass, bringing her right up to that precipice again.

She moaned and he dropped over her, his mouth on her ear as he thrust in and out of her. Fast and hard. "That's it, sweetheart. Come again for me."

His deep voice served as its own turn-on. She flew apart again. His arms wrapped around her, holding her tightly. With a few more strokes he joined her.

Their ragged breaths fogged the air between them. For a brief moment she worried awkwardness would instantly follow. Regret. He would look at her with cold eyes and everything would go back to before. They would return to captive and captor.

Except that didn't happen.

Reid rolled off her and left the bed to dispose of the condom. Then he returned, sliding under the sheets and pulling her against his side.

He curled her leg around him, his hand splaying over her hip. They were quiet for a long time. She fanned her fingers over his chest, enjoying the sound of his heart against her palm.

"It's been a while for me, too, you know," she whispered, her lips brushing the warm skin of his chest.

"Eleven years?" he returned.

She grinned and couldn't help the little giggle from escaping.

"I'm guessing I have you beat," he continued, his voice rumbling up under her. "Eleven years ago you were probably in high school."

"True." She sobered, thinking about that. Eleven

years was a long time to go without intimacy. "You really haven't been with anyone that long?"

He tensed under her. "I was no one's bitch if that's what—"

"I didn't mean it like that," she rushed to say, her hand smoothing his chest involuntarily. "It's just you're so hot . . . and virile. It's hard to imagine you not . . . doing it."

He was quiet for a long moment. "There were a few close calls when I first got to prison, but I quickly learned how things worked. I got in with a crew, made friends . . . allies. And watched my back. Every minute of every day."

"It sounds horrible," she whispered.

"Yeah, well, prison isn't supposed to be fun."

She propped her chin on his chest, looking up at him. "What did you do? To get yourself in prison?" she clarified. "What did you do?"

He paused before saying, "Murder. Sorry if you were looking for something more original."

He watched her, holding her gaze with an unreadable expression. She didn't look away, certain this moment was important. Her reaction was significant. He wanted to see if she would flinch. If she would recoil in horror.

Finally, she said, "I don't believe it of you. You're not a murderer. Not justifiably anyway."

A slow smile stole over his face. He leaned up, his hand gripping the back of her head, pulling her in, kissing her long and deep, stoking the fires again. Her body started to wake up, tingles sparking throughout all her well-used parts. She moaned softly into his mouth.

He pulled back and whispered against her mouth. "You have no reason to have that kind of faith in me."

"I'm a good judge of character." The moment she let go of that knife between them, she had placed her faith in this man. She wasn't wrong.

"Maybe you're just an idealist." His fingers played in her hair as he gripped her head, his fingers lost in the wild tangle.

"Am I wrong about you?" she challenged. Again, another long moment passed as she swam in the storm of his eyes, waiting for his response.

"No," he admitted, sounding almost reluctant to confess this to her. "I'm not guilty." He laughed once, low and rough. "Every criminal says that, though. I don't expect you to believe me."

She nodded once, a smile tugging her lips. "I believe you. I think I knew from the start that you were an innocent man."

"I didn't say I was 'innocent.' Only that I'm not guilty of the crime I was convicted for."

"There's a difference?"

He nodded. "I'm not innocent. I've done bad things. Before I went to prison and then, once I was in there . . . well, no one stays clean on the inside."

"But you're not a cold-blooded killer. You're not a rapist," she declared matter-of-factly.

He looked a little unnerved. His hand flexed in her hair, and she felt the strength in that hand, the power of his body pulsing beneath her. She knew that power firsthand, the stamina and intensity his body could inflict. Her girl parts kicked into gear again, turning warm and quivery. "And you knew that from the start, huh?"

She nodded, bumping his chest with her chin.

"How?"

"That first night in the house. You saved me. You could have hurt me and abused me in the worst way, but you didn't. You weren't like the others."

He settled back on the bed, sliding one hand under his head, revealing the delicious underside of his muscled bicep. "It feels like I've fought all my life to not be like those men. All I do is fight." He sighed, his hand tensing in her hair. "Eleven years and all I know is how to use my fists . . . how to break people. I don't think I'm that different from those guys. Not as much as I want to be, but I don't know how to *be* anything else. How to exist out here without being like that. God, I don't even know this world anymore. Or me in it. Guess it doesn't matter since I'm going back."

She swallowed a sudden lump in her throat. She didn't want him to go back to prison. He didn't belong there. He was innocent of murder. He shouldn't be in prison.

"So tell me what happened?" She threaded her fingers over his chest and resettled her chin over them. "How did you end up in prison for a crime you didn't commit?"

He took his time answering, as though formulating his thoughts. "After my grandfather died, I pretty much ran wild. Did petty crimes. Stupid shit. After high school things got more serious. I led a group of guys and we attracted the attention of Sullivan. He was rich, respected." He snorted. "He started hiring us to do things for him. Nothing too serious at first." He sighed, and she felt the heaviness of that sound drag through her.

Reid continued, "Then we started roughing up people for him. Knocking heads. Running drugs for him . . . and doing other stuff that didn't sit right with me. I could see what was happening. We were basically his thugs and things were spiraling. It was only going to get worse. I didn't want to go down that road. I told him I was pulling out. With my brother." Another pause followed, and she smoothed a hand over his chest. "He didn't like it, but seemed okay. Asked me to do one last job." He shook his head. "I should have been smarter."

"You were twenty years old."

He shook his head as if that was no excuse. "When I showed up, the security guard was dead, shot with one of my guns. Then the police were there before I could slip away. I was fucked."

"He set you up," she breathed, outrage and hurt dripping through her like acid. Rage filled her for this man she didn't even know.

He nodded. "Easy as that." His jaw locked and she knew he was thinking about his time in jail, all the years Sullivan had taken from him.

"So what are you going to do?"

Reid had escaped. He was out. Grace knew he wanted to see Sullivan, that's what he had been demanding from the start. A sick feeling rose up inside her, and now she knew why. She knew what he wanted.

"I'm gonna end him."

She swallowed against the sudden lump in her throat. Fear lanced through her. Fear for Reid. "I understand why you feel like that—"

"Do you, princess?" he snapped.

Stung, she started to pull away, sliding her hand off his chest and lifting up.

He snatched her hand back and put it where it was on his chest, holding it there. "Don't."

"You want to do this thing. Fine," she bit out. "But I don't have to pretend that I think it's a good idea."

"I'm sorry. You're right. You have every right to tell me what you think." He pressed his hand on the small of her back, urging her back down against him. His bright gaze locked on her, and her heart squeezed at the need she read there. Need for *her*. "You just can't understand, Gracie. You can't."

She nodded, the lump still there but not nearly as choking. "It's just . . ." She searched for the words carefully. "It's not going to go well for you."

This news didn't particularly rock him. He shrugged one shoulder. "This was never going to end well for me. I never planned on that." His thumb slid down her cheek. "And I never planned on you." His look was so intent and devouring as he uttered this that something inside her let go. Cracked and released. Another bit of her heart broke off and fell into his hands. "We don't have a lot of time together, so let's not spend it talking about this."

The truth of that went down in a bitter wash. This wasn't forever. He was destined for prison—or worse. And she had her own life waiting for her.

Stupidly, the backs of her eyes started to burn, and she buried her face in his chest. He was right. She was going to grab happiness with both hands. Seize her life. That's what she had vowed to do when she got out of here. It wasn't too early to start living that creed now. Even if this was destined to end, she would revel in the moment.

"Hey." He brought her face up again.

She blinked, determined that she wasn't going to cry. His scrutiny only made it worse. She knew he could see the emotion storming her features.

He shook his head, smiling tenderly as he threaded his fingers through her hair. "God, you're beautiful."

A hiccup of unexpected laughter escaped her. Heat crept up her face, and she fought the impulse to refute the compliment. "Maybe you're just not that particular," she teased. "You have been in prison for eleven years."

"I know beautiful when I see it." He ran a thumb over her lips. "'The curves of your lips rewrite history'."

She smiled against his tracing fingers, her chest swelling in awe, blown away at how this man, who should be coarse and unrefined, said such beautiful things to her—*about* her. "Where's that from?"

"Oscar Wilde. Never quite understood it before. Makes sense to me now. These lips . . . they do that for me. *You* do. You make everything somehow different. Even the past."

Except not different enough. Not enough to sway him from revenge. She fought back that bitter thought, not wanting to ruin the moment. He made it clear he would go after Sullivan. She would cling to now. She would have this with him—these precious moments.

Her fingers played against his chest, loving the texture of his skin, so smooth, but also scarred in places. "You read Oscar Wilde? Is he popular in prison?"

"Smartass." His chest purred under her fingers and she grinned. "No. I read *Dorian Gray.*"

She sent him a curious look. "In high school?" She didn't know how else he would know Oscar Wilde unless he'd studied him there. It wasn't exactly popular reading.

"In college. I got a degree through correspondence. Eleven years is a long time." He shrugged. "Figured I might as well do something with my time."

Stunned, she gaped at him.

"Try not to look so shocked," he said dryly.

She shook her head. "What's your degree in?"

"English. Figured why not? In prison, books were one thing I had access to. I might as well learn more about them."

She processed this, still marveling at the levels to this man.

"What about you, college girl? What did you study?" His fingers stroked up and down on her hip drowsily.

"I have a degree in astronomy."

"Wow. Look at the brains on you."

"Stop." She shoved at his shoulder. "I wanted to go to grad school but my father put a stop to that. He needed me. In the beginning, for his first campaign. Then he needed me during his first term. Now he needs me as we roll into his re-election campaign."

"And what about you? What do you need?"

No one had ever asked her that before. The fact that he did, this escaped convict, her captor . . . it made her wonder if everything she had ever thought about the world, about life, was wrong. Because everything she had ever been taught *should* have led her to believe that Reid was a waste of space.

The realization shook her, and for a moment she couldn't think of a response. Shaking off her stupor, she crawled over him, loving how small she felt over the great size of him. "Orgasms," she teased, desperate for levity. "I need those." She splayed both hands over his chest and centered herself, thrilled to feel him stirring beneath her.

He smiled up at her, showing off his rare dimples. "Is that so?"

She nodded cheerfully, pushing up and positioning herself so that her sex rested directly over his swelling manhood.

"Well. Coincidentally, I happen to be very good at giving orgasms." He tucked his hands behind his head as though he had all the time in the world, and looked up at her with smiling eyes. The sight of him like this did funny things to her heart. He was smoking hot any day of the week, but like this, smiling, he was devastating.

"Really?" She nodded in mock seriousness, tsking her tongue. "That's very good to know, considering that I'm in such dire need."

"Interesting," he mused, rocking his hips lightly and bumping her sex. Her lips parted on a small gasp. "Don't tell me your fiancé falls short in that arena."

Her smile slipped. The mention of Charles felt like a splash of cold water.

He watched her, his eyes suddenly intent. Before

she knew what was happening, he flipped her on her back, the great wall of him coming over her. "What's the matter? Reality isn't supposed to intrude? You said you're in dire need of orgasms. I can only assume you're not getting them from him."

Mortified, she glanced away, but he grabbed her chin and forced her to meet his gaze.

"I don't want to talk about him."

"Why not?" He angled his head, a dangerous glint in his eyes as he stared at her. "Feeling too guilty?"

"No." She wiggled under him, trying to get in a more comfortable position. Reid shifted to accommodate her, and the move only made her aware of his rock-solid erection. *How many times could he be ready in one night?*

She exhaled, trying to focus on the conversation and not how easy it would be for him to slip inside her. Even sore from earlier, her sex burned and throbbed at the sensation of him nestled along her core.

"If you're not guilty, tell me about him."

She wasn't guilty. She would need to have something real with Charles to feel that. She was embarrassed. She had led Reid to believe she and Charles were a real thing, when in reality they were just friends who mugged for the camera. Not very good friends either. She didn't want to confess the truth and let him know just how undesirable she actually was. Reid thought she was beautiful. She'd rather not let him know precisely how singular he was in that regard.

"Gracie." Still holding her chin, he trailed a thumb along her bottom lip, reminding her of those lovely words he had said about her mouth. *The curves of your lips rewrite history.*

Further proof that he thought she was desirable. Why dash the delusion?

"Talk to me," he prodded.

"I don't feel guilty because Charles and I aren't . . ." She swallowed. This was harder than she expected. "We're not real. Our relationship is a sham. Something cooked up by father to make me look more likable. To earn public favor." She smiled weakly. Saying it out loud made her feel all the more lame.

Reid stared down at her with that all-seeing gaze, and for the first time she knew he was seeing it all. Every bit of her with all her insecurities and flaws.

"You're saying you just dated this guy because your father wanted you to. For publicity?"

Cue mortification and flaming cheeks. She

nodded, adding dumbly, "Everyone loves a romance."

"So you haven't slept with him?"

"We've kissed. Made it to second base. Tried for third and that was a disaster. No sparks. Pathetic, right?"

"So you're telling me you're single." One corner of his mouth kicked up playfully, and she let loose a short burst of laughter before she slapped a hand over her mouth, quickly smothering the sound.

"Because right now that makes a difference," she joked with an exaggerated roll of her eyes. He'd already had his way with her and she had reveled in it.

He left the bed suddenly, and she thought maybe she had angered him, but then he was back, covering her body with his. She caught the glint of foil between his teeth, heard the sharp rip and understood.

He reached between them and rolled the condom on, his blazing gaze finding hers. "Fuck, yes, it makes a difference." He entered her in one hard thrust. "It means there's no one between us. No ghost of a boyfriend. Just us. And *sparks*. We have plenty of those."

She opened her mouth on a sharp cry as he started a fierce tempo. He took hold of her hips and lifted them, angling her so he was targeting the spot that made her shake and spots dance in front of her eyes. How was it that she could have known this man for so short a time but he already knew her body and how to play it like an instrument?

His mouth collided with hers, words a harsh mutter, "It means this is mine."

She wrapped both arms around his shoulders and buried her face in his neck, afraid he would see her response in her expression. *Because it was impossible.* Complicated and stamped with a fat, irrevocable end date on it. This connection they felt couldn't go anywhere. They both admitted that. They both knew it. Still, it didn't change how she felt.

He is mine, too.

TWENTY

DAWN TINGED THE room a purpling blue as he watched Grace sleep. The occasional lightning flashed against the curtain, followed moments later by a rumble of thunder. The storm hadn't reached them yet, but it was coming. Rain was rare in this part of the state, but when it happened, it hit hard.

Her eyelids flickered and he wondered at her dreams. Hopefully, they weren't anything like his. He'd only dozed, but images had infiltrated, haunted him in those fleeting moments. Images of Grace running. Gunshots. Blood. One moment he was standing over the body of the security guard from all those years ago, and then he was rolling him over and he wasn't the security guard anymore. He was Grace. Reid woke up shaking. After that, he gave up on sleep.

Watching her curled up on her side, the sheet wrapped around her naked body, he tried to figure out what the hell his next move should be.

Maybe there could be a way he could trick Sullivan into thinking she was dead. He winced, hating the thought of using her like that, though.

And what are you doing now if not using her?

The voice whispered insidiously through him. He'd taken her, enjoyed her (several times), and justified it all by telling himself that she wanted him, too. As if that were enough. As if that made it right. She was the sweetest thing he had ever touched. Beyond innocent. She was good and pure and deserved better than him. He needed to let her go before her heart became any more involved than it was. He knew she felt something for him and that it wasn't ego talking. A girl like Grace didn't sleep with a guy without some tender feelings.

He had to let her go. Whatever he had to do to get to Sullivan, he was going to do it without her.

Decision made, he contemplated the series of events likely to follow dropping her at the nearest sheriff's office. Once that happened, her safe return to the world wouldn't remain secret for long. Even if the media didn't immediately catch wind of it, with his extensive connections, Sullivan likely would. Reid couldn't lie and tell the bastard he'd done the dirty deed. He didn't even want to think about it.

He brought his hand up in the small space between them, trailing his fingers up and down the ladder of her spine, relishing the feel of her skin, the bump of every vertebra.

She stirred and he slid down in the bed, lifting the sheet to give him better access to her—and a better view. He wanted to remember everything about her. Even if Sullivan's men didn't gun him down, he was headed right back to prison. He wanted every moment with her imprinted on his mind, branded there forever so he had something to take out and hold when he was alone in his cell—the few brief days he had known freedom . . . where he'd lost himself in a woman who made everything else in the world fade away.

He curled alongside her body, her back to his chest, spooning her into his longer length. Another rumble of thunder rocked the air in the distance.

"I love rain and thunderstorms," she whispered into the thick space around them, letting him know she was awake without turning around to face him.

"They don't happen that much out here, but when they do, they're something else. It's like the wrath of God striking earth."

Her breath fanned against the pillow, rasping the cotton. He was so attuned to her. Every little sound and movement. He'd never felt this connection with another person. It was dangerous and scary as hell. Just another reason why he had to let her go.

"When I was a little girl in my bed at night, I would listen to the rain and thunder . . . watch the lightning flash from behind my curtains. It made me feel better."

"Why did you need to feel better?" His fingers brushed the silk of her hair off her nape.

She turned her head to look back at him, a ghost of a smile gracing her lips. "You think I have this perfect life."

No, he knew she didn't, and it knifed his heart to know she didn't. Because she deserved it. He smiled lightly at her. "It wasn't all castles, princess?"

Her look got faraway. "There were always castles with plenty of space to get lost in. Trust me, I usually hid. Until my father sent for me and then I would have to perform." She winced. "That might not have been so bad if he ever liked anything I did. If he didn't critique my every word . . . my everything."

He slid farther down on the bed, until they were nose-to-nose. "I'm sure the next time you see him there won't be any critique. He's just going to be glad to see you."

She sighed with deliberate drama. "It would be kind of dick of him to act any other way."

Reid chuckled. "He won't be acting."

Her laughter mingled with his and then faded. "It's going to be different now, you know."

He tensed, afraid that she meant because of *him* things were going to be different. He didn't want to hear that. Didn't want to know he'd fucked her up and affected her future.

"No. It won't. You'll go back to your life. You'll marry Charlie or whatever-his-name and you'll forget all about this."

She sat up abruptly, clutching the sheet over her amazing breasts and looking down at him like he'd just kicked her cat. "You mean forget about *you*? That's what you want?" Pain swam in those chocolate eyes. Pain that he put there, and he hated himself for that. "You *want* me to marry Charles?"

No, he didn't want her to marry anyone. But they had no future. She needed to forget him and move on with her life. She would marry that idiot and he'd soon realize what he had in her. How could he not?

She dropped onto her back with a huff.

He stared at her, waiting.

She sighed. "I don't want to marry him. Even without you, I'd reached that conclusion."

He tried not to smile or look as relieved as he felt. "What are you going to do, then?"

"Leave DC. Take some time for me. Maybe go back to grad school. Have you ever heard of the McDonald Observatory?"

He propped on an elbow and looked down at her. "Yeah. It's near here. Out by Fort Davis. Never been. My grandfather talked about taking us there. Never got around to it."

"I've never even been there either. It has some of the largest telescopes in the world. You have the darkest, clearest skies out here, did you know that? Excellent conditions for stargazing."

"I didn't know that," he replied, watching her, loving how rapt her expression was as she talked about stargazing.

"Can you imagine seeing a comet through one of those scopes? There's one called Seraphina, its next orbital period lands on New Year's eve. Only visible at an observatory, of course."

"Maybe you can go," he suggested.

She met his stare, almost challenging. "Maybe I will."

Silence swelled between them, full of things that needed to be said.

"I didn't mean to wake you," he finally said.

"Not your fault. I'm used to sleeping alone. Another body in bed with me throws me off."

He slipped his arm around her waist and pulled all her lush curves more firmly against him. Something swelled in his chest. She wasn't bound to some other man. Of course, she would be someday. Even if it wasn't Charlie. A woman like Grace, with all she had to offer, wouldn't stay single for long.

She rolled over and brought her smooth palm to his face. She held his cheek. "You're looking stern again."

"We have to talk about what's going to happen."

Her smile faded. "And what's that?"

"You need to go home."

From her expression, he guessed that was not what she expected him to say. "And what are you going to do?"

"I'm going to do what I broke out of prison to do."

"You're going to kill Sullivan," she said flatly, but damn if her eyes weren't full of disappointment.

He nodded once. "I have to do it."

"You don't have to. You're not a killer, Reid." She gripped his arm, her fingers pressing deep.

"He took eleven years from me. I don't think you realize just how bad a man he—"

"And you're not. Come with me. Let's go to the police together." Her hand slid up his arm to squeeze his shoulder. "We can explain everything to them . . . to my father—"

"Sullivan is powerful. He's got other powerful people in his pocket. There's not a chance in hell anyone is going to listen to me over him."

She reached between them, her hands cradling his face. "I will. I'll listen. I'll make others listen."

He gripped her hands and pulled them back down from his face, needing to be strong, needing to resist her pleas. "As soon as I show up with you, my ass is back in jail. And then my chance to get to him is done."

"But he wants me dead," she argued. "He won't see you without proof that I'm dead."

"The guy isn't going to let me get close to him. I realize that now. I'm an escaped con. It's too risky. He's just getting me to do his dirty work for him. If I had killed you, he would have probably ratted me out once I did his bidding."

"So what will you do, then?"

"I'll think of a plan. One that doesn't involve you."

"But if you set me free, he'll know you didn't listen to him. He'll be on the lookout for you."

"I'll deal with that. I know where he lives. I'll—" He stopped short and shook his head. "You know what? Doesn't matter. It's not your problem."

Her gaze flitted left and right and he knew she was thinking, plotting. "I'll stay here," she declared.

He pulled back. "What?"

"Leave me the keys. You got the bike running. Take that. I'll give you forty-eight hours to get to him and then I'll drive myself to the nearest sheriff station. You can tell him that you did it. That you killed me. He won't expect you to come after him. He'll think you're in his pocket. His guard will be down."

He opened his mouth to tell her that wouldn't help him, but his mind was racing. It just might work. He shook his head. No, he was finished using her. He wouldn't drag her into his vendetta. "No. The safest place for you is away from here."

She waved a hand. "No one is going to show up here. I'll be fine."

He hesitated, staring at her face, concern for her warring with his desperate need to destroy Sullivan. "Twenty-four hours," he finally said.

She smiled and nodded. "All right. I'll leave here in twenty-four hours." She slid her arms around his shoulders. "You know you're going to have to finally tell me where you've been hiding the keys to the van."

He fought to ignore the knot of uncertainty that he was doing wrong by her and murmured, "You might have to search me thoroughly."

Her hands dipped between them and closed around his dick, her eyes rounding in wonder. "Again?" she queried.

"One more time," he whispered, leaning forward to kiss her mouth. The last time.

TWENTY-ONE

*G*RACE FOLLOWED REID out into the yard. She shivered, rubbing her arms. The rain had stopped but it was still chilly, even with the sun breaking through the clouds.

He stopped in front of his bike and faced her. He stared at her for a long moment, his pale eyes catching the sunlight. There was something there, some emotion, but she couldn't name it. A slow smile lifted the corner of his mouth and he reached for her face, brushing a thumb down her cheek. "This time tomorrow. Promise me." He jerked a thumb toward the van. "You'll be heading east to the nearest county sheriff."

"Promise," she said, even though her throat deliberately closed up at the lie. He didn't seem to notice.

"Your heart is too big, Grace Reeves. You need

to find someplace where you want to be. Where your light can shine. Go to that observatory. I want to think of you there, watching your comet on New Year's eve."

"I will," she promised, this time not choking on the lie because she intended to do that. If this experience had taught her anything, it was that she couldn't go back to the way she was before. She wouldn't be going back to DC. Her old life was gone, and good riddance. Things would be different now.

She looked down at the ground and then back at him, wondering why she felt so awkward after everything she had shared with this man. Moistening her lips, she knew she had to try to reach him one more time. "I wish you wouldn't do this."

"I have to finish it."

She squashed that part of her that cried out: *But what about us? What about finishing what we have started?* Disappointment lanced through her. She turned her face away, unable to look at him in that moment.

"There was never any doubt of that, Gracie," he added. "I have to do this."

She snorted, crossing her arms. Because *this* was what mattered to him. More than anything else. He could turn himself in and try to prove his inno-

cence with her help. Or he could even flee. Run to
Mexico where he could maybe have a life. *No.* The
stubborn jerk wanted revenge more than either of
those options.

"I need justice—"

Her gaze wrenched back to him. "Oh, let's just
call it what it is. You want revenge."

He stared at her stonily, so much like the stranger
she first met that her heart ached. "Fine. Call it
that if you want. It doesn't change anything." He
took a step closer, the great wall of him encroaching on her space, giving her no way out around
him. "I don't want to say good-bye like this."

Her eyes started to sting. This was it, then.

She didn't know what was going to happen . . .
if he was going to walk out of this confrontation
with Sullivan or not. She was going to try to make
sure that he did, but she didn't know. Anything
could go wrong with her plan.

She uncrossed her arms and flung them around
him. He caught her up in his arms and lifted her
off the ground, his mouth claiming hers until she
was dizzy and breathless. He pulled back, still
holding her, and she resisted the impulse to chase
that mouth with her own.

"Good-bye, Gracie."

Her chest heaved. It was on the tip of her tongue

to insist that it didn't have to be good-bye. She could visit him in prison. She could promise him that. But staring at his resolute expression, she knew he would tell her not to come. He wouldn't want her to see him like that—as an inmate. A caged man. True, it would be hard. A bitter thing, but the idea that this could be the last time she saw him was even worse.

He set her down and walked away, his strides swift as he straddled his bike. It took two tries but he got the great beast of gleaming chrome started. He didn't look at her again as he pulled out onto the road.

Grace waited anxiously, her heart in her throat as she watched his bike fade in the distance. Satisfied that he was well and truly out of sight, she turned and raced inside, grabbing the keys and the stash of money he'd left her (in case she needed it) off the table.

Ten seconds later she was sitting in the van, turning the ignition and heading after him, careful to keep a good distance, well out of sight behind him.

She knew he was headed for Sullivan's house in Sweet Hill. She bumped along the unpaved road, determined to be there, too. When all hell broke loose, she was going to be there. She only knew she had to be.

This time when the police showed up, Reid wouldn't be alone. It wouldn't be like the last time, when he was a kid. She would be there to speak on his behalf. Even if he went through with it and actually killed Sullivan—and she was hoping he wouldn't . . . that he would discover he wasn't capable of murder—the world would know the truth. The world would know what kind of man Sullivan was and why Reid broke out of prison and went after him.

Whatever happened, she would be there. He wouldn't face this alone. Not this time.

OTIS SULLIVAN LIVED on the outskirts of Sweet Hill in a well-appointed community riddled with miniature lakes, bike paths, and golf courses. The houses sat on large lots, positioned well back from the road.

Reid turned down the street and then down a parallel side street, parking behind a landscaping truck.

From his vantage, he scanned the perimeter. A Lexus and two SUVs sat parked in the circular driveway. Two men stood beneath the shaded portico, on either side of the front door. Another two stood near the garage. One smoked a cigarette while the other paced a short line.

An attractive middle-aged woman in a pink tennis skirt emerged out of a door near the garage, a gangly boy in khaki pants and a crisp button-down shirt followed, his head buried in his phone. She said something to one of the men and then moved toward the Lexus. He opened the door for her.

Reid had followed Sullivan's career as much as he could from prison and knew that he was married and had a son. The picture-perfect family. A hard curse escaped him. While he'd been rotting in prison, this man was out here, killing, stealing, running drugs, and basically enjoying his charmed life.

Sullivan's wife and son climbed into the Lexus, backed out of the driveway and drove off. Reid dug his burner phone out of his pocket and punched in Sullivan. He answered on the third ring.

"It's done," he said.

"Good. Very good. Glad to see you still have it in you." Sullivan's voice rang with approval. "Now let's talk about the body . . ."

"Taking care of that. I'm on the way to you with her now."

"What?" Sullivan sputtered. "You can't do that."

"You have that fat house on Desert Lane, right? I'll be there soon."

"Do not come to my house, Allister. You hear me?" An edge of panic entered his voice.

Reid hung up, a grin playing about his lips. Now he only had to wait. And it didn't take long to wait for the rats to scurry.

A few moments later, as he'd hoped, the side door opened and Sullivan exited with two other men close at his sides. More men poured out of the house, taking positions around the perimeter, presumably readying themselves for Reid's arrival.

Sullivan and two of his thugs hopped in one of the SUVs, clearly in a hurry to get him away from the house. Sullivan wouldn't want to be at any location where a dead Grace Reeves could potentially show up. He wanted to hurt the president in the worst way by killing his daughter, but he didn't want to take the blame for it. The bastard would want to be someplace public and, more important, far away. Even if that meant he had fewer men guarding him.

Reid watched as the vehicle passed, then he started his bike and turned down the street, following the black SUV, keeping a careful distance as he trailed them through town. It was a short drive. Ten minutes later Sullivan pulled up in front of his office, a squat brown building.

Reid parked at the corner and climbed off his bike. Sullivan and his men went in through the front door, which was the point—letting himself be seen by witnesses. He was counting on his men back at the house dealing with Reid and the corpse he was bringing.

Reid checked his gun under his jacket, verifying it was still in position, tucked in the back of his jeans. Then he crossed the street and walked around to the back of the building advertising Sullivan Realty.

The back door was unlocked. He eased inside, making his way through an empty employee staff room. He rounded a corner, his hand behind his back, gripping his gun. He heard voices near the front, easily picking out Sullivan's ringing tones.

He stuck close to the wall, moving down a hall. His goal was Sullivan, but he knew he might have to take down his thugs, too.

His heart thundered in his chest the closer he inched toward the door where he heard Sullivan speaking. Inconveniently, he also heard another voice. This one in his head. Soft and familiar. *You're not a killer.* Damn it. It was bad enough she'd gotten beneath his skin. Now she was in his head, too, distracting him, softening him when he needed to be hard and calculated. When he needed to be the man he was at Devil's Rock, who kicked ass and took names and never thought twice about it.

He paused, squeezing his eyes in a tight blink. Exhaling, he let his head drop against the wall. *Christ*. He couldn't do it.

Eleven years he'd been dreaming about this moment and she'd ruined him.

TWENTY-TWO

*G*RACE STOOD OUTSIDE a nail salon just one block down the street from Sullivan Realty. She'd parked the van haphazardly in front of the salon, one tire rolled up onto the sidewalk. Several faces pressed against the glass, gawking at her. She'd made a spectacle of herself, running inside and using the phone to call her personal aide and give her instructions and her location.

She knew it was going to take a while for the Secret Service to show up, but she also knew they would contact the local police. Surely they would be here any second.

She paced in front of the salon, dragging a hand through her hair, her pulse hammering at her neck every moment Reid was inside that building. Where were they?

Damn it. She couldn't stand it. She had to do

something. Shooting a quick glance left and right, she darted across the street, her mind racing, trying to formulate a plan that wouldn't endanger Reid or herself.

As her gaze narrowed on the door that read SULLIVAN REALTY, she arrived at something that could work. Hopefully.

She would walk into the lobby and demand to see Otis Sullivan. Reid had gone around the back. Hopefully, the two had not come face-to-face yet. Or at least Reid had not committed murder yet. She would look Sullivan squarely in the face and tell him she knew who he was, what he had done, and that the police were on the way. It was over. There had to be witnesses inside that building that weren't criminals. He wouldn't harm her in front of them.

Nodding, convinced that this was a solid plan, she reached for the door.

Her hand never made it to the handle. A fist grabbed her by the hair and yanked her around. She yelped and clawed at the hand buried in her hair, her feet scampering over the ground, fighting for purchase as she was hauled back around the building.

"What the hell are you doing here?" a familiar voice snarled into her ear. "Shouldn't you be dead, you little bitch?"

She started to scream, but Rowdy's hand slammed over her mouth. He continued to drag her to the back of the building. There were other footsteps and she tried to twist her head to see who and how many she was up against.

Where were the police?

Once in the back gravel parking lot, Rowdy spun her around to face him. "Where the hell is he?" Zane and another guy she vaguely recognized as one of her abductors stood beside him. Rowdy jerked his chin at them. "Good thing we decided to come by right now and pick up the money Sullivan promised us for grabbing her." He turned his gaze back on her, full of blistering wrath. "Now answer my question. Where the fuck is he?"

"Who?" she hedged, bending her head awkwardly at his painful grip in her hair.

"Who?" Rowdy echoed, sending a quick smirk to Zane. "The bitch wants to play stupid." He looked back at Grace, cocking his head to the side, his bloodshot eyes wild. "You know what happens to stupid bitches? They get used for punching bags."

He cocked his fist and gut-punched her. She bowed over and dropped to the ground, pain radiating from her stomach and up her torso. Bile surged in her throat. She coughed. Afraid she was about to be sick.

"Rowdy—" Zane started to say.

"What, man? Sullivan wanted her dead and she's here." Grace looked up from the dark curtain of her hair. Zane met her gaze and shrugged helplessly, scratching at one skinny arm.

"I'm sure there's a reason—"

"Yeah, the reason is that your brother is a lying motherfucker. I told you we couldn't trust him. He ain't one of us anymore."

Rowdy looked back down at her, pulling a knife smoothly from his pocket. He flipped it open and nodded at the other guy, never taking his eyes off her. "Go get the truck."

Grace started to drag herself backward on the asphalt, indifferent to her palms scraping over the rough surface. Rowdy followed, moving in slowly. He didn't have to move fast. She couldn't even stand yet.

"Rowdy," Zane said, a shaky quality to his voice as he looked from Grace to the knife. "You gonna kill her here? That'll be messy."

Shaking badly, Grace heaved for breath, struggling to find her voice so she could scream. She wasn't sure if it was the lingering pain of being punched or if it was fear. Probably both.

Then she heard another voice. Gravel-deep and rich. A soothing balm to her terrified heart. "Drop the knife."

She twisted around to spot Reid, the most beautiful thing she had ever seen.

"Reid!" Zane cried out.

"Hey, asshole," Rowdy greeted. "We're just about to finish the job you were supposed to do."

"You really think Sullivan wants you to carve her up outside his office building?" Reid moved past her, closer to Rowdy.

"Yeah, Row," Zane chimed in. "Sullivan won't like it."

"Shut the hell up, Zane. Can't you see that he's just trying to protect her?" Rowdy nodded at Grace. "You like her, huh? Enough to turn on your old crew. Must be money between those legs."

Zane fumbled for his phone. "I'm calling Sullivan."

"You really went soft," Rowdy continued, looking at Reid again, his voice heavy with disgust. "Thought prison was supposed to make you tough." He shook his head and sent another quick glance to her. "She worth it? Turning your back on your crew? Maybe I'll have a go at her before I cut her throat. Should have done that back at the house instead of letting you have your way and go off with her."

Grace jerked at the sick words.

Reid took a measured step to the side, putting himself between her and Rowdy. "You gotta go through me."

Rowdy grinned then, revealing his yellowed, rotted teeth. "Nice. Finally. Some honesty from you."

"Reid," Zane choked, his expression one of bewilderment. "What are you doing?"

"Want some more honesty?" Reid asked. "I always hated you, Rowdy, just an inbred asshole with nothing up here." He tapped his skull.

Rowdy's smile slipped and he charged with an enraged shout.

The two collided, locked in struggle. Reid caught hold of Rowdy's arm wielding the knife.

Grace scampered back a few more feet and managed to stand as she watched, horrified, praying to God that Reid managed to avoid the swinging blade.

Zane watched, too, still wearing that dumbfounded expression on his face. Reid kicked Rowdy's leg out from under him and they went down hard with Reid sprawled over him.

The back door banged open.

Three well-dressed men emerged. Grace looked the one in the center up and down, eyeing his narrow face and cold eyes. It had to be Sullivan. He peered at Zane through stylish blue-framed glasses and demanded, "What's going on?"

As Zane stammered incoherently, gesturing to the fighting men, Sullivan's eyes locked on Grace. "What the hell is she doing here?" He blinked, looking her over. "And alive? She's supposed to be dead." He scanned the parking lot behind the building, clearly panicked. "Get her out of here," he barked, clearly a man accustomed to being obeyed. "Quick!"

His men made a move toward her, and then Grace heard the wail of sirens.

Her shoulders slumped with relief. Finally. Her gaze flew to Reid, who was still straddling Rowdy.

She looked back at Sullivan and said the words she had rehearsed in her mind. "It's over."

"The hell it is." Sullivan looked at his men. "Reeves isn't going to get away with what he did to me . . . to my nephew. He owed me and then he fucked me over when it was time to pay me back. He made a commitment to me the moment he took my money." His gaze swerved back to her.

"Kill her. Quick. And get out of here! Dump the body somewhere where it will eventually be found. None of the usual places, understood?"

Startled, she took a step back, bumping into Zane. His hands came up to close around her arms.

"Do it," Sullivan commanded, stabbing a finger at Zane, then scurrying toward the back door of his building.

Sullivan's henchmen looked back at Zane. "You heard him. Do it!"

Still gripping her arm, Zane reached into his pocket and pulled out a knife. He flipped it open, brandishing the blade. The door to the building thudded shut after Sullivan and his men.

"Zane," she whispered, eyeing the glinting steel. "Please, no. Don't."

"Zane!"

Grace looked up. Reid was standing, his boot on Rowdy's neck, pinning him to the ground. He clutched Rowdy's knife in his hand, his gaze locked on his brother. "Please, don't. You're not like the rest of them. You're my brother, man."

"You left me!" Zane exploded, his fingers digging into her arm like talons. "I was just seventeen. I had no one. They were the only ones there for me."

"I know. I didn't want to go . . . I shouldn't have fucked up. I should have never let you get mixed in with Sullivan. I should have been there for you."

Zane still held her arm, the knife pointed at her neck. The wail of sirens grew, getting closer.

"Please, Zane. Don't kill her. She's . . ." His eyes lifted and locked on Grace. "I love her. Don't take her from me."

Grace swallowed back a sob, her heart clenching. A thousand things raced through her mind and she wanted to say all of them. Especially if she was about to die. She wanted Reid to know she felt the same way about him.

Zane expelled a shuddering breath. "Shit, man." He let her go with a slight shove toward Reid.

She staggered away and started to close the last bit of distance between her and Reid, but everything felt like slow motion. Like she was moving underwater. *He loved her.* She didn't make it two steps before police and emergency vehicles roared into the back parking lot and exploded all around them.

She caught a glimpse of Reid being slammed to the ground, a gun pointed at his head.

She opened her mouth and screamed his name. Hands grabbed her, people surrounding her on every side, forming a wall and blocking her from seeing anything—from seeing him.

Grace continued to scream and fight, trying to reach him. She thought she heard him shout her name and then her knees gave out. The ground came up to meet her and her head went thick and fuzzy.

Everything went black.

TWENTY-THREE

GRACE WOKE TO a dark shape standing over her, sunlight streaming around him. She held her hand over her eyes, wondering if she had died. Was this it?

"Where am I?" She closed her eyes again and then reopened them. This time things were a little less hazy, the shape in front of her outlined against a wash of whiteness.

She blinked a few more times, processing the blue suit. Her gaze drifted up to a familiar face. "Daddy?"

"Glad to see you're with us again."

"Where am I?" she repeated.

"In the hospital."

She flattened her palms beside her on a bed and attempted to push herself up. She managed to eventually say, "What happened to me?"

"Don't strain yourself. You've been through an ordeal."

She frowned and lifted fingers to her pounding head. "Was I hurt?"

"You've been through a great trauma," he said, and she released a small snort. So like her father, the consummate politician, never answering a direct question with anything truly enlightening or helpful.

"How long have I been here?"

"Two days. How do you feel?"

Two days? She'd been unconscious that long? Her heart started racing. Ignoring his question, she demanded in a panicky voice, "What happened to Reid? Is he okay?"

"If you're referring to your abductor, then he's back in prison where he belongs."

"No!" She shook her head, ignoring the stabbing sensation in her temples. "You don't understand. He didn't kidnap me. Sullivan—"

"Sullivan has been arrested as well. We have several members of his crime network in custody. All have agreed to testify against him for reduced sentences."

"Oh." She relaxed somewhat. At least they got that part of it right. She just needed to straighten everything else out about Reid. She took a deep breath. "Reid Allister is innocent. Of all crimes.

He was sent to prison in the first place for a crime Sullivan—"

"Grace, you're upsetting yourself. Lay back down. Your mother is at the hotel. I'll call her. She's anxious to see you. This hasn't been good for her nerves."

"Damn it! For once listen to me!"

Her father's expression cracked for the barest moment, the handsome facade showing his astonishment that she would talk to him in such a way. "What's gotten into you, Grace? Clearly you're still suffering from shock. Let me ring the nurse to give you another sedative."

"*Another?* Is that what you've been doing? Drugging me? Is that why I've been in this bed for two days? Daddy, I'm twenty-six years old. I know you're the leader of the free world, but you don't own me." She let the irony of that statement hang there for a moment. "I'm a person with rights, and I'm done living my life for you."

He stared at her for a long moment, his blue eyes hardening. It was the type of stare that would normally have had her hastily apologizing before. But this wasn't *before* anymore. "Of course I don't own you, Grace. I never thought I did." He cleared his throat and looked to the door. "Dennis, if you would leave us for a moment please."

That's when she noticed her father's special agent in charge standing at attention a few feet away. Without a glance to her, the former special ops soldier exited the room.

Her father didn't waste time. Turning back to her, he said, "I understand you've been through an ordeal. Because of me. Because of who I am." He paused to take a breath and she blinked. This was the closest she had ever heard her father come to apologizing. He sounded almost contrite. "I never imagined anything like this could . . ." His voice faded away.

"I don't blame you, Daddy," she said gently, and she meant it.

Her father was a lot of things, but it wasn't his fault she'd been abducted. When evil men did evil things, it was no one's fault. Otis Sullivan was to blame. No one else.

He sighed and bowed his head. The sound was tired. He looked older standing there. "I'm glad to hear that, Grace." He dragged a chair up beside the bed and sank down in it. He patted her hand where it rested on the bed. "Truly relieved."

"Dad," she began after a moment. "I need to talk to you about Reid Allister."

He made a sound of disgust. "The man is exactly where he deserves to be."

"No, you don't understand—"

"There's nothing to discuss on the matter of Reid Allister. You'll only distress yourself further."

She crossed her arms where she reclined in the bed. "He saved my life."

Her father's top lip curled faintly, as though he had just tasted something unpleasant. "And what else did he *do* to you?"

She sucked in a slow breath. He knew. Of course he knew. He must have had agents out to the cabin by now. She winced. They would have relayed what they found there. Even if they hadn't found a half-empty box of condoms, her father could probably take one look at her and surmise the truth of it. But she loved Reid Allister and was *not* going to sit by idly and let him rot away in prison for the rest of his life.

"You can pardon him," she said calmly, not so much as blinking under her father's unflinching regard. "You have that power."

"And why would I do that? So my only daughter can ruin her life and be with a degenerate?" He shook his head slowly. "Not happening."

She propped up on her elbows in the bed. "Even if he's innocent?"

"Innocence is a relative thing."

She shook her head. "If you care about me at all—"

"I do care about you. I know I never say it. Your mother and I haven't been the most demonstrative with you over the years, but we love you. Believe it or not, I'm looking out for you."

"I know you think you are. But you're controlling. I'm twenty-six and can lead my own life. Make my own choices."

"And would one of those choices include being with Reid Allister?

She refrained from agreeing or disagreeing. "I'm done. I'm leaving DC. I won't be your puppet anymore."

His nostrils flared, the only indication that her declaration had affected him. "You're right, you know. I do have the power to pardon him." Hope started a slow whisper through her heart. "How badly do you want him to have his freedom?"

"You know I do."

"Enough to stay in DC?"

She sank back down on the bed as understanding began to penetrate. She gave a slow nod. "Yes."

"Enough to marry Charles?" he pressed.

She jerked back into a sitting position, outraged

and prepared to object, but the look in his eyes told her it was no use.

"You don't dislike each other," he reminded her sharply. "Charles was sick with worry while you were gone. He's a good man. You could be good together, Grace."

This was what her father did. He was a master negotiator. And he never lost.

"You would manipulate me like this?" she accused softly.

"I'm doing what's right for you." His expression was earnest, and she knew he thought that was true.

She gave another nod, feeling like she was sinking, falling, as she settled back down on the bed again. Falling into a grave. *Her* grave.

"Enough to promise never to see Reid Allister again?" The words hit her, landing like dirt over her grave. That was the final point to be negotiated. Maybe the most important one for her father.

She nodded once, hard. Thankfully, the boulder-sized lump in her throat blocked the sob that rose up in her chest.

"Say it, Grace. I'll have your word. You will never attempt to see Reid Allister again."

"You have my word," she whispered. She would

stay in DC under her father's thumb. She would marry Charles.

Her sentence had just begun, but it didn't matter because Reid would finally be free.

REID WAS BUZZED through a second set of doors. With his hands and ankles shackled, he walked with shuffling steps down the halls, a corrections officer on each side of him.

They usually didn't bother with the leg shackles, so he guessed they were taking him to meet with someone important. Probably the district attorney to talk to him about his testimony against Sullivan.

He was glad for the meeting. Whatever the reason, it was a nice break from segregation, where they'd had him ever since his return to Devil's Rock. He passed through several more doors until he was in an area of the prison he'd never seen before. Soon he was being led through a carpeted reception area, heading for the door marked as belonging to the warden. *Oh, shit.*

His mind raced, wondering what this could be about. Maybe it was about the riot . . . or breaking out of prison . . . or how much he'd embarrassed them by escaping, and they planned on keeping him in the hole for the rest of his life.

One of the bulls opened the door for him. Reid stepped inside. Immediately, he noticed two men in suits who were the size of NFL linebackers. It was impossible not to notice them. They were even taller than him. They sucked up all the space in the room.

"Have a seat," a voice intoned.

He looked over to a small sitting area. The President of the United States sat on a couch, a cup of steaming coffee in his head. His free hand motioned to the armchair across from him.

Reid moved slowly, as though expecting some kind of trap. Was this when one of those Secret Service agents forced him to his knees and put a bullet in the back of his head for fooling around with the president's daughter? For putting her life in danger?

Reid sank down into the chair, extending a small nod to the man who, in his opinion, had been a shitty father to Grace. He wasn't going to get a warm welcome from him. Reid didn't give a damn who he was.

The president stared at him for a few moments. "I understand I'm to thank you for saving my daughter's life."

Reid merely stared. Reeves was going to have to say more than that to get him to talk. He would have to make it clear why he was here.

Reeves continued, "Grace seems to think you deserve a pardon."

Of course Grace would be trying to get him free. She was good like that. Sweet. She believed in things like justice. She believed in him when no one else in the world did.

"What do you think my daughter deserves, Mr. Allister? Do you think she deserves you? Some lowlife degenerate who'll never amount to anything?" He waved an elegant hand in the air. "Who'll always wear the stain of this place on him?"

Reid finally answered him. "No. She deserves better than me."

President Reeves smiled then. It was fake and didn't reach his eyes, and Reid bet he did it every day and people bought into it. "Good then. I'm glad to see we're in agreement. As long as you agree that my daughter deserves better than you and you promise to stay far away from her, I'll see to your pardon."

Reid sat there for a moment, waiting for the rush of exultation to flow over him. Nothing. Without Grace, it didn't even make an impression.

"Mr. Allister." Hard eyes fixed on him. "Do I have your promise? Your freedom and you forget all about my daughter." His expression turned faintly mocking. "I'm sure that won't be that difficult for you to manage."

Reid's hands curled at his sides and it took everything in him not to lunge at the man. He didn't think Grace was one to inspire love and loyalty? Or maybe Reeves just thought he was incapable of feeling such dedication.

After a long moment, Reid nodded. Because Reeves was right. Grace deserved better than him. "Yes."

"Then you have your pardon."

TWENTY-FOUR

A SOFT KNOCK SOUNDED at her hospital door. She ignored it, scraping the inside of her Jell-O cup with a spoon, hoping whoever was there would just go away. Her mother, Holly, and Diana, her mother's personal aide, had just left, and her head was throbbing. She wasn't in the mood for more visitors. Hopefully the person would just go away.

Her spoon continued scavenging for the last bit of Jell-O. She probably hadn't had Jell-O since middle school. How had she gone this long without it? Especially black cherry. She was going to have to start adding it to her grocery list.

A rerun of *The Big Bang Theory* played on the TV. She'd seen the episode before but it still succeeded in distracting her. She laughed at Sheldon and wondered if Reid had ever seen the show before. Did they play it in prison? Did he have access to TV?

Hell. So much for distracting her.

The door opened. "Grace? Hello?" Charles stuck his head inside the room.

"Hey, Charles." She reached for the remote control, powering down the volume. He'd come by earlier with her mother, but she hadn't been alone with him since before . . .

Before everything.

Except now they were engaged.

"I brought you some breakfast tacos." He held up a brown paper bag. "The nurses here raved about them." He shrugged amiably. "Figured you should always go with the recommendations of the locals."

"Thanks, Charles."

He pulled a chair up and drew the bed tray closer, setting the bag on it. "Unless you want more Jell-O cups." He nodded at the empty cups littering her tray.

"Thanks, but I'll take the real food, please."

"Your mother said they should release you tomorrow."

Grace nodded, watching as he lifted a taco out of the bag and handed it to her. She opened the tinfoil and immediately the delicious aroma of warm flour tortilla, scrambled egg, and bacon wafted to her nose. "This smells like heaven." She moaned at her first bite.

At the stretch of silence, her gaze drifted to Charles. He watched her with a rapt expression.

She held her fingers over her mouth. "What?" she asked around a mouthful of taco. "You're not eating."

Nodding, he looked down at the taco in his hand, hurriedly unwrapped it and took a bite. She watched him curiously. He looked almost nervous, which he couldn't be. Charles was confident and charismatic. Never nervous.

"Good," he said approvingly, and took another bite. He glanced up at the TV, smiling. "This is a good one."

They ate in silence for a few moments. Companionable silence. Like before. That much hadn't changed.

"You seem . . . different," he announced.

Her gaze swerved back to him at this. A nervous tremor ran through her. *How could he know?* "Different how?" she dared asking.

Did he look at her and know she'd fallen in love with one of her abductors? That she'd slept with someone else and there had been sparks? Epic sparks. Once in a lifetime sparks. The kind she and Charles didn't have and never would have.

"I don't know." He shrugged one shoulder. "Stronger maybe?"

She smiled at that, a little relieved.

She felt stronger. It was a new day and she was a new Grace Reeves. She was glad he sensed that. "Tell that to my mother. She hasn't stopped hovering."

He smiled back. "She was worried. We all were." He paused and looked down at his taco. "I was worried, Grace."

"I know—" she started to say.

"No." His voice sounded almost pained as he cut her off. "*I* was really worried."

"Charles," she said softly, unsure what to say.

"I mean it." He lifted his gaze back up. "What we had was so comfortable. I realize that I took it for granted. I took you for granted."

She took another bite of her taco, chewing steadily so she wouldn't have to say anything right then.

"I know I went about all of this wrong, Grace. I went about *us* wrong. Your father has been calling the shots from the beginning."

"Well, that's what he does."

"Well, I shouldn't have let him. Not in this. Maybe that's why you and I never felt real." Abruptly, he put down his taco and stood up.

She watched him with wide eyes, her heart pounding like a jackhammer at her throat. He ran both hands through his well-groomed hair, sending the chestnut locks into uncustomary disarray. "Your father said you agreed to marry me."

Heat crept up her face. Did her father also explain that he had blackmailed her to get her agreement? For the first time, she thought about Charles and how he would feel if he knew she had been coerced. He couldn't like the idea. What man would?

Even knowing that, she didn't care. She did it for Reid. For his freedom. She didn't regret it. The choice was hers, and she did feel good about that at least. It was her decision. She was calling the shots. The very thing she had vowed to do when she returned to her family.

Charles cursed and looked away for a moment. She blinked. It wasn't like him to use language. "Charles," she started, pushing herself up a little higher in the bed. "Look . . ."

Her voice faded as he got down on one knee. She peered over the side of the bed at him, her mouth sagging open at the sight of him on bended knee. "I don't need anyone to propose for me. Not even your father. I'm quite capable of doing it myself. Grace Reeves, will you marry me?"

She stared, stunned.

He straightened and seized her hand. "I know this is probably not the most romantic gesture. And certainly not how any woman imagines a proposal." His lips twisted in a wry grin. "Over tacos in a hospital bed leaves a lot to be desired. But it's me that's asking this time, Grace. Not your father."

She cleared her throat. "I appreciate that."

"We can have something real, Grace. We can be good together. I believe it. Tell me you believe that, too."

Her mind touched on Reid and then shied away. It hurt too much. "I don't love you, Charles." She had to be honest with him. She couldn't go into this with him thinking she felt more for him than she did. She wouldn't do that to him no matter what she promised her father. She'd marry him, but he would know the truth.

"Do you like me?"

"Yes. Of course."

"Good, because I like you. I *more* than like you, and I think some day we could maybe even love each other. When I thought something might happen to you . . . that you might die—" He stopped and gave his head a swift shake. As though it was too unthinkable to say out loud. He pinned her with his gaze. "Say yes."

He knew she didn't love him. Despite his optimism, he knew she might never love him.

Reid's face flashed across her mind and she shuddered. It was all the incentive necessary.

"Yes."

TWENTY-FIVE

*R*EID WALKED INTO the diner where he was meeting Knox for breakfast before heading into work. It was New Year's Eve. His boss had offered him the day off, but he declined. As soon as he finished breakfast, he'd clock in like usual. Work kept him busy. His mind off other things.

He had a job working at a garage in Sweet Hill. Since he'd been pardoned, he'd started looking into graduate schools that offered masters in criminology. He was up for leaving the area. Starting fresh. There was nothing keeping him here anymore.

He'd been planning to meet with Knox for a while now, ever since he got out, but he'd been dragging his feet. For one thing, he'd promised to keep an eye out for North. Not only was Reid now free and unable to do that, but four years had been added to his sentence for the riot Reid had started. Talk about shit luck.

Knox spotted him from where he sat in a back booth and waved him over. Shrugging out of his heavy coat, he hung it on the hook outside the booth and slid onto the bench seat.

He reached across the table to shake his friend's hand. "Hey, man. How you doing?"

Knox shook his hand. A good sign, Reid guessed. At least he wasn't planting his fist in his face and cursing him.

"Doing great. You look good." Knox nodded. "Never thought I'd be sitting across a table from you on the outside, though."

"I know." He reached for the menu, his discomfort growing.

"I'm happy for you, man."

"How's your girl?" Reid asked dutifully. He knew Knox was with someone now. He'd mentioned it when they talked on the phone.

"Briar is great. Christmas was . . ." He looked away, his eyes growing suspiciously wet before he blinked them. "Never thought I'd have that again, you know. A girl to love. A real family Christmas with a tree and decorations. Huge turkey. Christ, she can cook." He shook his head. "The pies she can bake." He patted his flat stomach and grinned. "She'll have me fat soon enough."

Reid doubted that. His friend might be happy and at home on the outside, but he still looked hard and alert and ready to bust heads at a moment's notice.

"Never thought I'd have this, you know. Wasn't sure if I deserved it."

Reid nodded. "I know what you mean." Of course, he did. They came from the same place. Knox had spent seven years in Devil's Rock.

"Means there's hope for you." Knox grinned.

Reid's smile felt brittle.

Silence descended. The waitress came and took their orders. When she left, Knox cut to the point. "You see North before you left the Rock?"

Reid grimaced even though he had been expecting that question. "No, I was in the hole until my release."

Knox shook his head. "Last time I went to see him, he refused visitation."

"Maybe you should go visit Cross. He'll give you any news. Give North any messages."

"Yeah, that's a good thought."

Reid set his mug of coffee down with a clack on the table. "I'm sorry, man. I promised you that I would look after him."

Knox waved a hand. "It's not your fault. I might have been pissed at first but the fact is . . . no one can promise that in there. You can only try. You were a good friend to us when we first entered that place. The shit that would have happened to the both of us that first month if you hadn't stepped in . . ." He shook his head. "Man, forget about it. You don't owe us an apology. You're another brother to us."

Emotion punched him in the chest. Especially considering how alone he'd felt ever since he got out. Work, eat, sleep. That was pretty much the cycle.

A few weeks after his pardon, he'd actually paid his mother a visit. He didn't know what prompted him . . . what he was looking for from the woman who had never given him anything in life. He felt worse after seeing her.

The years had not been good to her. Most of her teeth were gone. Her greasy hair had thinned so much he could see her scalp through the stringy strands. He had to remind her who he was several times. She continually asked him if he had any money and even went so far as to grope his pockets when he stood up to leave.

When he left her trailer, he bumped into Gaby, one of the twins he used to fuck around with in high school. She was there visiting her parents. She was still hot. Jeans painted on and a skintight sweater that hung loose off one shoulder.

She invited him back to her apartment. He'd accepted the invitation, desperate to move on. Desperate to prove that what he felt for Gracie wasn't real. That it had just been circumstances. Their forced isolation and the constant threat of danger combined with the fact that he hadn't touched a woman in years. It had taken him ten minutes in Gaby's apartment to realize just how wrong he was.

The moment she stripped off her sweater and started a little strip tease, fondling her comically large breasts while licking her lips, he knew. He didn't want anyone but Grace.

"Like these babies?" she asked between licking her lips and tweaking her distended nipples. "My ex bought them for me. Best thing I got out of that marriage."

"I thought they were . . . different than before," he managed to say.

"Damn straight." She straddled him in her leopard print bikini underwear. "Bet you've got a lot of pent up energy." Her hand dove for his dick, grabbing it aggressively as she thrust her chest into his face, nearly blinding him with a nipple.

He jerked at her rough treatment, grabbing her wrist and trying to pull her hand off his dick. "Want to use this on me, big guy? I'm a lot better than I was in high school." She winked. "Have had lots of practice since then."

He tugged her hand off him and squeezed out from under her, dumping her on the couch. "I don't think I'm gonna be up to your standards, Gaby. Kinda rusty."

"Are you kidding me?" She blinked up at him, waving at herself. "You're passing this up?"

"I'm sure I'll regret it later." He was sure he wouldn't. "Nice seeing you, Gaby." And then he'd bailed. Ducked out of her apartment as fast as he could.

It had taught him a valuable lesson. Grace Reeves had in fact ruined him. What he felt for her had been real. Time hadn't dimmed his feelings. He couldn't even stomach touching another woman.

He had even stopped watching television. He needed to purge her from his system, and that included avoiding glimpses of her on TV.

Maybe it was the thought of the TV that had his gaze drifting to the box in the corner above the long counter. As though he had summoned her face, she was there. As beautiful as he remembered her. He stood from the table and drifted closer, drawn despite himself.

He shot a quick glance at the waitress behind the counter. "Hey, can you turn that up, please?"

The woman obliged and he heard the crisp voice of a reporter. "First Daughter Grace Reeves arrived yesterday with her family and fiancé . . ." The rest of the words faded away.

Fiancé. *She was getting married*. The sight of her looking sophisticated in a green skirt and a fitted black coat alongside some good-looking tool flashed on the screen. The guy was polished in a suit, his hair gelled and styled like he stepped off a magazine cover. So that was Charlie.

A panorama of the McDonald Observatory flashed across the screen. He refocused on the rest of the reporter's words. ". . . the observatory will be the location for the couple's engagement party tonight. An astronomy major herself, the First Daughter looks forward to witnessing Seraphina's comet tonight in the arms of her future husband, White House communications director Charles Hubbard."

She was going to the observatory. She would finally get to see out of her telescopes. He couldn't help smiling over that. *And she'll be doing it with some other guy*. A guy she didn't love. What the hell was she doing? *What the hell was he doing letting her do it?*

The waitress behind the counter smacked her gum and winked at him. "Got any New Year's plans, sugar?"

"Yes," he answered, turning for the door. "Yes, I do."

TWENTY-SIX

$\mathcal{I}$T STILL WASN'T that difficult to slip the Secret Service.

Grace knew she only had moments until they located her. The new special agents appointed to her were especially vigilant these days. She eased out a side door, escaping the din of the party and finding her way outside. Her coat was still inside and she shivered in her gown. She fell in love with the strapless blue satin the moment she saw it, but it wasn't equipped for outdoors or the winter. The two combined were a straight ticket to hypothermia. Another reason why she wouldn't be outside long.

She clattered up to the railing in her three-inch heels, wrapped her fingers around the cold steel and stared up at the darkest, clearest night she had ever seen. The stars were infinite. She exhaled, glad for the fresh air and silence even with the cold biting into her. Her eyes teared and she blinked, hoping she didn't ruin her mascara. Her hand shot out, dashing at her eyes.

She'd seen her comet, but it didn't matter nearly as much as she had hoped it would. She could only think that Reid should have been with her to see it, too.

"Did you see your comet?"

She spun around with a gasp at the deep voice. Her chest constricted as Reid stepped into the glow of the perimeter light. He looked amazing in dark jeans, the hint of a gray thermal shirt peeping out of his dark pea coat. His hair was a little longer. The winter wind whipped the dark blond strands.

"What are you doing here?"

"It's your engagement party. Didn't get an invitation." He shrugged as he advanced on her, walking slowly. "Figure it must have gotten lost in the mail."

A short, hard laugh escaped her before she could catch herself. "Don't," she whispered, pressing her fingers over her mouth.

"What?"

"Make me laugh."

"Why not?" He continued coming, stalking toward her with easy strides, his eyes fastened hotly on her face.

Her voice came out strangled. "Because when I look at you I only want to cry."

He stopped in front of her. "Yeah? Well, when I look at you I only want to do this."

His mouth crashed over hers and it was everything she remembered and more. His lips were hungry and brutal. His hands dove into her hair, messing the elegant updo. Pins scattered and she felt the heavy mass tumble down her back.

She broke away with a gasp, her heart pounding with a mixture of lust and panic. "Reid, stop! You have to go." She pushed at his chest and then reached for her hair. How would she explain her appearance?

"I'm not leaving without you."

She stilled, her eyes fixing on him. "What?"

"I was wrong to stay away." He motioned to the building. "You don't want to marry that guy."

"I have to," she whispered.

His eyes sparked. "What happened to the girl tired of doing what others wanted? The girl who was going to live for herself?"

She shook her head. "I promised my father."

"You promised yourself." He closed the space between them and seized her face. "You love me. I know you do. And I love you." He kissed her again, and she let herself drown in sensations again before breaking away.

"I can't!"

He stared at her a long moment before lowering his hands from her face. He shook his head, his eyes so sad and dejected it tore at her heart. "Then you're not the girl I fell in love with. I don't know who you are."

He started to back away, and every step felt like another shovel of dirt falling on her grave.

She shook her head and looked up helplessly to the sky. "I promised my father I would do what he wanted if he pardoned you." The moment the words were out, her gaze shot back to him again.

Reid froze, his face going pale. "What?"

"I told him I would marry Charles."

"For me? For my freedom?"

She nodded.

"Fuck that." In two strides he gripped her arms again. "I promised him if he pardoned me I would leave you alone."

"What? He went to see you?"

"Yes. Right before I was released." He shook his head. "I don't care what he does. I'm not staying away from you."

She nodded, tears blurring her vision. "Yeah. Fuck that."

He laughed, and before she knew what he intended, he tossed her over his shoulder.

She beat on his back. "What are you doing?"

"I don't expect you to get very far through the grass in those shoes."

She bit back a giggle and hit him in the shoulder. "You know kidnapping is a federal offense."

"I've beat it before," he replied, walking down the uneven slope of ground. "How does Vegas sound?"

"What?"

"We can drive through the night. Be married by the morning. It might be harder for the president to go through the effort of revoking my parole if I'm his son-in-law."

She went utterly still. Her silence must have worried him. He stopped and lowered her to her feet.

She shivered and he uttered a quick curse. Shrugging out of his coat, he slipped it around her shoulders. Beneath that endless blanket of stars, he took her hand and held it between them, looking almost nervous. "I know I don't deserve you—"

"You deserve everything," she quickly rebutted.

Still holding her hand, he dropped to his knees on the cold earth. "Grace Reeves, will you marry me?"

She exhaled and looked up, gazing at the lights of a million stars. Looking down again, she saw the same brightness in his eyes, in him, in the love reflected on his face. "I will." Leaning down, she pressed her mouth to his. "Now we better hurry before the Secret Service figures out I'm gone again."

"On it." Rising, Reid swept her up and carried her down the slope.

She leaned toward him to press tiny kisses to his throat. "Maybe we should head to a hotel before we start for Vegas?"

He turned his head and caught her mouth in a short, hard kiss. "Tempting, but not happening. The next time I have you in a bed, you're going to be my wife. And when the goons in the suits catch up to us, I'll be able to wave a marriage certificate at them." He nuzzled the side of her face with his mouth. "Because I'm not letting you ever go again."

Grace smiled. "I'm okay with that." More than okay. It sounded like a perfect kind of forever—one she had never thought possible. Never had the courage to seize for herself. Until him. Until he showed her courage. Until he showed her love.

Now it was real. And it belonged to them.

EPILOGUE

Ten months later . . .

*R*EID HURRIED UP the winding sidewalk, his arms full of grocery bags. He felt his iPhone vibrate in his pocket and gave a start. He still wasn't used to the damn thing. One of the many new technologies he was getting accustomed to since he and Grace had moved to Boston. Grace assured him it would make his life better. He didn't know about that. She was the thing that had made his life better. Technology, he could live without.

He took the three flights to the apartment he and Grace shared in graduate student housing. She had accepted her deferred offer, and he had applied and been accepted into grad school as well. He was getting that masters in Criminology after all.

Delicious aromas wafted from their apartment,

and he knew Grace was still hard at work in the kitchen where he'd left her an hour ago. Classes let out yesterday and she had sent him to the store three times since then. She swore that his first Thanksgiving was going to be perfect. He told her they could order a pizza and it would still be the best Thanksgiving he ever had. Because he was spending it with her. *His wife.*

Even her parents coming to dinner didn't dampen his happiness. They had come to terms with their marriage. If they didn't love the idea, they accepted it. He suspected her father might have helped with his admission to grad school. Probably figured it was better having a son with viable career choices.

Reid used the weight of his body against the door to hold up the grocery bags as he unlocked it. Grace was taking a fresh pan of corn bread out of the oven as he walked in, her dark hair pulled up into an adorable ponytail. He set the bags on the table and moved into the kitchen. Ear buds dangled from her ears. He came up behind her and folded her into his arms.

She yelped and whirled around, whacking him with a potholder. "Reid!" She yanked the buds from her ears. "You scared me!"

He plucked the potholder from her hands and tossed it down. "Just like old times. You beating me up."

"Ha! I seem to recall you chasing me and tackling me down."

He cocked his head to the side and looped his arms around her, bending his knees so they were eye level. "I also seem to recall that I was naked then."

She considered that with an expression of seriousness. "True. This isn't a total recreation of past events."

"Oh, I'm all up for getting naked."

"Big surprise." She giggled. "I've got to start on the cranberry sauce for tomorrow."

"You can take a break. You deserve it. So do I." He lifted her up in his arms. Her legs immediately opened and wrapped around his waist. He carried her into their bedroom with both hands cupping her ass.

"Just a short break," she said against his mouth as they fell together on the bed.

He deftly worked free the buttons of her blouse. "Of course. An hour. Two tops."

"Reid!" she gasped as his teeth sank down on her earlobe.

"Yes, Mrs. Allister?" he breathed into her ear,

his tongue playing over the tender flesh he had just bit.

"Why are you still wearing clothes? I thought you had an affinity for being naked."

"Baby, it's my favorite thing when I'm with you." Grinning, he stood back and started stripping off his clothes, his movements rough and anxious, his breath coming fast and hard. And that wasn't the only thing that was going to come fast and hard if he didn't get inside her quick.

She scrambled back on the bed and made quick work of getting out of her clothes, those beautiful breasts thrusting out as she reached behind her back to undo the clasp of her black bra. Her dark eyes devoured him as she crawled on all fours toward him on the bed. "C'mon. What are you waiting for?"

Then they were tangled up in each other on the mattress. Ten months and it still felt new. It would never get old. Every time with her felt different, better than the last.

He entered her with a hard thrust, bare-skinned. Grace hugged him like a glove. Nothing separated them and it was the sweetest, hottest thing. They'd ditched the condoms shortly after the wedding. They planned to ditch the birth control pills in a few years. The idea of Grace pregnant, carrying his child, snapped the last of his control. He pumped harder, lifting her hips and angling her just right so that she flew apart, screaming his name.

A few more strokes and he followed, finding his own climax without barrier. That was sweet, too. Something he had only ever done with Grace. Something he would only *ever* do with Grace. This was it. For both of them. Real and forever.

He snuggled up beside her, loving her naked curves nestled against him. Gradually her breathing slowed and evened.

"That was amazing," she murmured.

He smiled smugly. She said that every time. Because it was true—for both of them. "Aren't you glad you took that break?"

She nodded. "I need to get back to the kitchen. I have two piecrusts to finish."

He hugged her closer. "It hasn't been an hour yet."

"Reid, my parents are going to be here in the morning."

"See. Plenty of time." He started a trail of small, nibbling kisses down her throat.

She moaned softly and melted against him. "You're very persuasive, Mr. Allister."

"You promised me a perfect Thanksgiving."

"But that's what I'm trying to give you," she protested.